THE MADRAS MANGLER

Usha Narayanan

Happy reading!
Usha

JUFIC BOOKS

First published in India 2013 by Jufic Books
An imprint of Leadstart Publishing Pvt Ltd
1 Level, Trade Centre
Bandra Kurla Complex
Bandra (East) Mumbai 400 051 India
Telephone: +91-22-40700804
Fax: +91-22-40700800
Email: info@leadstartcorp.com
www.leadstartcorp.com

Sales Office:
Unit No.25/26, Building No.A/1,
Near Wadala RTO,
Wadala (East), Mumbai – 400037 India
Phone: +91 22 24046887

US Office:
Axis Corp, 7845 E Oakbrook Circle
Madison, WI 53717 USA

Copyright © Usha Narayanan

All rights reserved worldwide. No part of this publication may be reproduced, stored in or introduced into a retrieval system, or transmitted, in any form, or by any means (electronic, mechanical, photocopying, recording or otherwise) without the prior written permission of the publisher. Any person who does any unauthorised act in relation to this publication may be liable to criminal prosecution and civil claims for damages.

This is a work of fiction. The contents of this book are the expressions and opinions of its author.

ISBN 978-93-82473-64-0

| Cover Design | Fravashi Aga |
| Layout | Chandravadan R. Shiroorkar |

Typeset in Calibri
Printed at Repro India Ltd, Mumbai

Price — India: Rs 195; Elsewhere: US $10

*To Sriya, for being comrade, confidante and cheerleader.
And my cats for their Zen-like calm.*

About the Author

Usha Narayanan has worked as a teacher of English, creative director in advertising agencies, jingle-writer, corporate communications manager, web editor, journalist, leadership skills-trainer, green volunteer and head of copyright permissions in e-publishing. She is a gold-medallist with a Master's degree in English Literature. She also has a diploma in creative writing from the University of Hawaii. You can visit her at her website: www.ushanarayanan.com

Acknowledgements

A big thank you to the following people for their tremendous help:

Srinath, for several innovative concepts that enhanced the book considerably.

Kumaran, for brainstorming ideas and providing insightful feedback.

Hema and her husband Sampath, for always standing by me.

The big guns, Swarup Nanda and Madhavi Purohit, for their flair in spotting new writers and introducing them to the world. Suchita Vemuri, for meticulously editing my manuscript. Fravashi Aga, for her evocative cover design. And the entire publishing team, for their valuable contribution.

Prologue

She was asleep, in her warm soft bed in her room in the college hostel. Next to her with his head on her pillow was Cuddles, her stuffed bear, his golden fur now faded to a dull brown. Her cupboard was filled with cool clothes. Her layered hair-cut brought out her eyes. And she'd met the hunk who made her want to sing into her hairbrush like Taylor Swift — *You belong with me*. A sunny smile lit up her face. Life was good, so good.

And then, in just an instant, it changed. She plunged head-first into a nightmare. *You are dead, dead, dead*, a voice echoed in her brain. *No I'm not*, she screamed, though she couldn't hear her voice. Why couldn't she hear her voice? She couldn't see either. *Why can't I see anything?* Then she felt the pain. Her head felt like it would shatter, as if someone was pounding it with a mallet. *Go away, leave me alone,* she shouted, trying to push the hammer away. But she couldn't. Her hands wouldn't move. She tried to lift herself, move away from the attacker. But her body lay still, as if disconnected from her brain. Her heart was bursting through her chest, a terrible pain seared through her body.

It's a nightmare, it's just a nightmare, she told herself. Sweat poured down her face as she willed her body to move. But it would not obey. She gagged, bitter bile flooding up from within, choking her. She tried to turn her head to vomit it out, but could not. Her head would not turn, her mouth would not open. She could not breathe. *God, I'm going to die!*

Panic sliced through every nerve. *I'm pretty, I'm young. And I have so much to live for.* She listened to the silence. *I can't be dying. See, my brain is still working*. The voice did not answer. What was it planning to do? Why didn't it say something?

Who are you, where am I? Somebody save me. Someone. Anyone. Where was everyone? She had friends, many friends. Why weren't they here to rescue her? Did they know she had been buried alive? She heard something. A scratching sound. She lay still, like a cornered mouse, waiting for someone to stomp on her head and smash it.

He stood watching, smiling. Her hands were flexing, trying to break the bonds that tied her to the bed. He saw the ring on her finger, with a ram's head on it. Her slim legs were bound too, so she could not move. A dirty rag was stuffed into her mouth and her eyes were blindfolded. She had been reduced to a quivering mass of flesh, just the way he wanted. Like all the girls he had brought here before.

He dropped to his knees, lifted her foot. Felt her muscles clench in terror. He ran his fingers over her toes, then around the ankle. So pretty, at least for now. He fastened a delicate silver anklet on her. First one and then the other. His mother's anklets. He loved the sound they made when the girls twisted in pain and fear.

She was at his mercy, ready to be moulded, with a knife if necessary. She would become his Perfect Bride. Immaculate, beautiful, submissive. A loving human doll who would heal him, making him whole again.

Or she would die. Slowly, painfully.

1

What was that? Kat stopped to listen. She had been on her way to the canteen when she heard the voices. She was a second year student doing her Master's in Visual Communications in SS Padmaja College, located in a Chennai suburb. The college was part of a deemed university built on a 400-acre spread on GST Road, the road leading to the airport. The university was adding assorted courses every year, fed by the ambition of parents who invested their life savings in the education of their children. There were currently 25,000 students here, studying everything from biosciences to medicine, computer science to chemical engineering, fine arts to management.

It must be the ragging of new students, she thought, as she hurried towards the dark corner of the campus, which she normally avoided. It was close to the perimeter fence through which anti-social elements sneaked in once the sun had set. This was where the coke-heads gathered to smoke, drink and broker deals. Moneyed juniors were dragged here, bullied and made to pay for their drinks and drugs.

Last year, when she joined the college, she had been asked some crude questions and made to dance to a film song. The ragging was not so bad that year probably because of the excesses that had taken place the year before and the gory finale. A girl who had been paraded nude around her hostel by her seniors had thrown herself off the top floor and landed in a bloody heap on the ground. There had been a media furore. TV reporters had talked endlessly about ragging being 'an inhuman form of physical and psychological torture'. Parents and freshers had held up placards asking that the culprits be brought to justice. Activist groups had gheraoed the Principal.

But then it had all died down, as these things usually did. The management had swung into action to warn students that they would be expelled if they continued with their agitation. They paid a huge sum to the parents of the dead girl so they would withdraw their case. Anti-ragging squads were formed to assure parents that this would not recur.

But here it was again. A girl's voice rising in a screech. "Please. Please let me go."

A male voice imitated her in a falsetto. "Please, please let me go!"

Jeers and loud laughter followed.

Kat realised that the easiest course of action would be to ignore the girl's desperation and leave her to her fate. Or simply inform the college office and go on her way. But that was not the way her mind worked. She could not stay silent when she saw someone being exploited. She was an optimist, believing that there were many right-minded people just waiting for someone to show the way. Maybe she could frighten the goons off with threats. Or make them believe the police had been informed and were just minutes away.

She skidded on something as she hurried through the shadows under the trees. It was an empty whisky bottle, rolling away from under her feet. She grabbed at a bush to steady herself, scratching her hand on the thorns. She should have run to her room and brought a torch, but then it might have been too late to save the girl.

The loud laughter was nearer. She stopped and peered out from behind a tree. Three girls and two boys were cowering in front of a group of hoodlums wielding assorted weapons. One was swishing a wicked, curved knife in the air as if planning to behead someone. Another was armed with a cricket stump. Kat recognised the ringleader in the faint light of the lamp from the perimeter fence.

Ugly face. Crocodile eyes. Leer. Red streak on forehead. Pink shirt. Gold chains. A final-year BA student for three years now. Jambu.

The victim was a tiny girl with her hair in an oily plait. Wearing a *salwar kameez* splashed with huge flowers and pink plastic slippers; looking like someone who was in the big city for the first time. Her body was shaking with loud sobs and she swayed, almost collapsing on the ground. One of the thugs dragged her upright with a tattooed arm round her waist, pulling her close to his body. She squirmed, trying to get away from him, flailing with weak arms.

"*Anna*. Please Anna," she pleaded to Jambu as she realised she was in desperate trouble.

"Oh, Anna? You call me brother? You touch my heart," said Jambu, putting a hand on his chest. The girl looked at his face with a quiver of hope.

"Pull off her *dupatta* Mari," Jambu barked. The man holding her pulled it off even as she wailed in fear. The henchmen hooted.

"I'm not hero. I'm very b-a-a-a-a-a-d man," said Jambu, dragging out the word for effect. Must be a dialogue from one of the Tamil movies playing in the mall nearby, thought Kat. "Now come here... sister," he said.

His men were salivating, exploding in whistles and catcalls, taking drags from the joint they passed around.

The girl took two tiny steps forward, choking with fear.

"Come, give kiss," said Jambu.

She shook her head violently from side to side.

"Oh, you don't know to kiss? Mari, show her."

Mari bent to pull her face closer and kiss her. She shrieked and ran from him, brought up short by two other goons.

"Okay, you choose. Kiss me. Or take off your top. What you say, Mari? Good choice, no?" said Jambu.

The girl's eyes darted around, looking for an escape route. The men stood in a ring around her, waiting for the strip show with doped eyes and crazed faces. She ran two stumbling steps away from Jambu, but Mari grabbed her. He stroked her cheek as she reared back from him.

"Poor girl. Don't know how to take off top?" asked Jambu. "Mari, help her."

Mari grabbed her kameez, ripped it off. She moaned and clutched pieces of it over her white cotton vest. One of the new boys yelped in fear.

"Whack him Rahim," said Jambu, without taking his eyes off the girl. Another of his men jumped into the act. He yanked the boy's rucksack off his back and shoved him against a tree. He pulled a tennis racket from one of the outside pouches of the rucksack and held it aloft like a trophy.

"Play tennis?" asked Jambu.

"Yes, sir. My brother bought it in London," said the tall boy, now hunched over in fear.

"Rahim, show him how to play."

Rahim took the racquet and started raining blows on the back of the boy. The racquet broke and the strings sprang loose. The boy whimpered. Rahim emptied the rucksack on the ground. Books, certificate folders, a photo frame — assorted things tumbled out.

"Sir, please, please…" pleaded the boy.

Rahim poured some whisky from his bottle over the pile. Then he lit a match stick and dropped it on the pile. The boy struggled, but was held fast by two goons. Tongues of flame started to burn everything up.

"Any more noise, Rahim will cut your throat," said Jambu.

Rahim grinned and wrapped his curved knife round the boy's throat.

Jambu signalled to Mari. "What? Waiting for *muhurtham*? Pull off her clothes man. I take her first. You watch."

The girl started howling as Mari pulled on her vest. The garment tore as she tried to hold on. Kat was frantic. This was much worse than she had expected. She needed to call for help. Where was her cell phone? She searched her pocket with frantic fingers. Nothing, except her room key. She was a fool. A bloody fool.

The girl ran a few steps before Mari caught her again, like a cat playing with a mouse it had maimed. She screamed louder now, a tortured sound. Mari pulled off her vest, revealing her white bra. Kat could not take it any more. She sprang from her hiding place. "Leave her alone, you bastards. Why are you torturing her?"

They turned to look at her. She saw Jambu's whisky-sodden face and knew he was beyond all reasoning. She took a step back.

"Aha, Jhansi Rani," said Jambu. "Come, join the fun. Where your beautiful friends? Not come?"

"Let her go. I'll complain to the Principal," said Kat.

"To Principal?" Jambu guffawed. "You don't know? Principal in my pocket. College Board in my pocket. My father's college. Two more colleges in Thanjavur." His words were slurred, running one into the other.

She turned to run. If she was lucky, they would be too sozzled to catch her and she could get some help. The problem was that there were hardly any people on campus at this time of the year when the academic sessions were just beginning.

Too late. A giant with a shaven head stood blocking her way. She pushed at him. He slapped her hard, grabbed her arm and dragged her to Jambu.

Jambu sat back in his folding chair. "More girls, more fun," he said. "Mottai, strip her."

The giant, nicknamed 'Mottai' because of his shaven head, bent over Kat. She recoiled as she smelt the *ganja* on his breath. He grabbed her T-shirt to rip it off.

"Help! Somebody help!" she shouted.

2

And then it happened. A muscular figure rushed into the clearing, positioned himself with his back to a tree and surveyed the scene. He assessed the motley crowd in front of him, frozen in stances that revealed aggressor and victim. A giant with a shaven head, preparing to tear off the T-shirt of a pretty girl. A boy cowering in the grip of a man with a long, curved knife. Another girl with her clothes in tatters, a tattooed arm holding her close. A bully with a knife, next to the man lounging in his chair, probably the one in charge.

Three of the men turned to face the intruder, forming a loose line in front of their leader. They stood with their arms dangling by their sides like apes. Heads raised, confident that they had the advantage of numbers and arms.

Five men. He had to be quick. Plan his moves. First, take out the giant holding the girl, standing between him and the others. By then, the rest would be upon him like a pack of hyenas. One blow for each, powerful enough to knock them out. One of them would probably run, once heads started hitting the ground. That was the way it was, most times.

He took two strides forward and addressed the shaven headed giant. "What's your name?"

"My name?" The goon turned to face him.

"Never mind. Mottai it is," the stranger said. His voice dropped. "Now listen."

Mottai leaned forward. The stranger let fly with a heavy boot to the groin. Mottai collapsed in agony, howling. The stranger followed up with a driving kick to his side. Mottai was out cold before his head smashed into the hard ground.

The newcomer pivoted on the balls of his feet to face the three thugs now advancing on him. He yanked off his jacket and threw it towards the girl trembling in her torn clothes. "Sure you want to do this?" he asked the thugs. "You want to fight for scum like him?" He pointed to Jambu.

The three stared at him. Three hundred kilos of meat. One of them with a machete. The other two armed with a cricket stump and a knife.

"You know, bullying college kids doesn't make you tough," he said. "Pick someone your own size." No answer. He hadn't expected one. "So, bring it on. I don't have all day," he said. And it was true. He had about two minutes to finish here or he'd be late for his appointment. And he couldn't go there with a bloody lip and a torn shirt either.

The three men moved forward in a rough line. He stepped forward to meet them. The guy with the machete lunged at him, swinging his weapon back, aiming for the intruder's arm. But the stranger was faster. His boot drove right through the man's knee. Smashing the kneecap, tearing through the joint, pulverising the ligaments, knocking him into a howling mess on the ground, his leg twisted at an impossible angle.

Even before the thug hit the ground, the stranger had sidestepped to face the second man who was coming at him with his knife. His body erupted in a quick flurry of moves to take down the thug. First, he whipped his head back, to avoid the sharp edge of the blade coming at him. Then a powerful uppercut to the goon's jaw with his left fist, while his right hand grabbed his wrist, forcing him to drop the knife. Then a kick to the thug's knees brought the man tumbling face down to the ground.

The newcomer kicked the knife away from the man, pivoting to face the third attacker who was rushing forward with a raised cricket stump. He greeted the attacker with a vicious head-butt to the face, sending him staggering back with dazed eyes, blood flooding out of his nose. Turning tail, the goon ran off through the trees.

The stranger turned to the first two. A professional did not leave his enemy soldiers in fighting shape. He kicked out and broke the wrist that had wielded the machete. Another kick splintered the other goon's ankle.

One minute in all. The avenging hero saw that Mottai was still unconscious and turned to face the leader. The man was fumbling at his waist belt, pulling out a pistol. Still confident that he would win. He bared his stained teeth in a grin as he raised it, savouring the thought of bringing down the intruder. He extended his arm to point the gun at the stranger's face.

But the stranger was no longer where he had been a few seconds back. He had barrelled forward, lashing out with a vicious chop at the man's gun hand. The gun boomed. The shot went wide, the muzzle blast blinding him. The stranger continued forward, crashing into the goon with his shoulder, sending him and the gun flying in opposite directions. As the thug crashed to the ground, the man kicked him, a solid blow to the side of his head. He followed up with a kick guaranteed to break his ribs. The gang leader gasped and spluttered, racked with blinding flashes of pain.

The newcomer looked for the gun, moved to pick it up. A country pistol. He crushed the barrel under his foot, making sure no one used this gun again. He looked up, dusted off his shirt, patted down his hair. Nodded to the dazed spectators.

"Take care then," he said, striding off the way he came.

3

Kat had just returned to college from a crazy summer vacation in Puducherry, some 160 km from Chennai. Annamalai, her father, was away most of the time in the Middle East, managing his business deals. Her mother, Shyamala, began and ended her day searching for a bridegroom for her daughter. She networked with friends and relatives and pored over endless matrimonial websites. Looking for a man with a fat pay cheque to cosset her daughter for the rest of her life.

"We should have got you married when you finished your degree," she complained. "But you wouldn't listen. You had to go to Chennai for your Master's. Now you're in your second year, and all the best boys are gone."

She makes it sound like a clearance sale, thought Kat. *Unless you go to the showroom on the first day, you will be left with the cast-offs.* Kat hated her mother's insistence that the groom should be wealthy, which was why she kept coming up with the weirdest of options. Like Gopi Boy, for instance.

"15 lakhs a year in his own business, Kathoo. He hires out vehicles for funerals," said Shyamala.

"First you saddle me with a name like 'Kathyayani', then shorten it to 'Kathoo'. Now you want me to marry an undertaker?" Kat gnashed her teeth. She read out the details from the website. "His name is Gopi Boy. What kind of name is that? He looks like 'Bheem Boy, Bheem Boy' in Kamal Hassan's movie. What's his weight? 100 tons?"

"Look, he's sent a video." Shyamala said as she clicked on the link.

Kat watched in morbid fascination as Bheem Boy did his version of 'Show and Tell'. Pumping weights, displaying his car, bedroom, kitchen, the row of hearses standing ready for people to die, his mother. He flashed his teeth to mark each new scene. Some 45 teeth, bleached a bright white.

"What's with his teeth, ma?" whispered Kat. "Do you think they glow in the dark?"

Shyamala glanced at her face and quickly clicked on the 'Decline' button before moving on to the next prospect.

"How about this one Kathoo? Citibank. Three lakhs a month."

'Kathoo' read out the man's specifications for the bride. "Must look like Kareena and dance like Katrina? Did he even look at his own face? Shut this down, ma. Now."

Kat was growing tired of the process. And her mother's belief that money could gloss over a multitude of faults. But what was she to do? She did not want to hurt her mother when she was trying so hard to find the best man for her daughter. And she herself had not been able to find that special someone.

"Ma, why don't we take a break from this for a while? Maybe I'm destined to have a love marriage," she said. Her mother began to sob. *God, she keeps bringing on the histrionics like Kirron Kher in 'Devdas' or 'Main Hoon Na'. But with Tamil sub titles.*

"Girls your age in our family are all married," said Shyamala. "Your cousin Anjali...."

Kat knew this one by heart. "She married the man aunty chose for her. She had 2.5 children the next year...."

"Only two children Kathoo," her mother protested. "Two years apart."

"Her husband is vice president at Pepsi. Bought a big apartment in Besant Nagar," Kat continued the recitation. And then slipped in the clincher: "Do you know the man hugs all the pretty girls in sight?"

"What? He hugs girls?"

"Yes, ma. He hit on me at Babloo's wedding. Made a total ass of himself."

"I have to tell Anjali at once," said her mother. "Ask her to get the apartment transferred to her name."

Kat had to laugh. *Show me the money.*

An uneasy silence prevailed in the house over the next few days. Shyamala realised that Kat would rebel if she pushed too hard. Her little girl was beginning to have very strong opinions about things and was not afraid to express them.

And then, just one week before she had to return to college, Shyamala made a last ditch effort, setting her up on a date with Gajendran. "No profile, Kathoo. Just go meet him. His father owns GG Silks," she said.

"What's he studied? Does he smoke? You know I hate smokers."

"Ask him yourself. Even if he smokes, you can make him stop, no?" Shyamala was insistent. "If this comes through, we don't have to spend one paisa on sarees. Maybe they have a jewellery store too."

"So how will I know him when I meet him? I don't know what he looks like." *Just let me get this over with,* she thought. *And then I'm off to college again.*

"Don't worry. He saw your picture and is dying to meet you. Just make sure you wear a silk saree."

This was too much for Kat. "You know nothing about this man. He could be a drunken fool or a rapist for all you know. And you want me to deck myself up in a silk saree?" She kept her voice low but her expression said it all.

"Okay, okay," said her mother, backing down. "Wear what you want. As long as you meet him. Please Kathoo, do this for me."

"Yes ma," said Kat. "But listen. This is absolutely the last date you're setting up for me. I have my own plans for my future and am not going to get married to some ass just to please you."

So here she was in the restaurant, dressed defiantly in casual pants and T-shirt. The idiot was already half an hour late and she was damned if she was going to wait any longer. She pushed back her chair, ready to leave.

"Hello." The rough voice made her jump. She looked up and saw a no-neck monster with a bullet-shaped head and a mouthful of *paan*-stained teeth, standing inches from her. Her first reaction was to scream, but she controlled herself with difficulty.

"Gajendran," he said, as if he was a bus conductor announcing a stop.

"He's not coming?" she asked, though she already knew the answer.

"I am Gajendran," he said as he dropped into the chair opposite her. "We'll order?" She recoiled as she took in the total picture. His shirt was white with bright swirls in red and yellow, and he was wearing shiny blue jeans with metal embellishments. The top buttons of his shirt were left open, revealing a hairy chest. His voice was loud and uncouth. His mouth moved as he read the menu. And he seemed totally unaware that everyone in the restaurant was looking at him and laughing. She was embarrassed to be seen with him and wondered if she should simply get up and leave. Or fake a heart attack.

Does ma know? she wondered. *Can she be such a complete wretch? Why do I keep ending up with Tom, Dick and Harry when I'm looking for tall, dark and handsome? Tom the terrible, Dick the dick and Harry the... well, hairy.*

She ordered a sandwich, something she could push around on her plate for a few minutes before getting up to leave. The man was unperturbed, ordering course after course and eating with both hands, a sight she found strangely fascinating.

"You should eat more," he told her. "I like girls with big figure. Like Namitha."

And why should I care, you hippo?

Fried rice. Butter chicken. *Naan.* Roast potato. *Ras malai.* Ice cream. Kat was stunned at the size of the man's stomach. And his ego. He talked non-stop about his successes. The combined turnover of two showrooms. His 'phoren' cars. His trips to 'You-rope'. The girls who wanted to marry him. The actresses he'd dated.

"Shall we go on a drive? To get to know you better," he leered, after he'd burped a few times. Kat had a splitting headache and insisted on being dropped home. But he had other ideas. He parked on a deserted road and then leaned over to pull her close and kiss her.

Kat saw the horrible face coming nearer. "Bastard," she screamed and pushed him away. He fell back at the unexpected attack, banging his head on the steering wheel. She jumped out of the car and ran down the nearest alley. She cowered there, hearing his car take off. She then hurried to the main road and hailed a cab idling at a hotel entrance.

Never again, she swore. She would never trust her mother again. She would find a guy for herself or stay single. She'd be a hotshot script writer in a couple of years. She could take care of herself — like her friend Lolita. Did Lolita care about anyone? She lived her life the way she wanted to. And to hell with everyone else.

4

Lolita was at BigBen's. The mega store prided itself on having the latest in everything from around the world. Electronic items, couture, furniture, jewellery. The lighting was subdued and warm. Spotlights in the ceiling shone down on imported mannequins draped in expensive designer clothes. The assistants were soft-footed, unobtrusive. The jewellery counters were lined with velvet, displaying exquisite creations in gold and silver.

Lolita tried on a pair of pretty earrings and looked at herself in the mirror. With her straight dark hair, porcelain skin and hazel eyes, she looked like she'd come straight off a 'Welcome to Italy' poster. Till you noticed her snooty expression and her T-shirt which said 'I don't give a...', followed by pictures of a rat and an ass.

One of her classmates had modified Lalitha to Lolita, after the character of the girl who seduces a professor in the famous novel. This Lolita too could coax professors into giving her top marks so she could retain her scholarship. The male ones, that is. Female professors hated her guts, and her skimpy clothes.

Grow up ladies — I'm stopping at nothing, Lolita wanted to say to the disapproving hags. She moved her head from side to side, watching the diamond earrings dance. 'Don't you wish your girlfriend was hot like me?' she hummed under her breath. *Dare I pocket this? No, not now. The assistant is looking right at me.* She put the earrings back on the counter and walked away.

'The face of an angel and the body of a slut.' That's what a guy had said about her on Facebook. She didn't care. He could have added 'the hands of a sorcerer', for that was true too. Her dexterity helped her shoplift without anyone noticing: a skill she found invaluable in her struggle to survive. The nuns in her school would be horrified if they found out that this was what she had learnt from the book on card tricks that Mother Superior had given her one Christmas.

The reason she'd come to the store today was because of an email she had received, saying that she'd won a gift hamper of cosmetics. A promotion from the store's fashion club. But some idiot had goofed. The store assistants had no idea what she was talking about. Her trip would be a waste of time.... Or maybe not.

She moved to the costume jewellery counter. *Oooh — this chain looks great. With all those pretty-coloured stones. Costs a bomb though.*

She couldn't afford any of the stuff here. Then why did she come? It was just that everything here was so perfect. Making her feel she could solve all her problems if she just had this awesome shirt, or that sexy perfume. Moreover, she had a reputation to keep up. She'd told the girls that she had rich parents in the US. She needed to parade a few expensive gifts they were supposed to have sent.

She'd pulled off the heist easily last month, when everyone, including the sales girls, had been busy gawking at her pretty friends. Minx had tried out exotic perfumes. "Mmm — I love it! But is it too expensive?"

Kat had yearned for a tube of deep red lipstick. "Maybe I'll wear it when my mother's not around."

Moti worried if a new eye shadow would suit her dusky complexion and ranted about the guy who'd asked her if she'd tried 'Fair & Lovely'.

And while they chattered, Lolita made her move. She had set her sights on a charming pearl bracelet, thinking it would look amazing on her wrist. A rush of adrenaline had overwhelmed her rational brain. Her hand flashed forward to pick up the bracelet and slide it into her pocket in one smooth move. She had managed to get away without arousing suspicion, taking a deep breath of relief when they made it outside without being stopped.

And today, could she repeat her success? Would she be able to pull it off when her friends were not around for cover? What if she were caught? The cops would handcuff her, parade her through the mall. She'd be dismissed from college. Her friends would shrink from her. Then the police station, fingerprinting, jail. Her one escape route to a normal life closed forever.

She took one step away from the jewellery counter. Then she returned, unable to resist. The earrings and necklaces were suspended from the branches of silver-painted jewellery trees. She chose several pairs of earrings, tried them on and left them scattered on the counter. These were small in size and easily hidden. The sales girl would probably keep her eye on them. She then pulled out a few random chains and bead necklaces, tried them on, and dropped them in a messy pile.

She had noticed that the sales girl at this counter was sloppy. Busy making gooey eyes at the young assistant at the counter across the aisle, when she should have been putting the discarded items back in their places. Now the sales girl moved away to attend to an overdressed, middle-aged woman who wanted to see an expensive piece locked under the counter.

It was now or never. Lolita's heart pounded. She felt hot eyes burning her back. She looked around casually. No, no one was watching. She'd already checked out the security cameras and worked out the angles. She knew how to use her body to shield her actions. Her hand flashed. The chain with the pretty stones disappeared into her pocket. If someone caught her, she'd pretend to be astonished. Look puzzled and ask, 'How did it get in here?'

She took a few steps away. Her stomach churned. *Why am I doing this? Should I put it back?* But she could easily get caught when trying to put it back. Better to move quickly to the exit.

"Excuse me, miss!" The voice stopped her in her tracks. She turned, her heart thudding.

"Can I interest you in some perfumes?" asked the sales girl at the perfume counter. She shook her head and continued walking. *The store is big enough to bear some losses. They deserve to be ripped off for the prices they charge.* She moved swiftly through the lingerie section, and collided with a wall of stone. She looked up and gasped.

5

The man was stunning, like a Spanish movie star. A tanned, craggy face. Five o'clock shadow at noon. Long, thick hair and a body she would like to see more of, dressed in a smart pair of jeans and pale blue shirt. The man was sizing her up too, his eyes so piercing she knew he would cut through her lies. Her forehead felt clammy. *What does he want? Did he see me stealing?*

"Good evening! I'm Aryan, the manager here. Hope you like the stuff in our store."

"Yes, yes I do," she stammered.

"I saw you checking the jewellery. Find anything you like?"

Is this a trap? Should I tell him I am thinking of buying the chain? But how would I explain hiding it in my pocket? Maybe she should take control. "Actually, there's something you can help me with," she said, taking out her cell phone and showing him the email she'd received. "No one here seems to know about this free hamper that I was promised."

Aryan checked the email and apologised for the mix-up. "I'll definitely look into the matter," he said. When he stepped aside, Lolita took a deep breath and exited the store. *What was that about? Was he suspicious or am I being paranoid? What the hell have I gotten myself into?*

****

Moti was still in her village, wishing she had not come home during the college vacation and had chosen to visit one of her friends' homes instead. She hated her father and her surname — Motwani. The idiots in college had shortened this to Moti or Fat Girl. No one now remembered that her first name was Siya.

She stared at her reflection in the mirror. She was wearing one of her usual earth-coloured kurtas. Loose clothes, chunky beads, bracelets... none of these succeeded in drawing attention away from her plump figure. Add to this her dark skin and husky voice and her cup of sorrow was full to the brim. No wonder her father was desperate to get her married to that lout Balwan.

"Who will marry this fat girl?" he had shouted at her mother. "Balwan wants her. And I want to keep the business in the family. That's why I got our Seema married to his *bhai*."

Moti was hopping mad as she heard him from the next room. *Is he a Tata or an Ambani? He has a small business selling bricks and tiles. And his wonderful partners Balwan and Bittu are running the business into the ground. Drunkards.*

"But Balwan is not a good man. He went to jail for beating a girl. And he's 12 years older than our daughter." Her mother was trying to save her daughter from a fate similar to hers. She was a sad shell of a woman, who had never left her village, not even seen Nagpur, just 50 km away.

"What? Arguing? Going to run away like your daughter? Slut."

Moti heard loud slaps and her mother's cries. She rushed into the room and stood between him and her mother. "Stop it, papa. Why are you beating her? Yes. I ran away from this hell. And I made a stupid mistake coming back."

Her father raised his hand to hit her. His cell phone rang. "I have to go see Bhaiyya," he said when he disconnected the call.

"He's sinking fast. I'll come back and deal with you." He pushed past her, dragging his wife with him.

Why did I come now? wondered Moti. *How foolish to expect my father to have changed in a year.*

She'd run away the previous year when her father had fixed her marriage date. She'd stolen the money they'd set aside for her wedding as well as her few jewels, boarded the Tamil Nadu Express, stayed awake the entire night in a crowded compartment, and arrived at Chennai's Central Station 17 hours later. By then, her mother had found her letter, cried the entire day, and prayed to her gods. Clutching her meagre belongings and using her broken English, Moti had found her way to the house of the only person she knew in the city. A friend who'd moved here the previous month and promised to help her. The girl's father had pitched in to arrange a scholarship for Moti through the Lions Club. Soon after that, the friend left for her own college in Manipal. And Moti set off in an auto to SS Padmaja College, her home for the next two years.

She got off at the college gates, clutching her battered suitcase. Her hair was in two tight plaits and she was dressed in one of her good salwars. Or so she'd thought till she saw the other girls in short skirts, skinny jeans and scrunched tops, jabbering away in English.

The campus was huge. A large sprawling building in the middle with shiny marble steps. Other big buildings around a central quadrangle. A marble fountain with water dribbling over a mermaid and plump cherubs. *The marble looks greenish*, she thought, *as if it could do with some scrubbing.*

Where do I go now? Can anyone here speak Hindi? She could speak very little English though she could understand it to a fair extent. She had been really lucky to get in through the 'reserved' category. She saw some older people shepherding their wards and guessed that these were parents of the new students. She followed them into a huge hall with counters and long queues in front of each. *Which one now?*

A girl stumbled against her, dropping her papers on the floor. "Sorry," she smiled up at Moti as she crouched to pick them up. Moti bent down to help her, happy to see a friendly face.

"First day?" asked the girl.

"Yes."

"Come, let's stand in line," said the girl, leading the way to the farthest queue. The queue moved forward in fits and starts. When Moti produced her certificates, the surly clerk told her she needed to submit notarised copies. Moti was flummoxed.

"I don't have," she stammered. "Where to get? Help?"

"If I have to help you and the two hundred students behind you, I'll be here till next year's admissions. Get out of the way and let the others register."

"But, but...," Moti's eyes filled with tears.

The clerk revelled in his temporary powers and was happy to find someone who could not talk back. He turned the screws further. "We're closing in an hour. If you don't get it by then, you'll go to the bottom of the waiting list. There are so many students eager for the seat. I can't hold it for you."

I'll lose my seat? After this entire struggle? Where will I go? Moti's stomach churned. *I can't go back to the life I ran from. I'll kill myself rather than get married to that drunkard and have his children.*

And then the girl she'd spoken to earlier, standing behind her in the queue, stepped forward.

"You can't dump her because she doesn't have some copies," she told the clerk. Her voice was loud and clear, her mouth set in firm lines. "I'll raise hell if you try anything like that. I've noted your name and will track you down even if you've closed the counter. You'd better wait till I come back with her notarised documents or I'll raise a stink."

She completed her registration and then took Moti with her to get the signatures necessary to complete her admission process. When it was all done, she went with her to the canteen and got her a cup of coffee. "By the way, my name is Kat," she said. "I think we're going to be great friends."

Kat wangled a room for Moti right next to hers in the hostel and helped her settle down. She took her under her wing, tutoring her in English, taking her shopping at inexpensive stores, and treating her to a flattering hair-cut. The two girls became inseparable, watching Rajini movies as well as '3 Idiots' and 'Delhi Belly' again and again.

A year had flown by. Then Moti had made her ill-advised trip home to meet her mother, only to realise that nothing had changed. Her father was still the tyrant, willing to sacrifice his daughter to keep his business cronies happy.

Moti had fallen into a deep sleep after her father left to visit his sick brother. A fierce knocking on the door woke her up. She staggered to her feet, assuming that her father was back home with her mother. She opened the door.

Balwan. With red eyes and a whisky bottle in his hand. She tried to slam the door shut. And failed.

6

Balwan shoved her inside, bolted the door and grabbed her.

"What are you doing? Get out! Papa is not here," she shouted.

"I know *pyaari*," he replied. "Your papa told me you would be all alone. And I could make use of my property." He laughed, showing his jagged teeth. She gagged at his sour breath.

"Is he a pimp?" she screamed. "Don't you dare touch me or I'll scream." She yanked herself free and retreated till her knees hit the bed. He lurched forward and pushed her onto the bed and rolled on top of her. His rank sweat made her retch. His slobbering lips moved across her cheek towards her mouth. She shoved him away, lashing out with a vicious kick to his groin. He fell back, wheezing in pain. She ran to the door and fumbled with the bolt. He grabbed her from behind, turned her around and punched her in the face. One huge paw grabbed her by the throat, while the other ripped her salwar.

"You are asking for this, aren't you?" he said. "Once I show you I'm the master, you will behave. Or you can burn yourself to a pile of ashes like Bela. I don't care."

Bela? The sweet fifteen-year-old had committed suicide two years back. Was it because this monster had raped her? Moti's vision dimmed as he choked her. She would not give up. She would find a way to hit back. She made desperate arcs with her hand, hoping to find something she could use as a weapon. There was something behind her. She grabbed it, brought it up and forward in a vicious arc. It hit his temple with a crack. She saw that it was the walking stick her father used when his rheumatism got bad.

He dropped like an ox, blood gushing from the deep cut on his forehead. The metal casing on the tip of the stick had slashed him. She gasped for air and crouched, drenched in sweat, ready to hit him again if he tried to attack. He didn't budge. She bent down to see if his chest moved. She could not be sure. Her heart thudded. Her vision blurred. She felt like throwing up. What if she had killed him? She had to get away. Now. But first, she must get her things. Her purse and cell phone. What else? She closed her eyes tight, opened them again. Then she stepped around the body on the ground, looking at it with horror.

Time passed in a haze. She finally emerged on the dirt track leading out of her village, carrying her airbag over her shoulder. *Please God, let me catch the last bus out of town. And make it to college without getting caught.*

****

Back in college, the doors of the Principal's office opened to admit a visitor. The man was six-foot tall, lean and toned, clad in an impeccable shirt, trousers and tie.

"Vir Pradyumna," he said, extending his hand. "Though I go by the name Vir. Folks back in the US couldn't quite handle the full version."

"Of course, of course," nodded Belliappa, the Principal of Padmaja College as he shook Vir's hand. "Please sit down. Will you have some Coke or coffee?"

"I'd love some coffee," said Vir. "Tastes so much better than the swill they serve in the States."

The Principal's belly wobbled as he chuckled. Vir tried hard not to stare. The man's body seemed a mere prop for the huge belly, covered by a hideous striped shirt. He sat behind his massive desk, with his hands folded over his stomach, looking at his visitor with protruding fish eyes. A few files, two phones and framed pictures decorated his desk. The walls of the room were plastered with more pictures, of Belliappa greeting the President, various Chief Ministers and celebrities. *Like a pizza place in Times Square,* thought Vir. There was a teakwood shelf behind the desk, with huge tomes lined up in height order. *Are there any pages inside those shells?* he wondered. The books looked pristine, untouched by human hands.

The peon entered in response to the Principal's buzzer. "Get Sir some good coffee from Iyengar's Coffee, not the sugar syrup from the canteen," he told him. And then to Vir: "I've travelled everywhere — US, Europe, Russia. This doctorate is from Romania, for my outstanding contribution to education." He turned a framed certificate on his desk towards the visitor. *One of those sham institutions which sell degrees no doubt,* thought Vir.

The Principal continued his boasting. "The College Board was very happy that I agreed to take up this position. I do what I can. So many impressionable young minds to mould!"

Vir nodded with a smile. *That's not what my research turned up. Didn't you pay a few crores for the post? And recoup your investment and then some, at admission time?*

"Now tell me how I can help you," Belliappa said, satisfied that the man was suitably impressed.

"I'd like to submit a proposal to start a new Master's course in criminology and forensic sciences at your college, sir. As you know, many top universities in the United States offer this already. Maryland at College Park, SUNY-Albany, Penn State. There is a growing demand for criminologists to tackle the challenges facing law enforcement today. We need to create professionals in criminal justice policies, forensic pathology, blood splatter analysis, DNA analysis, ballistics. Train them to tackle cyber crimes like hacking, financial theft, espionage, copyright and privacy issues. I'm talking to several top colleges in Chennai on this, including IIT Madras."

"IIT, IIT. Our college is the best and the biggest. We are leaders in placements, infrastructure and faculty. When will you people see beyond IIT?"

When you stop selling your seats for money, I guess. Looks like I hit a nerve there, Belliappa.

The Principal continued his diatribe. "You NRIs have your head in the clouds. But in India, parents will not admit their children in new-fangled programmes. They want them to become engineers, doctors, programmers. The Board won't approve your course either. Please understand — here, we are not like America."

The man opposite him remained unruffled. *Plan B then,* he thought. He shrugged and stood up to leave. "You're right, of course, sir. Thank you for setting me straight. I'd thought of compensating you for your guidance, but...." He turned to the door.

"What... what kind of compensation?"

Vir stopped. *Just as I thought.* He turned back to face the Principal.

"Not a whole lot. A few lakhs, maybe ten for starters."

"Please sit down. Maybe I should help you. I feel bad that you've come all the way from the US...."

Vir smiled as he took his seat. *Will you walk into my parlour, said the spider to the fly.*

The peon came in with the coffee. Belliappa pounced on him. "How much time to get one coffee, man?"

"There's some fighting sir. Some man from outside hitting our students. Boys hurt badly, sir."

"An outsider?" asked the Principal. "I've been telling the Board we need to have proper security. Where is Hari? Call him." He turned to Vir, saying, "You see how it is. Managing students is very difficult. Not like before."

"So many thousands of them. Even checking their attendance must be tough, I'd think."

"Yes, they ask friends to give them proxy attendance. Rascals."

Hari came in while Vir was making a request. "Before I take my leave, could I take a tour of your campus facilities, sir?" he asked.

"I'll see if I can find one of my staff members," said Belliappa.

"How about one of your students, sir? It'll help me see things from their perspective. This girl looks capable." He pointed to the group photograph on the Principal's desk featuring several glum students and one beaming principal. *Like a Hardy surrounded by Laurels,* he thought.

"Well that's Kathyayani. She's in charge of the upcoming culturals. Hari, see if you can find her and then come back to see me."

Vir was happy. *Piece of cake. What a gullible dude. Did all the work himself. All it took was some flattery....*

Kat was in fact already in the office building. She had been busy comforting the newbies, reassuring them after their ragging encounter with Jambu. She had taken the girls to their hostel and retrieved the sports jacket from the girl who'd been assaulted. The jacket had an Armani label. She'd better leave it in the Lost Property office, in case the man came looking for it. But the door was locked. She turned back, wondering what to do, when she was intercepted by Hari.

"The Principal wants to see you," he said.

What did I do? she asked herself. Had someone seen her at the fight that evening? But she had only tried to save a new girl. The Principal couldn't pull her up for that. Or maybe he wanted to ask her why she hadn't reported the incident. Her thoughts were chaotic as she knocked on the door of the office and entered.

"I want you to take our visitor round our campus," the Principal said to her. "Show him our excellent facilities."

The visitor set down his coffee cup, stood up and turned. She looked up at his face as he towered over her. Blood rushed to her head. Her mouth fell open.

7

It was the man whose jacket she was clutching in her hand.

She was aware that the Principal was saying something but couldn't make out the words.

"Hi, I'm Vir," he said, shaking her hand. Kat's heart was pounding so loudly she thought he must be able to hear it. *Thump. Thump. Thump.* She heard Rihanna singing "Hey boy, I really wanna be with you."

He smiled. *A perfect smile, reaching all the way to his eyes,* she thought. *A square jaw with a cleft.* She had noticed his powerful body earlier when he'd demolished the goons.

"This is Kathyayani," said the Principal.

"Kathyayani ... an unusual name," said Vir. "It suits you," he added, looking directly into her eyes. *Reminds me of Vidya Balan in that film I saw in New York. Parineeta — that's it. The shy and lovely Indian woman. Lustrous hair. Big expressive eyes.*

"May I?" he asked, extending his hand to take his jacket.

"Yes, of course," stuttered Kat, handing it over.

Belliappa's head was swivelling from one to the other, watching the interplay. "Your coat? How did she get it?"

Kat's eyes widened. *I can't get him into trouble for saving us. What do I say?*

"Miss Kathyayani thought I looked like a terrorist. She took my jacket away to check," he said.

"No, of course not....," she stammered.

"Just kidding," said Vir. "She was kind enough to clean it for me. The crows on your campus are very well-fed," he smiled. "And have deadly aim."

The Principal did not have patience to unravel this. "So, let's meet again soon, Vir," he said, standing up to indicate that the meeting was over.

"Shall we?" asked Vir to her, gesturing towards the door. As they stepped out of the office, Kat noted the way he moved. Light on his feet, like a boxer. She realised she had no clue who he was or what he wanted to see.

But she had something to clear up first. "My friends call me Kat," she said.

"A pleasure meeting you again, Kathyayani," he repeated. She glared.

"What does BB want me to show you? Who are you? I mean...." She stopped. *Did I sound rude?*

"BB?" he enquired.

"Big Belly — our principal. Oops!"

"Don't worry. Your secret dies with me." His grin flashed.

He's as hot as Edward, she thought. That was Edward Cullen, the vampire who vied with the werewolf Jacob Black for the love of Bella, in the 'Twilight' fantasy series. Kat had read all the books several times and watched the movies too. She loved the way Bella took on terrible foes to protect the people she cared for.

"Have you had yourself checked for fugue?" Vir's voice broke into her thoughts.

"What?"

"You know — fugue? The dreamlike state you enter when you lose your memory?"

"I know what the word means!" she snapped, though she had no clue. "I don't have to be checked for anything."

They had now emerged from the building and entered the quadrangle with the fountain.

"You want to see our campus? What exactly?" She tried to get her act together.

"Maybe we should do this some other day. I don't think we want to encounter our friend the goon, right? What's his name? How's he allowed to run tame like this?" asked Vir.

"That's Jambu. His father owns Jambu Distilleries. He's the money behind the college."

"But still, I'd think someone would put him down. Like a rabid animal."

"Doesn't happen that easily. Ragging is much too common this time of the year," she said. "The victims are too scared to complain. And everyone pretends it's not happening — unless someone dies."

His cell phone rang and he excused himself to answer it.

"Sure, of course." He sounded delighted. "Dinner at eight tonight at the Taj Connemara. Count me in," he said. Taking a few steps away, he continued talking in a soft voice.

Is it his girlfriend? He seems mighty kicked. But how does it matter to me? I just met him and don't know anything about him. Could be a serial killer for all I know. I must stop behaving like a stupid heroine in a stupid romance.

He came back towards her, took a look at her face and said, "Yes, my briefs have pink bunny rabbits on them. Always bunny rabbits."

"What?" her eyes flew to his face. "I didn't ask about, about...."

"You didn't? My bad," he chuckled. He put out his hands in front, palms raised. A gesture of peace. "Sadly, I have to rush off now. Can we meet up again soon? Here's my card."

He jotted down her cell phone number, shook her hand and walked briskly away.

Kat stood staring at his receding back. *Seems in a hurry all the time. Maybe he's brought his girlfriend to meet his parents. Wonder what she's like. A French babe with an accent and a slinky body. Or a Swedish blonde with rosebud lips and high cheekbones. Or maybe an Indian American who cooks a mean kabab and biriyani. And what does he mean talking about his briefs? Patronising ass! He thinks I've fallen for his dimpled charm.*

8

Moti had managed to catch the last bus to Nagpur after leaving Balwan senseless on the floor.

She barely remembered the long journey to Chennai as she relived the horror of the encounter. Back in college, she kept wondering how long it would be before the police tracked her down and arrested her. Then she would be charged with murder and thrown into a prison cell with killers and thieves.

She began to look haunted, unable to eat or sleep, jumping at every sound. Kat saw how disturbed she was and persuaded her to confide in her. The story came out in bits and pieces, leaving Moti drained and in tears. Kat was horrified at what she heard but pulled herself together to reassure her friend, telling her she and her parents would help if the cops came for Moti.

But when a week passed without incident, Moti began to hope that she was safe. Perhaps Balwan had been merely stunned and managed to limp away, ashamed to tell the world that he had been knocked down by a girl. Or maybe he'd given up on her and found someone nearer at hand to torture.

She was now on her way to their hideout, an abandoned shed deep in the thicket behind her hostel, with her classmates Minx and Deepika. Kat had found this shed when she'd dragged her friends with her to rescue a kitten she'd heard in the bushes. They had not found the kitten, but stumbled on a place where they could relax and gossip about the latest happenings in college.

Lolita was already there, smoking inside the shed, lounging in her torn jeans and a T-shirt printed with a raised middle finger.

"I can smell smoke. Who is smoking here?" The warden's loud voice startled her. Lolita darted outside to stub out her cigarette. Moti and the others came out of hiding, doubled over with laughter.

"You're just too good Moti," said Deepika. Moti had imitated the warden's voice to perfection.

"So it was you?" screeched Lolita, jumping on Moti and shaking her. "Fool, I wasted a good smoke."

"Don't get historical," said Moti.

"That's hysterical, you moron," said Lolita as she started laughing too.

"You know, I saw the warden sneaking out through a gap in the fence to meet her boyfriend," said Deepika.

"Who? Bhadrakali?" Moti's jaw dropped. The warden was a hated figure, as are most wardens, and they got back at her by mocking her heavy use of *kajal* and red lipstick. Moti couldn't imagine anyone wanting to date the warden and wondered if it was another of Deepika's tall tales. The girl was a terrible gossip and they were afraid to say anything in front of her. God knows which of their secrets she had already ferreted out.

Deepika was chattering away on another topic already, telling Lolita about the fight she'd missed that afternoon in the college canteen.

Amar, Subu and Rakesh were a trio of nerds who called themselves 'Asuras', putting together the first letters of their names. They were forever lurking online, and sending sleazy IMs and friend-invites on Facebook. They downloaded pirated software and porn and were always playing games on a network of computers in their rooms. Kat swore that she smelled them before she saw them: booze, cigarettes, sweat-stained clothes.

Amar had ragged Moti, making a rude joke about her appearance. "She's the missing link between apes and men," he'd said.

Moti had winced, but Minx, who was with her, turned to swear at him. Rakesh threw a Coke can into the metal dustbin behind her and cackled when the clatter made her jump.

"Are you scared? Do you want to hold my hand? Or anything else?" he asked.

And that was enough to rouse the sleeping Minx. Soft and pretty on the outside, her mouth was like an AK47 spewing venom. "Were you up all night to come up with that one, creep?" she pounced on him.

"Why are you fighting for Moti? Is she your friend? Or *girl*friend?" Subu chipped in.

"You've got to be the reason God created the middle finger," snapped Minx, flipping him one.

Rakesh moved closer. The group hunted in a pack, like hyenas. "Come on now, whisper those three little words to me. You know you want to," he said.

"Go. Fuck. Yourself."

"Oooh," hooted the boys.

Minx turned to Moti and said, "Looks like the toilet didn't flush. Let's come back later."

They stormed out. The boys exchanged high fives, proclaiming: "You don't mess with the Asuras."

Now in the hideout, Minx checked her laptop and saw a message from Rakesh. "Are you a 34 or a 32 pretending to be 34? Or should we check your bra?" She swore and showed the message to Moti.

But when she really thought about it, she realised that college was so much better than home, despite all these creeps. "I get far fewer lectures here than I get from Sushil and his mother Kanta," she told Moti.

"Your boyfriend Sushil?" Deepika was agog. The girls sat back, ready to enjoy one of Minx's nasty take-offs.

"Well, Kanta aunty has a bad case of verbal diarrhoea," said Minx. "Did I tell you how she ranted when she found out I'm moving from Delhi to Chennai?"

"Minaxi, what is this college shollege in Chennai?" Kanta aunty had asked.

"It's only for two years aunty," Minx had replied politely. *Why don't you go chase your own tail, you nag?* she'd thought.

"I was hoping to hold my grandson before I die," Kanta said next.

"Of course you will Aunty," she replied. *So am I a vending machine for babies?* Wasn't it enough that her own mother had her breast-beating sessions? About Madrasis, their food, their climate, living in a hostel, leaving Sushil?

Her mother viewed Sushil as a 'catch' on the matrimonial market. He was a TV reporter after all, with his own show and tons of money left by a wealthy father. But Minx did not like his playboy reputation and his dominating nature. He kept insisting that she stay in Delhi adulating him, if there was even such a word. And when she refused to listen to his objections, he'd tried to make her jealous.

"You know, I've been asked to get married over a hundred times," he'd said.

"Yeah, but your mother doesn't count," she'd replied.

"Don't think I'll wait for you. Lots of hot girls are dying to date me."

"Well, I've got one for you. But the zoo's refusing to let her out," she'd snapped.

And that was the end of that conversation.

She had dreaded a renewal of all the whining when she went to Delhi at the end of the first year. But luckily it was a lot quieter this time. Her annoying younger sister Arpita had gone to Kashmir on an excursion. Her father, a school headmaster, seemed to be working late almost every day. Even her mother was strangely silent.

Until one day when the dam broke. It seemed Dad had decided to get the spotlight on himself with his midlife crisis. This particular one was an Anglo-Indian girl named Lily who was a junior teacher in his school. The dour older man had seen this young thing looking at him with admiration, seeking his help to fill in tax returns and choose courses to further her career. Used to leading a drab, conventional life with a stolid wife, the man found the attentions of the young girl in a skirt as cataclysmic as moving from Jagjit Singh to Justin Bieber. Now the hours that he should have devoted to his thesis on 'Development of special cryogenics for dark matter experiments' were diverted to wooing Lily.

Soon, evidence of his dalliance mounted. Unexplained absences, receipts for hotels and jewellery, and a new interest in combing his scanty hair over the bald patch on his head. And in the true tradition of Hindi movie mothers, Minx's mother had cried into her dupatta and not spoken a word to her husband.

So, luckily for Minx, and not so luckily for her family, her mother was not so obsessed with her. The nagging disappeared and Minx took advantage of the break. She came back refreshed, ready to take on the Asuras, and the Devas if need be.

Her cell phone beeped. It was Kat.

9

The event that would turn their lives upside down had taken place earlier that day, in a desolate yet picturesque corner of Chennai. Munusamy, occasional construction worker and permanent drunkard, had opened his eyes with difficulty. He had straightened his legs and heard the clatter of the whisky bottle rolling. A flock of cranes was wheeling above the shallow waters of the Adyar River. The sun was beating down on him. He grimaced and closed his eyes. His head pounded.

"Get up, you worthless fellow," the voice was insistent. Someone was shaking his shoulder. He opened his eyes again. His wife Ponni, with their toddler on her hip. "Get up. You said you'd go to work there today." She pointed to the huge building coming up across the river at MRC Nagar.

"Let me be. I have to sleep," he said, trying to draw his *lungi* over his face.

"Drunken fool. Wasting money on arrack when we don't have enough for food."

Choice abuses followed, forcing him to sit up. He had collapsed in a stupor at the foot of the Broken Bridge, his usual drinking spot. It was a kilometre from Olcott Kuppam, the slum where he lived. Ponni knew he would be there, or maybe their mongrel Karuppa had brought her. Where was the dog, he wondered. He normally stayed within a few feet of Ponni.

Karuppa, named after his dark coat, was swimming across the shallow waters in the river, carrying something in his mouth. He trotted up to them, shook his body dry, splattering them with polluted water from the river.

"Drop it Karuppa. You can't eat fish from this river. It's poisonous," Ponni scolded.

Karuppa dropped his offering at their feet. She looked at it and screamed. Munusamy's liquor-sodden brain registered what it was after a few seconds. A bloated, decomposed arm, the finger nails showing traces of red polish.

"*Aiyyo, aiyyo!* What is this?" he shouted.

A fisherman who had walked into the water to spread his nets came running up. "What? What is it?"

Two young men smoking ganja in an auto parked along the dirt track joined the group. Karuppa stood in the middle, wagging his tail, delighted with the attention. An excited discussion sprang up.

"Must be someone who killed herself in the river," said one of the young men. "Did you see anyone jump in?"

"How can you kill yourself in two feet of water? This looks like it's been soaking for a while," said the fisherman.

"Maybe the girl was murdered here," said the other young man. "Some people said they heard a *bhoot* screaming in the night."

"Call the police, you fools," said Ponni. "Let them find out if it is a suicide or murder."

One of the young men pulled out his cell phone and called the police station. "Sir, dead body sir. Broken Bridge. Come at once."

Ponni pulled Munusamy aside, whispering to him: "We have to get away. The police will harass us, asking questions as if we killed her."

She dragged him away down the track towards the slum. Karuppa picked up the sodden arm, unwilling to leave it behind. Ponni swatted him on the head and made him drop it.

Soon an Inspector arrived on his motor bike. He pushed the limb around with a stick and then made a few calls. Deputy Commissioner Reddy arrived in his jeep, bouncing through the deep channels that served as drainage canals for the slum. He sent a few cops to speak to the slumdwellers, but they came back after a perfunctory enquiry, saying no one had heard or seen anything. These people were familiar with police procedures and did not want to get involved in a long investigation.

The firemen came next, to dredge the water and look for the rest of the body. The divers struggled to sift through the sludge in the river and finally managed to pull out a corpse. There was a gasp as they realised this body had both its arms intact. There must be another body in the water. The divers plunged in again.

One more body, this too with both arms intact. The divers settled down to a long, horrific morning. Another body and yet another. A huge crowd had gathered to watch and wonder. Someone had called the TV stations. Reporters descended in full force like the jackal-headed army of Anubis. Wielding cameras, lights and blathering mouths that ran at incredible speeds. The camera vans were unable to cross the drainage canals cutting across the rough track and the crew shifted their equipment to autos that ferried them to the scene.

Senior reporters told their studios to blur the faces of the bodies as the cameras zoomed in. The tabloid press had no such concerns. *Snap. Snap. Whirr. Whirr.* The excitement mounted with each additional body dragged onto the bridge.

Pia, the livewire News1 TV reporter was struggling for words to describe the horror. She'd already run through 'macabre', 'gory', 'ghastly' and 'fiendish' to describe the scene.

"The police are shocked by the number of bodies. This is something that Chennai has never seen before. The city is conservative and the people here are known to be law-abiding," she said.

"You are right Pia," said the anchor in the studio. "Our lines are jammed with callers saying how shocked they are to hear of a serial killer here, for the first time in Chennai. This could well overtake the 19 skulls found in the Noida mass murders. Do you think Chennai will beat that record?"

"It could, of course," said Pia, looking very excited. "The stench is terrible. I can see people who came to see the bodies running away once they see the mangled faces. Or throwing up on the sands. The bodies are bloated after being in the water for a long time."

"And you were saying that they have been weighted...."

"Yes, with huge stones and scrap metal to make them stay under. And all the bodies have tattered scarves tied around their necks."

The anchor nodded, looking suitably solemn, as if he had secret knowledge of sinister and violent mysteries he would reveal if they kept watching.

"Very strange indeed," he intoned before switching to an interview with a guest in his studio. "We have Mr. Murthy, forensic technician, to tell us more about bodies and the stories they tell. Mr Murthy, are these corpses what you would call 'floaters'?"

"No," said Murthy. "Floaters are bodies which float to the surface after they decompose, due to the formation of gas collecting below the skin and in the body cavities. Then the bodies rise."

"How long does that take?"

"It depends on several factors such as water temperature, currents and the size of the victim. A body will float after 8-10 days in warm water and 2-3 weeks in colder water. But these bodies are not floaters and have risen to the surface only because the water level has come down."

"So, will the post-mortem reveal the cause of death and the time?"

"That depends on the state of the body. Hopefully, the body is not too damaged for forensics to provide useful information."

The camera zoomed in again to the anchor's sombre face. "We seem to have a monster in our midst," he said. "And it could be someone we know."

10

The girls had rushed into the Common Room in response to Kat's ominous message.

"You asked us to come running, to watch TV?" Minx's voice rose.

"Shut up and watch," snapped Kat.

The entire female population of the hostel seemed to be gathered in front of the television at one end of the long hall. The other end of the hall where the girls normally read magazines, played cards or ping pong, was completely deserted.

A male reporter was speaking about the day's big news. "Seven bodies have been found so far near the Broken Bridge across the Adyar River. The firemen are still digging through the slush looking for bodies. Here's Deputy Commissioner Reddy, answering our questions about this gruesome discovery."

Reddy composed his face into a ponderous mask as he faced the barrage of questions.

"Is this the work of a serial killer?" asked a reporter.

"Could be, could be," replied Reddy. His small eyes glinted as he looked at the media representatives jostling for a vantage point.

"The man has emptied a bucket of talcum powder on his face," commented one of the cameramen. The others laughed, happy to talk about anything other than the mound of rotting corpses.

"Must have dressed up for the cameras," laughed another.

"We have set up two teams to look into this and have started the process of identifying the victims," said Reddy. "The perpetrator will soon be behind bars."

The camera cut back to the studio. "Stay tuned for our continuous updates on this breaking story," said the anchor. "Coming up next, our exclusive interview with the director of 'Death Warrior 7 —Eastern Terror', the first Hollywood movie to be shot in Chennai."

One of the girls reached up to switch channels. An excited young man in a suit was midway through his 'exclusive report', again on the killings. "One of the victims has been identified as Ranjini, first year student of history in Swarnakamal College. She was reported missing two months back."

The screen filled with the face of a girl with smiling eyes and a mop of curly hair, who looked like she could still be in school. A wave of fear ran through the watching crowd. The horror had become more real when one of the bodies acquired a name and a face. The camera zoomed to the wailing face of the mother as she waited with her relatives outside the morgue. A lecturer from the victim's college said that Ranjini was a quiet, sincere girl and that it was terrible to hear about her death. Behind her stood a group of crying students who were identified as Ranjini's classmates.

"All the victims are in the age group of 17 to 25," continued the reporter. "Parents of girls who were reported missing earlier, are rushing to the morgue to find out if their daughters are among the victims. Several parents are saying that they are afraid to send their daughters to school or college. The police have asked the public to contact these phone numbers if they have any useful information." The control room numbers scrolled across the screen.

"The city is anxiously waiting for the killer to be identified and apprehended. The media is doing all it can to help the police bring these terrible murders to an end."

The camera panned to show special editions of newspapers with banner headlines. 'MONSTER ON THE LOOSE!' 'WHO IS THE LADY KILLER?' 'EXPECT MORE MURDERS!'

The channel cut to a commercial break. Someone turned off the TV and the girls gathered in groups to discuss the news in subdued voices.

"This is terrible. This could have been our college. It could have been one of us," said Minx.

"What should we do? Stop going out anywhere?" asked Kat.

"Maybe buy ourselves pepper spray. Didn't they say they were going to make these cans available to women?"

"That's not going to stop this killer. We need to take self-defence classes. Kick the guy where it hurts most," said Kat.

Minx's cell phone rang. It was her mother. "Oh God, she must have been watching the news," she said. A shrill volley of words could be heard streaming from the phone. Her mother having a panic attack. Minx moved the phone away from her ear and gestured to her friends to come listen.

"What is happening there *beti*? So far away. I told you it's not safe. But you won't listen. Tomorrow I'll see your face on TV. Then what I will do? Your father is always busy, busy. What does he care?"

She stopped mid-rant. They heard some whispering on the other side and then her sister Arpita, an obnoxious 14-year old motormouth, came on the line.

"Minx, if you get killed, can I have your GAP cardigan and top?" she asked. "Also, your Paige jeans and your fake Dior handbag?"

Minx heard the sound of a hard slap followed by a screech. Thankfully the phone went dead. Her mother had found someone closer at hand on whom to vent her angst.

"Guess someone left the cage open," said Minx. But her heart was not in it.

Kat's phone beeped. "My mother, of course," said Kat, after taking the call. "She wants to drive down to make sure I'm alright. I managed to convince her that we are all safe. She's simply got too much time on her hands."

And too much money, thought Lolita. *Poor little rich girl. She has a father rolling in money and a mother who thinks the sun rises out of her daughter's backside. And then she complains.* Lolita's mother had no TV, and might never get to hear about this. And even if she did, she couldn't afford a trip here.

11

At the other end of the city, the man was watching TV too. He could not remember how many bodies were out there now. Ten? Or was it eleven? They had missed one body he'd dumped in the Adyar River. Idiots. How many had he killed in all the cities he'd been in? He clicked through the pictures on his computer. All the girls were so pretty, so afraid. With a gag across their mouths, their eyes popping out. Dreading the horrors yet to come. Ready to do anything if he would only set them free. Anything. But he couldn't do that, could he? They had to pay for their sins, with their blood and bone and tissue. And then... then they had to die.

He checked his favourite website, to see if they had any new pictures of girls being strangled, stabbed, dismembered. The urge to kill was upon him again.

****

"May I come in sir?"

The waiter brought in a platter of butter cookies sprinkled with candied orange bits and placed it on the table along with a pot of rich dark coffee. After a refreshing session in his private Jacuzzi, Vir had been gazing down at the city from his terrace. Then he'd settled down to some TV viewing in his plush suite on the top floor of the Taj Coromandel Hotel. He reminded himself that he had to get an apartment on rent soon, perhaps a service apartment; or he'd get a whopping hotel bill. But with all the hours he'd been putting in at work, he had not found the time.

The serial killer was top of the news on national TV as well, with the channels putting their big guns on the job. Ujwal Taneja, the head of News1 TV, was hectoring Deputy Commissioner Reddy in Chennai. He was notorious for his interview tactics, which were modelled on the attack patterns of a Rottweiler. He counted among his career bests the time when a lady Chief Minister had walked off in the middle of one of his questions, calling him several unprintable names.

"Mr. Reddy, Mr. Reddy," he was shouting now at the top of his voice till the cop stopped mid-sentence. "Is it true that the police found three other bodies earlier, killed in the same way?"

"Yes," said Reddy. "The ligature marks showed they had also been strangled with the silk scarves tied round their necks. We have been checking to see where these scarves were bought so that we can identify the killer."

"So you have known about this serial killer for some time but kept it from the public?"

"We have been pursuing various leads...," Reddy started, but was again cut off.

"But didn't you file these complaints as disappearances, deliberately hiding the truth from the press? Doesn't the media have a right to know, Mr. Reddy?"

My God! Why is he riding down the main street like Clint Eastwood with all guns blazing? And why do they all shout? Vir stabbed at the remote.

The leader of the Opposition Party in Tamil Nadu, Charan Raj was being interviewed on the next channel. Vir had met him for dinner after leaving the college, as he had wanted to establish a working relationship with the CM-in-waiting. He knew how important such connections were if you wanted to operate in India.

Charan Raj was taking advantage of the mood in the city to rip into the ruling party. A consummate politician, he knew that the safety of its women folk was a major priority in every society, and particularly in this city. "Innocent young girls being killed. People living in fear. And what are the police doing?" he asked. "We demand that the government resigns today. We demand a CBI enquiry."

Vir's cell phone beeped.

"Watching the news?" asked Bishnu. "The shit's hit the fan as you can see. We need you here. How about I pick you up in ten?"

Vir got busy putting together all his notes before meeting Bishnu's team. As he selected and copied the files, his mind travelled back to the day he'd first met Bishnu, his junior by two years at Yale's Department of Psychiatry. They had bonded so well that when he moved on to College Park, Maryland, for his Master's in Criminology and Criminal Justice, Bishnu had followed suit. Those were the golden days, when Rima had been with him too. God, it still hurt to think about her.

After his studies, Vir had stayed on in the US to work with Interpol. But Bishnu was determined to join law enforcement in India. Vir had tried to dissuade him, making a last ditch effort even as he was dropping him off at the Baltimore Washington airport to catch his flight.

"So, why this patriotism? This 'back-to-the-roots' obsession?" he'd asked.

"Girls are prettier there, haven't you noticed?" asked Bishnu.

"Really? But I thought blondes were more your thing."

"And there's good old cricket," said Bishnu. "You should come back too."

"Thanks, but I prefer baseball," said Vir as he gave his friend a bear hug. "Keep in touch."

Vir had gone on to build a solid reputation in criminal investigation, specialising in victimology and criminal profiling. He'd just closed the case of a professional killer who operated across three countries and was busy receiving thank you calls from various cities when his cell phone buzzed. But this call was from India. Bishnu asking for help.

"My first case of a serial killer," said Bishnu. "College girls killed and dumped in rivers. And we're getting nowhere."

"Send me the files. I'll try to see what I can do to help."

"Bro, I have a better idea," said Bishnu. "When's the last time you came down to India? I've got a Special Ops budget I can splurge."

"You want me to come down there?" Vir paused to think. It was an interesting idea. "Well, there's a lot of leave owing. Let me see what I can do." It would be nice to help Bishnu establish himself, he thought. His junior's initial stint in the Indian police force had been difficult as he had faced a lot of resistance to implementing the systems he had learned in the US. He had started making progress now in his newly established unit.

Vir found it far easier to get away than he'd expected, as he'd not started a new case yet. He found himself on a plane to Chennai in just a couple of days and landed to a boisterous welcome. Bishnu told him he'd be working undercover along with him.

Vir had already begun working on the killer's profile based on the modus operandi, crime scene and choice of victims.

He had been putting together his tentative conclusions when the city had woken up to the horror of seven bodies surfacing at once. The media had begun to train their lights on every step and misstep of the police and the stakes had suddenly gone up. Bishnu and his team were on tenterhooks as this was their first major case and they needed to prove themselves.

As Vir left his room now with his laptop, ready for the brainstorming at Bishnu's office, he had a bad feeling in the pit of his stomach. It looked like the killer was warming up and there was worse to come.

12

Bishnu drove into the Taj to pick up Vir and saw the paparazzi clustered outside the huge glass doors. He entered the grand lobby to find several foreigners chatting near the reception counter. An ardent Hollywood buff, he recognised some famous faces and realised that the crew of 'Death Warrior 7' was staying here. A swift glance around told him that Vir wasn't down yet. So he strolled up to the edge of the group, catching the eye of a huge guy who looked like he could give Stallone a run for his money. The man turned a friendly smile on him when Bishnu greeted him with a casual "How's it going?"

"Wonderful," said the man. "Though the heat's something else. We're shooting on Island Grounds you know and I keep escaping to my van whenever I get a chance."

"Yeah. Took me time to get used to the heat too, after just a few years in the States," said Bishnu, as he extended his hand and introduced himself.

"Jeff," said the other.

Soon they were chatting easily with each other and other crew members gravitated towards them. There was a general buzz of conversation and bonhomie, with the director inviting him to drop in on their sets. Bishnu offered to show them the city's hot spots. Mandy, the pretty blonde who played the heroine's friend, said she wanted to shop for Indian silks. Bishnu was only too ready to escort her.

When he found out that Bishnu was in law enforcement, the director joked and said he could do with some help in navigating the red tape. "The paperwork's driving me crazy, especially the forms in the local language," he said.

The lift pinged open and Vir stepped out into the lobby. Bishnu took his leave from the crew and walked up to him.

"Talked yourself into a role yet?" Vir asked as he took in the film-making equipment the crew was lugging.

Bishnu smiled. "Ready to go?" he asked.

The valet brought the car to the portico and they got in. Bishnu drove out of the gates of the Taj while Vir ragged him about his small car. "Didn't you say you were a big guy in your organisation?" he asked.

"A flashy Lamborghini isn't going to help me stay under the radar. I'm in the undercover unit, remember?" said Bishnu.

The car sped onto Anna Salai, and Vir looked around, noting the changes that had taken place in the years he'd been away.

"No Safire Theatre now, right?" he asked. "I remember watching movies at Blue Diamond with Rima. Just one ticket and you could watch continuous shows throughout the day. Though sometimes you'd watch the ending first and then the beginning. But we didn't care."

He fell silent as old memories came flooding in. He had found himself thinking increasingly of Rima ever since he'd returned to India. Her smiling eyes, her soft lips, and her perfume that was a delicate blend of rose and lavender. Strange how his sense of smell seemed to work as an emotional time machine.

Bishnu glanced at him but remained silent. He well remembered the dark days when he'd thought his friend would never emerge from the trauma of losing Rima. Bishnu himself had been devastated as he'd been captivated by Rima's warm heart and sparkling beauty and been a happy third on their outings. He kept asking Vir to see a grief counsellor so he could come to terms with the loss, but his friend had just thrown himself deeper into his work, refusing to share his feelings with anyone.

Their car drove past Spencer Plaza. "The first mall in Madras, isn't it?" asked Vir, pulling himself back from the past. "And yes, I know it's 'Chennai' now and I have to stop saying 'Madras'."

Traffic was crawling. A water tanker ahead of them splashed water on the road each time it inched forward. A bike cut across from the right lane to the left, wobbling unsteadily. Vir saw a man with his wife behind him, a baby sandwiched between them. A boy perched between him and the handlebars, crouching so he would not obstruct the father's vision. No helmets in sight. An auto inched past on the left, half on the road and half on the pavement.

"The driving here would beat the F1 races hollow," said Vir.

"Yeah, if you can drive here, you can drive anywhere in the world."

They turned left on Binny Road. "We're going to the CBI office, right?" asked Vir.

"No. To HATCHET, my Ops Centre. Just set it up. Wait till you see it."

"HATCHET? What's that?"

"High-risk Anti Terror Cyber Hazard Extermination Taskforce," Bishnu rattled off.

"Not SMERSH? Sounds like someone's been freaking on Bond movies."

"Well, it was my idea. Took me six hours to come up with it. Rom, one of the boys, wanted to call it 'Bazinga'. "

"Of course." Vir stifled a laugh.

Bishnu turned right after crossing Connemara Hotel, following the bend of the river. There were large bushes on the bank of the river to their left, and big buildings to the right. "This is our scenic route," he said.

"I didn't know it was a date," said Vir.

"Right. Just the two of us and a quiet place by the river."

As they enjoyed the banter, Vir realised that Bishnu was to him the younger brother he'd never had. If he had to pick someone to work with, he would top the list.

They stopped at a check post where they had to show identification before the barrier was lifted. They drove further down, past the Electricity Board office. A thin, gangling figure was walking along the road. Bishnu braked to a halt next to him and the man got in. No hellos, nothing. Vir thought it was rather peculiar.

Bishnu continued speaking, "Did you see my email on the seven bodies in the Adyar?"

Vir flashed his eyes at the passenger, wondering if they should talk in front of him.

"Oh, introductions. Romeo, meet Vir," said Bishnu. "Vir, meet Romeo. The guy gets his daily dose of sunlight by walking to Ethiraj College every day to meet his girlfriends."

"Girlfriends?" Vir smiled as he stretched out his hand between the front seats to grasp the passenger's hand. The guy's like a college kid himself, geeky-looking with glasses and an earnest air, he thought.

"The college has two shifts with two different sets of girls," Romeo explained, with a sheepish smile. "And please call me Rom."

Bishnu took a right turn through an arch into a narrow road and drove up to an innocuous white building behind some trees.

"Three guards," Vir observed. "The guard-to-gate ratio is pretty high here."

The guards stared at him. Bishnu smiled at them and said "My guest. He'll be getting his ID today."

They nodded and let them through. The building seemed abandoned but the walls were high, particularly in the back. Bishnu drove behind the building and pulled up next to a shutter. He pressed a button on the dashboard and the shutter went up. They drove in. Vir had a quick glimpse of what seemed to be an automated parking system. He expected the lift to go up but it went down instead. They were in total darkness.

"Absolutely the worst date I've ever been on," he said.

"Are you wearing your seat belt? It gets a little bumpy at the end," said Bishnu. He pressed another button and the interior lights came on. The lift moved pretty fast and then the north doors opened into a tunnel. Vir saw more lift doors next to theirs. Access from other places, he thought.

They drove into the tunnel, lit by green lights that gave it an eerie look, as if they'd entered another planet. The smooth curved walls stretched ahead to infinity. Cameras on the roof swivelled to follow their movements. A Mercedes with dark tinted windows sped past in the opposite direction. Security guards seated in recesses in the wall monitored the cameras and checked the vehicle numbers. The sleekness of the set-up gave it a futuristic feel, on par with the best he'd seen in the world.

"This is cool! Like something out of a spook movie. Where are we?" asked Vir.

"300 feet below the Cooum riverbed," said Bishnu.

They came to a parking lot with several cars in the slots. "All these people work with you?"

"No. There are several other divisions," said Bishnu as he parked and led the way through a door in the wall into an air-conditioned lobby. An elegant blue board identified the place as the visitor control centre. Rom swiped his card and went on ahead. Vir went through the security process: identification documents, fingerprints, iris scans, photo, ID card. He swiped his new card to follow Bishnu into a spacious office with glass walls separating different departments. His first impression was that it was all chrome, gleaming consoles and high end equipment. The place was humming with an air of quiet efficiency.

"Here are the maths guys working on faster algorithms, though they are not for public consumption," said Bishnu, waving at the men working on digital white boards. "We also have our own crypto-mathematicians." They moved on, with Bishnu giving staccato descriptions of the work going on. "These guys block scams on the Sensex, and prevent the inflow of terrorist funds. This one's our anti-hacking squad and the next is the anti-terror unit."

He opened a door to the right of the central corridor. "This is my domain. Everyone on my team's been briefed about you. This is Sasha, our equivalent of the US President's nuclear football."

Sasha was a slim young woman in a lime green jump suit who looked him over with a quick glance and nodded.

"We have the fastest computers here," said Bishnu. "Totally standalone. No data sharing. No hacking either, as the best hackers are on our team. That's our cover. A state-of-the-art facility to protect the nation's cyber security. Very few people have even heard of HATCHET."

He pointed to the man seated at a desk in the farther corner. "That is Keegan. I don't know half the things he does. And if I were to tell you what I know...."

"You'd have to kill me. Got it." Vir grinned.

Keegan was in his mid-thirties, with a spare tanned face and a military bearing. He looked through them as if he were in a parallel universe, engaged in a galactic mission.

"We have our own shooting range and a gun library where we can replicate a shooting," said Bishnu. He waved to two youngsters engaged in a serious discussion in front of a bank of computers at the far end. "Let's not disturb the twins. They get real nasty when we do that. You can meet them later. They were ranked second and third in the IIT-JEE entrance exam. Dropped out from IIT after a couple of years as they thought our work was more fun."

"They don't look similar. Fraternal twins?" asked Vir.

"Nope. We call them twins because they speak their own language. Geek speak."

Rom was at his computer by then, staring at a Sudoku screen. "And then there are leftover guys like this one," said Bishnu. "Don't know why we are paying this bozo to crack the Sudoku code on company time."

"Maybe because this bozo is far better than anyone else in digital intelligence and crime analysis. And saved your ass at least a dozen times in the last few years," retorted Rom. His words came out in a rush, as if speeding to keep up with his thoughts.

"And, as you'll notice, he's got the biggest ego you've ever seen," said Bishnu.

"Did you know that soon after they started building Madras in 1639, a woman's body was found floating down the river past Fort St. George?" asked Rom, pulling up an old map of the city. "That was Chennai's first recorded murder. They thought it was a suicide, till one of the bystanders spotted blood on the clothes of the 'rescuer'. Turned out he'd murdered the woman with the help of an accomplice. The two were hanged on a gibbet."

"And why are you telling us this?" Bishnu cocked an eyebrow. "Are you saying that Reddy, the man in charge of our current pile of corpses, is the serial killer?"

"Scoff away," said Rom. "You need brains to realise that they formulated the first rule of criminal investigation 500 years ago."

"And what is that?"

"Look beyond the obvious."

"Ooh, that's a good one," said Bishnu, and led Vir forward again. "Rom's a wiz in cryptanalyzing coded communications. Financial information, stock transactions, business deals, foreign military and diplomatic secrets, legal documents. As you can imagine, we have an almost bottomless database with all this stuff."

Vir could see from Rom's easy banter that there were no hierarchies here, no egos. The team comprised a hand-picked bunch of experts focused on producing results. Bishnu had already told him about the genesis of the unit. How the government had seen the need for it several years earlier, when terror attacks had caught them flat-footed. But setting it up had taken time and lots of money. The unit could now source the best people from around the world without floundering in red tape.

Bishnu's own room was spacious, brightly lit. Glass walls on three sides. A projection screen and a white board on the wall behind the desk. A few files and a laptop on the table. A large flat-screen TV with the sound muted, tuned to a news channel. A coffee maker from which Bishnu filled two mugs that he brought to the table.

"Ten corpses till now," said Bishnu, his face turning sombre. "And seriously, what have we got?"

13

"First, let's get organised. Put together everything we know. Establish the timeline for the killings," said Vir.

Bishnu called in the other team members. They all filed in, with their notes and laptops, ready to pitch in with the results of their research and pick up new directions for their search.

"Okay," said Bishnu. "The seven bodies found in the Adyar River are actually earlier kills, starting around six months ago. They are too decomposed for any accurate findings. The killer probably thought they would remain hidden because of the weights he'd used."

"Perhaps he's a newcomer to the city, not aware that the water level rises during the monsoon and falls in summer," said Vir.

"The other three bodies are later kills which floated to the surface as soon as they decomposed. He has not bothered to weigh these down," Bishnu continued.

"So, his later kills were the ones you found first. That's when you called me down to assist," said Vir.

"Yes, two bodies in the Cooum, close to our office here. We were able to clamp down before the news hounds sniffed it out. The third was in the Buckingham Canal."

"And the cause of death was identical?"

"Yes, strangling. The ligature marks show that the silk scarves tied around their necks were used for killing."

"I heard Deputy Commissioner Reddy going live on TV saying they were checking the silk stores for leads. Why did you release this info?"

Bishnu's face turned red. "We told him to keep it under wraps so we don't tip off the killer. And then the guy blabs it to the media. He's a loose cannon who loves the cameras."

"Let it go for now. What does the autopsy reveal?"

"Death due to compression of the carotid arteries. Fractures of the hyoid bone in the neck."

"What's the kill frequency?"

"The last three floaters — every 10 days. The others were about one every month. He seems to be upping the ante now. Challenging us to find him."

"Any ideas on where the actual killings took place?"

"The number of murders in the city has been increasing, even in crowded areas. Victims often live in flats where you'd think the neighbours would have heard something. But these are mostly murders for gain. An open door, a woman alone, a knife across the throat, jewels snatched. There are several gang murders too."

"But an apartment within the city wouldn't suit our killer, would it?" said Vir. "He needs time and uninterrupted privacy, so he can torture, kill and then dump the bodies when the city is asleep."

"So he'll need a secluded house or shed, somewhere in the suburbs where development is still in progress," said Bishnu.

He brought up a Chennai Metro Area map on the screen. "But here's the problem. We're looking at 1189 sq. km. The city of Chennai plus 16 municipalities, 20 town panchayats and 214 village panchayats. That's a lot of area, and we don't have complete computerised records yet."

"Let's see if the profile I've come up with will help you," said Vir. "Serial killers as you know are my special area of interest. We're looking at a man in his prime with a lot of hostility toward women, as you can see from his choice of victims. Studies show that several such killers are from broken homes and have a history of psychiatric problems. You must understand he's quite intelligent, or he would have been caught long ago."

The team nodded as they followed his reasoning. "He could be a narcissist who longs for an emotional bond but is unable to sustain a relationship," he continued. "He fakes warm feelings for a while, but erupts into violence when he is no longer able to pretend. The more intimate the relationship, the more aggressive and hostile he becomes. Psychologists have found that the distinguishing characteristic of serial killers is that they are ready to cross the line and turn their twisted fantasies into reality."

"According to research," said Rom, "these killers have felt powerless in real life which is why they crave total control over their victims in their fantasy world. They are often interested in fetishism, voyeurism and violent porn."

"That's right," said Bishnu. "Going by this profile, the three D's are important to our killer. Dependency: the victim has to rely on him for every moment of life. Dread: she is terrified by the pain and torture. Degradation: she has to beg for her life and tell him she will do anything to please him."

"So, probably a man with severe childhood trauma linked with violence. Someone who has gone through years of abuse and hates himself," said Rom.

"Why not a woman?" asked Keegan. "These days women are increasingly fit. They work out and take up physically demanding jobs."

"Granted," said Vir. "Though a female serial killer is less likely, statistically speaking. Our killer is likely to be someone with a job that lets him roam around choosing victims, arranging for the kidnapping, etc. Or he's someone with a measure of authority, able to move about freely."

"His choice of weapon reveals his desire to show the world he's in control," added Bishnu. "The scarf is an extension of his power. We will probably find that he collects trophies of his kills, which may be body parts."

"These trophies may also be videos and photos of the victims," said Vir. "Each time he plays his tapes, he relives the pleasure of the torture and the kill. Now, moving on to victimology, what do we know about his victims?"

"The girls have nothing in common," said Rom, "except that they were all studying in college. The colleges are in different suburbs of the city. No similarity in socio-economic class and hence fewer chances of their belonging to the same circles."

"Maybe the guy is someone connected to colleges in some way," said Bishnu. "Like a placement consultant or a computer services guy. He is a familiar figure on the campus and is able to blend in."

"Possible," said Vir. "Make a list of visiting faculty, service providers and the like in each college and check to see if there are any common names. Also look into recent killings here to see if we have missed any other victims. Find out from your counterparts in other cities if they have similar cases. Look closely at suspects who were questioned in those. Check if the victims were drugged."

"Why does he strangle them and then leave the scarf tied around their necks?" asked Rom. "Why give away his murder weapon?"

"The woman is the object of his desire but she also makes him feel frustrated and inadequate. It is this inner conflict that makes him strangle her and then try to cover up the mark on her throat, as it mars his mental image of the ideal woman," said Vir.

"The scarves are all silk ones," said Bishnu. "The twins are analysing the fibres and also trying to track down the designer in case he recalls any customer who specially orders them."

"Any progress?" asked Vir.

"Let's ask them," said Bishnu. A minute later, the twins joined them.

"Hi, I'm Umang," the lanky, long-haired guy introduced himself to Vir. "I've been working on the correlation between the deterioration of silk and the post-mortem interval. We know textiles are subject to differential decay depending on composition, dyes, surface finishes, and treatments. As opposed to synthetic fibres, natural fibres like silk are readily degraded by the action of micro-organisms and lose their sheen. Their weave structure weakens. Also, putrefactive changes in the human body produce a considerable amount of heat. This heat, as well as the insect activity that decaying tissue would draw, accelerates the decomposition of fabrics in a forensic context."

"What did I tell you about geek speak?" said Bishnu to Vir, as Umang paused for breath.

"I know that the Adyar River is heavily contaminated by effluents and sewage," said Vir. "Must have made your task difficult. Were you able to come up with anything useful?"

"Our best guess is that the bodies have been in water for a period of between three and six months. We also looked into the design, and Punit here made a trip to Kancheepuram to meet the senior designer of Nallathambi Silks."

Punit was short and stocky, with sharp eyes behind thick-rimmed glasses. "The old designer I spoke to is still pretty sharp. Says he has been working on the looms for 60 years. He says the designs on the scarves, featuring mangoes and *zari* dots, are pretty old. From 30 years ago or more. Perhaps you can still find them packed away in mothballs in the cupboards of older women. Some people place orders for them in order to make offerings to the goddesses in the temples. But these orders are for sarees, not scarves."

"Looks like our killer has a penchant for the traditional," said Bishnu. "He must be having access to a cache of these old scarves."

"Another important detail to be noted is that there are no signs of sexual assault on the victims," said Vir, glancing at the post-mortem reports. "Even on the Cooum bodies which were discovered soon after they were dumped."

"As we were speculating earlier, perhaps the killer is a female," said Bishnu. "Or, a man whose motivation is not lust, but anger, thrill or the need to dominate."

"Like Ted Bundy," nodded Rom. "He said he wanted to 'own' the victim, as if she were a potted plant, a painting, or a Porsche."

"Yes. Bundy killed 30 women in seven states in the US," said Vir. "And our killer could be well on his way to match him, unless we stop him."

14

It was past ten in the night and the Padmaja College campus was still buzzing with activity. In fact, this was the time the students chose to make their own, to do what they wanted without the supervision of parents or authorities. They had their meetings, worked on their group projects, hung out with friends, networked on Facebook or surfed the internet.

A student was working on his laptop in his room. Fingers danced across the keyboard and words appeared on the screen: "Who's the ugliest Moti in college? Oops, is that the answer already? Are you thinking of the fat one with the man's voice and the big body? Vote now. Vote as many times as you want. Let the fun begin!"

A cartoon pig in lurid pink appeared on the screen. Moti's beaming face was superimposed on its head. A big piece of cake appeared in one hand and a crown in the other. Photos of other overweight girls popped up. The fingers tapped away to create a new website. A few quick clicks on the picture of the pig and the poll showed that Moti had received eight votes.

"Great, it's working," purred the student. "Now for the hyperlink to be emailed to all the students. Aha... it's done!"

Another room, another student logging in. "Check this out," said the guy to his friends. They crowded round the screen.

"Awesome, let me go first." There were more clicks, followed by raucous laughter.

Moti's score was now a huge 2860. She was trailed by Nisha, a plump student from the Biology section, with 165 votes.

Minx was the first among the friends to see this site. She clicked on the link she had received and turned pale. "This is awful!" The buzz was spreading fast. Moti's score topped 3000 even as Minx watched in dismay. She rushed to the next room carrying her laptop and woke Kat up. They scrambled to Moti's room. Maybe she hadn't seen it yet.

No such luck. The site was open on Moti's screen. Moti looked at them, her eyes brimming. Kat put her arms around her while Minx sat on her other side.

"I try so hard to lose weight. But I was born fat. I'll always be fat," sobbed Moti. "Who hates me so much?"

"We'll find the bastard and make his life hell," said Minx.

"Who can it be?" asked Kat. "Must be someone who can do coding or whatever."

"It's Rakesh and the other creeps," Minx said. "They probably think they're the next Zuckerberg."

"Who? The Facebook guy?" asked Kat.

"Yes. He had a poll to vote for the sexiest girls, remember? But these pervs are not going to become billionaires, they're going straight to jail."

"But why do you think it's them? It could be anyone," said Kat.

"Oh, stop it!" said Moti. "I'm worried about something else. How do I show my face in class after this?"

"If anyone dares to say anything, I'll rip them to shreds," Minx spat out. "Anyway, tomorrow's Sunday. No classes. Let's take a break from all the weirdoes and spend the day at the mall.

Lolita was saying she needed to go there to pick up something."

"But you've not finished your paper and it's due on Monday. You've not even started, have you?" Kat objected.

Minx shrugged. "Our Profs are crazy. I'll be damned if I'm going to kill myself studying. College is supposed to be fun, not a place to slog like slaves."

After her friends left the room, Moti sat dejected, watching the scores mount as more students voted her Queen Pig. When she went to bed finally, she could not sleep. She'd come such a long way in the last year, but a cyber bully was sending her spiralling down the drain again.

She would have been in worse shape had she known that more trouble was coming her way. Balwan had boarded the train in Nagpur, still looking a little battered. The crude scar on his temple was painful, reminding him of the girl who'd got away. He had to bring the slut back somehow, even though he would be lost in a strange city where people spoke an unknown language, and he knew only the name of Moti's college.

The whistle blew to indicate the train's departure. His bhai Bittu, who had come to see him off, pushed some money into his hand. "You can't let the woman get away. You must make her pay," he said.

The next morning, as he was jolting along in the train, plotting his revenge, the girls were on their way to the mall in Minx's bright red Polo. She was driving in her typical hit and miss way, endangering man and beast alike.

Deepika piped up with her version of '20 Questions'. "Isn't this the car Sushil gave you for your birthday? When's the engagement?"

But Minx was not playing. She shut her up with a terse "Don't go there."

The girls stopped at an ice cream parlour near the mall to have their favourite gelato. As they slurped it down, they were unaware of malevolent eyes watching them through binoculars from a terrace opposite the parlour. *Look at that fat girl. Just spilling out of her tight clothes. Why the hell is she eating ice cream? I'll have to take a knife to her. Cut off the blubber, or chop off her tongue so she can't eat so much. Then I'll whip her into shape so I can look at her without cringing. Fools. Don't you realise time is running out?*

The girls got into the car again and drove into the mall. The watcher came down to the ground floor, jumped over the wall, crossed the lane and entered right behind them.

15

Aryan, the manager of BigBen's, saw the girls enter his showroom. He had sent an email to Lolita asking her to collect a gift that evening, as an apology for the earlier goof-up. Everything in Lolita's life was going downhill these days and she was happy that something nice was coming her way. She had done badly in Professor Lakshman's paper and was afraid she'd lose her scholarship, unless she convinced him to add extra marks. The tuition fees and the hostel fees added up to a hefty sum that she had no way of paying. The problem was that the professor was a strict, no-nonsense type with no inclination to flirt. However, this had not prevented her from trying. She had shocked the professor by going to his room late in the night to try and coax him to help her.

"If you want to say something, do so in the department during college hours," he had said with a stern face. "Not in my room at night."

"But sir, I wanted to talk to you alone. I'm very worried about losing my scholarship."

"Then you should have studied harder."

She brought on the tears. "But I can't pay the fees. I'll have to discontinue my studies."

He remained unyielding, moving to the doorstep and gesturing her to leave. "You're lucky I'm not reporting you to the College Board," he said. "Leave immediately." He slammed the door shut behind her.

What was she to do now? She couldn't ask her friends for money. She would have to confess that she had lied and that her parents were not in the US. That her mother was a cook at a convent, and that her father had deserted them. How would they treat her then? They'd never be able to forgive her for the airs she'd given herself.

She looked at her friends who were browsing the western wear collection at BigBen's, unaware of her problems. What was she going to do?

"Excuse me, could you come to my room for a minute?" A smooth voice interrupted her thoughts.

Lolita looked up, distracted. *He's hot and he looks familiar, but who is he?*

"Aryan, the manager here?" he prompted. "I sent you the email about the gift?"

"Oh yes," nodded Lolita. *It seems so long back when I lifted stuff from his store. I've even forgotten that I came to the mall today just to collect my gift.*

He took her to a plush room furnished with a glass-topped table and some comfortable chairs. An assistant brought them coffee. The walls had framed pictures of models strutting their stuff, with their usual surly expression. "You seem worried. Anything I can help with?" he asked.

Not unless you want to pay my fees, she thought.

When she didn't answer, he changed the topic. "So what are you studying? I assume all of you are from the same college."

"I'm doing my Master's in Viscom. SS Padmaja College," said Lolita. "We just completed a horrid set of papers and I'm really tired."

"Retail therapy is the best pick-me-up," he smiled. "And I get the pleasure of having you in my showroom."

God, he's cute, thought Lolita, perking up. *And he seems to like me.* "So when did you join here as manager?"

"Just last month, after a stint in the army," he replied. "Before that, a degree in Maths. Always been fascinated by digits."

"You're not from around here, are you?" she asked.

"I'm from Mumbai. My parents live there. Mother's a darling, and father's a bank manager. Real prim and proper." He made a face. "What about your family?"

"They're in the States. Dad's a software consultant," she said, sticking to the story she'd told everyone in college.

"And here's your gift," he said, pulling out a gift-wrapped package. "A goodwill gesture from the store and me, to make up for not giving you the free hamper."

"Thank you," she said as she opened the package and saw the snazzy new cell phone. "This is awesome. Something that will be really useful."

"I saw your phone when you showed me the email," he said. "Pretty weather-beaten."

"So true." She turned the full force of her smile on him.

"You know, you are different from the girls I see here every day who spend a fortune on a single party outfit. You seem to know the value of money, despite having rich parents in the US. I really admire that."

She basked in the warmth of his words and the expression in his eyes. They talked casually for a few minutes and then she stood up to leave. He came with her too, seeming reluctant to let her go. And when she introduced him to her friends, Minx wiggled her eyebrows and mouthed a "Wow!" Moti was won over when he complimented her on her outfit. Kat got her share of praise too when he told her she looked lovely in a saree. He noted down Lolita's cell phone number and gave everyone his business card. As he accompanied them through the electronics department, they saw all the television sets blaring the news and stopped to watch.

"The last of the bodies has been identified," the TV1 reporter Pia was saying. "Chitra Biswas, a student of Malar College." The passport picture of a girl with a thin face and huge eyes flashed on the screen.

"This is terrible," said Aryan. "What kind of pervert would attack innocent girls?"

"Deputy Commissioner Reddy is here to give us an exclusive interview," said Pia.

Reddy's smirk was missing and the lines on his face seemed more prominent. There were dark circles under his eyes, and his usually well-groomed hair was unkempt. "We have identified the last of the victims and are interrogating a few suspects. I can assure the public that our teams are making good progress," he said.

His team had indeed been working hard all that week over *murukku* and coffee from Hotel Saravana Bhavan — but not on solving the case. They had been trying to come up with a name for the serial killer.

"We should give him a nice name, sir," his assistant Joshi had said. "Like Chennai Casanova or Lady Killer."

"We can call him Kolaveri Kabali, sir. That song 'Why this kolaveri' is very famous," said Constable Muthu.

"How about Sicko Strangler?" Reddy suggested. He was planning to drop a catchy name for the killer in his next interview so that all the channels picked it up.

He brought his attention back to what the reporter was saying: "National channels are sending their top people here to track the story. The Madras Mangler is making news even in foreign countries."

"Madras Mangler? Don't they know 'Madras' has been changed to 'Chennai'?" Reddy complained to his friends over a Scotch in his apartment later that evening. "I had so many good options lined up." His wife had gone to her mother's house for the delivery of her fourth child. He was hoping that this one would be a boy. Maybe he should tonsure his head as an offering to the gods, but how would he look on TV with a shaven head? He had to be careful about his appearance these days, as he was constantly on the news.

16

It was very late, maybe past one in the night. When he'd come back from school, she'd not been home. No dinner either. He'd changed out of his uniform, swallowed some bread after soaking it in hot milk and sugar. Sometimes there was nothing at all to eat and no money to buy any food. He'd check the rice bin where she sometimes kept some change. She locked the big money in the steel cupboard whose key she always carried. Must have quite a stash, judging by the gifts and jewels her customers showered on her. All those slimy politicians and pot-bellied businessmen. He had seen her stealing a bundle of cash from one of the customers when he passed out. "He has so much black money, he'll never find out," she'd whispered.

Where was she? She must be out at one of her parties. Dressed in a see-through chiffon saree with a blouse that plunged so deep it made him feel embarrassed. Sometimes he confronted her when she was leaving, asking her to stay home with him. Make dinner, ask about school. Do what other mothers do. But she slapped him away, asking him, "Who will pay for our food and our flat if I don't go out? Your father?"

Who was his father? She'd never told him. Even on the day she'd taken him to hospital after her drunken boyfriend had beaten him senseless, calling him 'Bastard' all the while. Why did she wear the silver ring on the second toe of her foot? As if she was a virtuous woman like the heroines in the old movies she watched. Simple, devoted to their husband and children. Wearing silk sarees and with their hair in a long plait.

And the way she abused him, in the foulest of language, asking him to keep out of sight when she came in with one of her customers. "They all want young girls. I don't want them to know I have such a big son," she'd said. She was drunk most of the time now, flying into rages. She had held his hand over a flame once because he'd disobeyed her, and beaten him when he screamed in pain. Told him his father had left them because he thought his son was a worthless sissy.

He'd learned to keep out of her way, hiding behind the door of his small room, watching as she staggered in with another drunkard. She'd laugh loudly, whisper in the man's ear, and guide him to her bed. Her son listened to the man's lewd comments and then to the creaks of the old bed that assaulted his ears through the paper-thin walls. Worst of all was the tinkle of her anklets. The way they went on and on as she tumbled on the bed with a new man every night.

He'd watched her and her lover one night when she had been too drunk to shut her door. It had then become a compulsion, a disease; though he hated himself for wanting to see her in bed with one man after another. It drove him mad, and made him want to kill her. This evil woman had betrayed everything that was sacred to motherhood.

17

Kat and her friends were caught up in classes, submissions and project work. Fear of the serial killer had faded to a dim corner of their minds like a toothache that you forget till it rises up again like a demon from hell.

Professor Lakshman was piling assignments on them and making sure they did not take short cuts such as copying from the internet or from their seniors.

"That man has the memory of an elephant," grumbled Lolita. "And he's still not forgiven me for visiting him in his room. As if I made a pass at him."

"As if you wouldn't," said Minx. "My problem is with Annabelle. Like other visiting faculty from abroad, she expects us to match her students in the US in our 'thirst for knowledge'. Doesn't know we specialise in memorising stuff and care only about getting the degree."

"Speak for yourself," said Kat. "Why does the US President pick so many Indian Americans for his team if we're all such morons? I'm more worried about our culturals. I think I'll have a nervous breakdown even before Sabrang takes off."

Their culturals were modelled on Saarang, given the principal's obsession with IIT, and it was the high point of the year. Colleges from all over the country participated and the events were covered by all the mainline media.

"This should be the best festival anyone has seen. Better than

IIT," Belliappa had said at a meeting of the Festival Committee. As always, Kat was the first choice to head the committee, given her excellent organisational skills. Moti was her lieutenant, ready to pitch in with a sunny smile. The open-air theatre would be the venue for all the major events held over a long weekend. Minx and Lolita were the showstoppers for the fashion show and were neck-deep in costumes and choreographers. Lolita was coordinating with Aryan, whose store was one of the main sponsors. Or at least that was the reason the two gave for spending quality time together every day. Deepika was busy practising for the dance contest, hoping to impress Pony Verma, the diva among choreographers.

The Asuras were out in force, slathering themselves with cheap body spray and goop in their hair, making the girls retch. Decked up in psychedelic shirts and cheap blazers, they lurked in dark corners, hoping to get some revealing shots they could drool over.

"So, will you treat us to a wardrobe malfunction?" Rakesh asked Minx, braying at his own wit.

"Why don't you first fix your brain malfunction?" she snapped.

"Poor girl," said Amar. "So frustrated because her boyfriend ditched her."

"Hey! Why don't you come back when you've finished evolving?" she replied, wondering how the Asuras always knew everyone's affairs.

Subu slunk away, deciding to come back another day.

The culturals went off without a hitch however, thanks to Kat's meticulous planning. Minx was crowned Miss Catwalk by Reggie, the ace cinematographer. He gave her his card and told her she had the potential to become a model or a film star. "Everyone's looking for fresh faces now. I can introduce you to some directors and producers," he said. Deepika had taken first place in dance but was disappointed that Pony Verma had not been able to make it.

The next day, Kat and Moti took some well-deserved rest, chattering away about everything that had happened and clicking through the photos taken at the festival. Belliappa had called Kat that morning to congratulate her and preen over the wide press coverage that the events had received. Kat was telling Moti about it when her cell phone rang.

"It's Vir," said Kat, looking at the display. And then: "Hello?"

"Hi, Kathyayani?"

"Yes?"

"This is Vir. I'm sure you remember me."

"I'm sorry, I don't know who this is." She didn't want him to know she'd been longing for his call.

"Okay," said Vir. "Do you remember the self-absorbed guy who ditched you when he got a phone call?"

"Oh Vir, how are you?" She heard him chuckle. *Good sport.*

"Wondering if I could get you out for coffee today. Talk about my plans for the college. That is, if you aren't busy sketching a nude dude."

"Nude dude or rude dude? Hmm," she paused. "Well, okay. The main gate this evening? At seven?"

Kat disconnected and looked at Moti with a huge grin on her face. "Now, what shall I wear?"

"Let's check your wardrobe. Or better still, Minx's," said Moti.

That evening, in a mint green floral print top and slim fit jeans, she looked delicious, more Kat than Kathyayani. Vir greeted her with a once-over and a "Wow!" under his breath as he got out of the car to open the passenger door for her. She liked his old-world gallantry and the way he looked in distressed jeans and a pale blue shirt.

"What's that you're reading?" he asked her when they started moving again. He'd seen her nose buried in a book while she was waiting for him on a bench outside the college gates. She showed him the book. "The Screenwriter's Workbook, by Syd Field," he read out. "You're an English major then."

"Nope. My father thinks Lit students can only become teachers. Typical businessman. I'm doing my Master's in Visual Communications."

"Planning to enter the big bad world of movies?"

"Yes, mom."

"Ouch," he grinned. "But isn't rom-com oversaturated?"

"You should be careful, you know. Your prejudice is showing," she said.

"Okay, let's start again. What genre of movie do you have in mind?"

"Thriller," she said and smiled.

Beauty, brains and spirit, he thought.

"Your turn," she said. "What were you doing in our college? You never got round to telling me."

"I'm planning to start criminology courses in colleges here. So I'm checking out infrastructure, student interest, etc. You know the drill."

"You're a detective then? Planning to set up a bureau to vet prospective brides and grooms? I think you really should meet my mother," she laughed.

"I was thinking more on the lines of forensic sciences, cyber crime," he said. "So, tell me. Are you getting married soon, to a guy your mother chooses?"

Here he goes, needling me again, she thought. "Yes, I'm engaged. To a rich guy with tons of money and three saree shops."

"Really? You're engaged?" He seemed at a loss for words.

She started giggling. He looked at her and smiled. *She got my wheels spinning, the little devil. I should stop underestimating her.*

"What about you?" she asked. "Time to settle down too?"

"I'm not too sure, but my mother thinks I'm nearing my 'Use by' date!"

There it is, she thought. *His lopsided grin that will turn any girl to mush. Handy trick, that.* "So that wasn't your girlfriend on the phone the other day?" she asked.

He shook his head. "No, no girlfriend. Yet." He turned to look at her. "I'm hiring, though." She did not take the bait. "The phone call was from Charan Raj, the Opposition leader," he continued. "I met him for dinner and he promised to help speed up my paperwork."

He drove through the gates of a plush hotel, then guided her to the lovely poolside cafe. The pool was the colour of jade, and the surface shimmered as though it had been sprinkled with gold dust. She nibbled on the pastries that were iced in pink, glazed with sugar, or drizzled with cream. He ordered a silver pot of rich black coffee, and a plate of fresh fruit: mango wedges and strawberries arranged in the shape of a smiling sun.

"So what's the latest in Chennai?" he asked.

"Everyone's het up about the serial killer but the cops seem to be chasing their tails. Why haven't they roped in the expert from the US?" she teased.

He was not listening. "Oops," he said, looking past her to the entrance, picking up the menu card and holding it up to cover his face.

18

Kat paused, fork near her mouth, to check out the couple who'd entered. A young man with his hair in spikes, wearing a suit with a flamboyant blue scarf round his neck. And holding onto his arm was a size zero blonde on stilettos, with full-blown lips and a brief cocktail dress that seemed a size too small. The two walked past to sit at a table further inside the cafe. Vir switched to the seat next to Kat, so that he had his back to the newcomers.

"Hey buddy, you should know better than to try and hide from me," said a voice as an arm dropped on his shoulder. The young man who'd just entered was smiling down at him. Not too tall, the stranger had the lithe grace of a man who was in good shape.

"Oh hi," said Vir, looking resigned. "I should have known I couldn't shake you off. Kat, meet Bishnu. Bishnu — Kat," he performed the introductions.

"We did our criminology program at the same time in College Park, Maryland," said Bishnu to Kat, dropping into a chair. "I was his junior by two years."

"Two years in age. About 10 in mental age. You should have seen him, he was like a whale then," said Vir.

Bishnu smiled. "This guy was a lady killer then and I can see he's still the same. Did he tell you he aced all his papers? Graduated summa cum laude?"

"I should get some tips from him then for my script," she said.

Vir chipped in. "Our young friend specialises in girls with nothing between their ears."

"But you've got to admit, she's got plenty elsewhere," said Bishnu. The two turned to look at his date, who looked like she was in her own world. "Mandy's the heroine's bff in 'Death Warrior 7'. Heard about the shooting on Island Grounds? Tons of action, stunt men, fast cars. Even a helicopter."

"Yeah, I saw it on the news. I used to love the Island Grounds and the trade fair," said Vir. "Huge *papads*, cotton candy, ferris wheels and carousels."

"Or as we *desi* folks call it, giant wheels and merry-go-rounds," said Bishnu. "Melting Man is still around, and Haunted House. There's a new Chandramukhi stall. You've heard of Rajni's film, right?"

"So, are you pitching for a role then?" asked Vir, rolling his eyes at the other's bright silk scarf. Bishnu grinned.

"You're blood brothers, huh?" asked Kat.

"Yes, like Butch Cassidy and the Sundance Kid," said Vir.

"George Clooney and Ryan Gosling," said Bishnu.

"I was thinking... more like Dumb and Dumber," she said.

Bishnu flashed her a smile, saying "You be careful with this guy now. He's not used to girls with spunk." She smiled back at him, thinking there was something very appealing about him.

"We were just talking about the serial killer who's terrorising the town," said Vir. "I think she and her friends need to learn some self-defence tactics."

"I'd *love* to teach you some tricks," Bishnu butted in. He pulled his chair closer to hers and said: "Maybe I can get you an internship with the Hollywood crew. You could help them with local colour, mediate with people here. *And* get pointers for your script. What do you think?"

"Whoa, man. Back off," said Vir.

"It's like that, is it?" said Bishnu as Kat blushed. "Okay, she's got some pretty friends I can teach, right? Give me a call when you fix something up." He stood up. "Back to Mandy. And let me tell you that you're wrong about her," he said to Vir. "She's studying to be a lawyer. This acting stuff is to help her pay the fees."

"Reese Witherspoon in 'Legally Blonde'. I get it," said Vir.

Bishnu waved and walked away. Vir turned back to Kat and a disturbing thought crossed his mind as he looked at her fresh face. *She fits the profile of the killer's victims to a T. I can't lose her like I lost Rima.*

He remembered the first day he'd met Rima. Her parents had moved in next door and he'd wandered around their house while his mother chatted with her parents. Rima was playing with her doll's house, and invited him to have tea with her dolls. He was taken in by her huge eyes and her mop of curly hair tied up in a pink satin bow. He found himself sitting opposite her as if mesmerised, holding a delicate porcelain cup in a grimy paw. Pretending to drink, listening to her chatter away.

She had joined his school and become his best friend, gradually becoming the love of his life. He'd protected her from bullies, escorted her wherever, whenever she needed to go. When he left for the States to do his undergraduate studies at Yale, she had coaxed her parents to let her go too. A talented painter, she had taken up a programme at Yale's School of Art. The two had grown closer, bonding further as they found their feet in a land far from home. There was no drama, no passionate declaration of love. But they knew they wanted a life together, a family, and a house with a white picket fence.

And then that fateful day wiped everything away as if it had never existed. She left him with a kiss, to attend a workshop on sculpture in a neighbouring state. And never returned. She did not make the promised call once she reached her hotel. His frantic calls were not answered either. The hotel said she had not checked in.

Dark days followed. He waited for the call from the police telling him she had been found. Maybe caught in an accident, lost her memory. He told himself she was smart. Alert. She would not take a lift from a stranger or venture out late in a strange city. She was safe, she had to be.

And then he got the news that he'd been dreading. She was dead. Murdered by a serial killer who lured young women by pretending to be injured and needing help. She had been betrayed by her generous heart and her eagerness to lend a helping hand. She had become just another victim in the cops' files. A passport picture with all the colour and life leached out. And then a body on the cold slab in the morgue, with a peculiar greenish tinge on her face as she lay waiting for him to claim her.

He had accompanied the body home and sleepwalked through the funeral. He was burdened with guilt, afraid to look at her parents' faces, though they had not openly blamed him. He stopped eating and talking, retreated into himself. Then he returned to complete his studies, determined to make it his life's business to track down killers like the one who had bludgeoned Rima. It had been his first encounter with evil, with men who could destroy love and life without a pang of remorse. And now, he needed to stay the course, hope that he would achieve his catharsis by hunting this killer down.

19

"Penny for your thoughts," Kat's voice broke into his grim thoughts. She had been watching the despair on his face, wanting to reach out and smooth the lines that furrowed his forehead.

He looked at her and saw the concern in her face. He smiled and continued with the quote she had started: "A nickel for a kiss. A dime if you tell me you love me."

She blushed, looking away in confusion. He resumed talking again, drawing her out about her college, her friends and her plans. She realised only much later that he had hardly spoken about himself.

"I heard your culturals went off well, under the expert supervision of Miss Kathyayani," he teased.

"Where did you hear that?"

"Your principal's added me to his mailing list and sent me an update on how it was the biggest and the best."

"Yes, it went off well, despite the likes of Jambu and other creeps."

"Want me to pitch in again?" he asked, flexing his arm. "But seriously, you and your friends should keep away from him. He's really the dregs."

"Why, did you find out something about him?"

"He's a suspect in several cases of murder for hire. Supposed to be the bully boy for the ruling Samaj Sevak Party, and rumoured to have killed an investigative reporter who exposed his crimes. An eyewitness saw him kill the reporter by slitting his abdomen, pouring petrol into the cavity and setting it alight."

She shuddered. "The witness was also killed, wasn't he?"

"He disappeared and his body was never found," he said. "So trust me when I say you should keep away from him. Can you do that for me?'

She nodded. *He seems to really care. Makes me feel so safe. Maybe I should drop a hint to Mummy about him. But she'll have a million questions to ask, about his caste, income, family. And I don't know if he's interested in me in the same way. After all, Bishnu said he's a lady killer.*

He looked at her with amusement, thinking that she was cute when she went off like that into her own world.

Kat was suddenly struck by another thought. She'd been so busy with the culturals she'd not noticed something rather unusual. Mummy dearest had been silent for a couple of weeks now. No early morning calls. No shortlisted profiles. Was she cheesed off after Kat's rant about Gajendran, her last date? It was a short journey by bus to Puducherry, but not one she made often. She decided she would descend on her without warning, and find out if there was anything afoot. Her crazy mother was capable of fixing up her marriage and then using emotional blackmail to make her agree to it.

****

There were several buses to Puducherry throughout the day and it was easy enough to get tickets on a week day. When she rang the bell, her mother Shyamala came to open the door, and gave a start of delight on seeing her. She fussed over her and rushed to the kitchen to start cooking her favourite dishes. "You have become so thin and dark," she said. "Stay here over the weekend and get some rest. Your father will return on Sunday and will be happy to see you."

"I really can't, ma!" said Kat. "I have a lot of assignments that I need to submit. I just wanted to check that you were alright, as you haven't been calling much these days." She looked carefully at her mother's face as she said this. Her mother looked away without saying anything. *Is she hiding something, or am I being paranoid*, wondered Kat.

"I'll put together some goodies for you to take back with you," said Shyamala. "And I bought you a beautiful chiffon saree that you can wear to parties. Just wait till you see it!"

Kat feasted on some delicious food that almost made her wish she was still living at home. She went to lie down in her bedroom and was soon fast asleep. When she woke up, she went looking for her mother, ready for some fragrant filter coffee. She saw her mother in the living room, standing with her back to the door, talking to someone on the phone.

"Yes, I'm so happy," Shyamala said. And then, "It's better if she doesn't know."

"Is it Daddy?" Kat asked as she entered the room.

Her mother turned around with a start. "No, no," she stuttered. She hung up the phone and rushed off to the kitchen saying she would make her some coffee.

That was strange, thought Kat. *What's the big secret? It's not like she's having an affair, like Minx's father.* She felt a vague unease as she made her way back to college again. Something had changed, but she was not sure if it concerned her or whether she should worry about it.

20

Vir had called for a meeting at the HATCHET premises to discuss a theory that he hoped would advance their investigation of the serial killer. The team members gathered in Bishnu's room for the presentation.

"I've been working with Rom to create a mathematical model to help us predict the likely location of his next kill," said Vir. "It's based on geographic profiling, one of the latest techniques used abroad. You might have heard of Rossmo's theory and of later models like Dragnet and CrimeStat. Rom, please take us through the case of Ramirez, the Railroad Killer."

Rom projected Ramirez's picture on the screen followed by a map of Kentucky, Texas and Illinois. "The red dots on the map mark his kill sites," he explained. "As you can see, all his killings were near railway tracks indicating that he was an itinerant drifter. Investigators were able to narrow the suspects down to a Mexican immigrant who'd been in trouble with the law for years. Fingerprints found at the crime sites confirmed that Ramirez was the killer and he was caught and jailed."

Vir took it up from there. "Our model uses several of the same principles, but modified to suit Indian realities. It needs to satisfy three criteria to be relevant. First, it should accurately predict the site of future crimes, better than the control algorithm can. Second, the predicted area should be compact so it helps us zero in on the killer. And third, it should produce fast results." The team members were paying close attention, taking notes for future reference.

"Other factors to consider," Vir continued, "are the location of the crime and the profile of the victims. These are critical because the location of a crime is likely to be near the killer's normal activity space. Some killers operate in a narrow area while those who use a vehicle have more mobility. Here we have a 3-D map colour-coded for easy understanding," said Vir as Rom moved to the next frame. "The light coloured areas are those with a high probability of becoming a kill scene. The darker areas suggest a lower probability. We impose the danger zones over a street map on which the crimes are marked, indicating the 'fingerprints' of the killer's mind."

Rom projected a map of Chennai, divided into 64 grids.

Vir continued. "This is the crime map we put together, to analyse crime incident patterns, specifically homicides. This shows the different modes of killing, using a gun, knife, strangling or other means." The map morphed to show fewer action spots. "This map focuses on just strangling deaths over the last six months," he said. "The blue dots indicate the kidnap sites and the red dots show the dump sites. What strikes you first when you see this map?"

"Basically, all the kidnap sites are in the immediate vicinity of campuses, and the dump sites are rivers," said Bishnu. "But more important to our investigation, this map shows that he strikes only once in a college. Maybe he thinks it's too dangerous for him to return to the same spot again."

"Yes," agreed Vir. "We've designed a software program that conducts spatial and statistical analyses and can interface with a Geographic Information System. Of course, as there is no such system here as yet, Rom has done much of the work himself. In fact, he's even sacrificed his daily walks to Ethiraj College."

Rom's face turned red as everyone smiled at him.

"But how reliable are these predictions?" asked Umang. "I've heard it said that they are simply subjective interpretations dependent on the investigator's expertise."

His partner Punit piped up with his own question. "And what do you say to the accusation that these are elaborate cons to hype up TV shows like CSI?"

"I wouldn't go so far," smiled Vir. "But I agree... this theory is still evolving. Algorithms are not absolute truths, they have their limits. But they work well in serial type crimes, because we can see patterns more easily when there are more crimes to analyse. I've used these models extensively over the last few years and found them very helpful."

He nodded to Rom who now took over the presentation. He projected the next map on the screen and explained what it represented: "This map shows via colour codes and graphs the likely location of the killer's base. Now, using our algorithm, we predict the likely location of the killer's next attack." The team watched as he zoomed in on GST Road. The names of some colleges on that road began to flash.

"SS Padmaja College. That's where Kat studies, isn't it?" asked Bishnu.

"Yes," said Vir. "She or one of her friends could well be the killer's next target."

21

It was cool under the trees where Kat was waiting for Moti at Appu Kuttan's 'cool drink' shop, set up in a corner of the campus. Appu was short and squat, invariably clad in black pants and white shirt, waddling like a penguin as he scurried to attend to his customers. Though he'd started small, he'd soon expanded his business with some judicious greasing of management palms. Now, in addition to tea, coffee and soft drinks, students could binge on chips, chocolates, samosas and gaudy pastries topped with hideous pink or lemon yellow icing. Cigarettes were hidden under the counter. And a motley bunch hovered behind the shed when they were looking for some 'inspiration'. Grass!

There was a phone on the counter next to Appu's cash box, from where students could make STD or ISD calls. As their cell phone signals were erratic, several students used this facility. Rough tables and benches had been nailed together to provide seating, all painted a bright blue. A *shamiana* provided shade.

Kat and Moti were making a half-hearted attempt to work on their group project over Cokes when Kat's cell phone rang. "What? An accident? Are you hurt?" she exclaimed. And then, "Don't worry. I'll be there in 10 minutes."

Minx had driven to the library some time earlier to borrow some chick flicks. As usual, she had been driving too fast. She saw the cow in the middle of the road a little too late and wrenched the wheel to the left. The car skidded on the sandy edge of the road and crashed into a *neem* tree. She was flung against the windshield as she wasn't wearing her seat belt. She blacked out.

A bunch of students on their bikes recognised her car, ran up and lifted her out. They called an ambulance and admitted her in hospital. She had been revived by the doctors who insisted that she undergo a battery of tests.

When Kat and Moti hurried into the hospital, a stout, bespectacled doctor was reading Minx the riot act. "Not wearing your seat belt. Driving too fast. You've been very lucky, my girl," he was saying. "But I want to keep you overnight for observation. The nurse just called your parents and I've spoken to them."

Her mother called at once, in a tizzy. "How are you, beti? I'm so worried. The doctor told us there is no danger. But I'm coming to Chennai to see you. Sushil is bringing me," she said.

Sushil took the phone from her to ask Minx how she was feeling.

"I'm so sorry. I wrecked the car you gifted me," she said. "I feel so guilty."

He was very nice about it. He had never grudged spending money on gifts for her. "Don't worry about it now. Focus on getting well," he said. "I'll take care of all the insurance stuff when I come down."

Kat saw that Minx was a little shaken but otherwise unharmed. They sat with her for a while, brought her some food from the hospital canteen and returned to college. Their project report was overdue and Minx assured them she was fine on her own. In fact, by the morning, when her mother arrived, Minx was eager to leave the hospital. But first she had to endure her mother's 'I-told-you-so's.

"Didn't I tell you not to move here Minx? Now look what happened," said her mother.

Blah blah blah. Here we go again. Her head started to pound.

"Your father's very upset. He thinks he should have been stricter with you."

Oh, so that's what he's doing with Lily. Trying out new parenting techniques.

"What kind of place this is — only Madrasis and serial killers."

Yes, not as safe as Delhi where there's a rape every 18 hours. Tell me about it.

"Sushil's mother Kanta was in tears. Told me to bring you back with me," said her mother.

Minx had had enough. "Who is she to tell me anything, ma? Tell her I'm not dying to marry her son and sit at home!"

Her mother gasped and stared at the doorway. Sushil had entered just in time to hear the outburst.

His face was angry. "Did I tell you to sit at home and do nothing?"

"You didn't. But your mother did!" she replied. She mimicked his mother's tone exactly: "What is this college-shollege, Minaxi? I want to see my grandson before I die."

"What's wrong with that?" he snapped. "You should be happy she still feels that way about you. I'm fed up with your tantrums. In fact, I'll be taking the first flight out. Aunty, you can come back with me now or come later. And don't worry, I've taken care of the insurance for the car."

He charged out of the room, with Minx's mother running behind him, apologising for her daughter's behaviour. Lolita, who'd just come in to visit, stopped to gape at the two agitated figures.

Minx's mother stopped Sushil by clutching his arm. "*Beta*, meet Lolita, Minx's friend from college." She was hoping he would calm down, given some time. It wasn't easy to find such a rich and handsome husband for her daughter.

Lolita had seen him on TV and thought he looked even better in person. He stopped to greet her, his eyes widening as he took in her good looks.

"Excuse me, I'm rushing off to the airport. It was nice to meet you," he said as he turned to leave. Minx's mother followed him like a poodle, yapping at his heels.

Lolita continued to Minx's room. "What was that?" she asked her. "Why is Sushil storming off?"

Minx was sobbing quietly. The shock of the accident was catching up to her after the argument with Sushil. "I blasted Sushil's mother and he got angry. My mother is upset too."

"Can't blame her," said Lolita. "Sushil's rich and cute. Mind if I take him if you're done?"

Ever take a day off, slut? thought Minx. "Yes, take him. And don't bother talking to me again."

She turned her face away and started weeping again. *Will Sushil ever forgive me?*

22

Moti saw the photo as soon as she woke up from a restless sleep. Someone had pushed it under her door during the night. She picked it up and gazed at the close-up of four grim faces. Her hand trembled and the picture fell face down on the floor. She stared at the message scribbled in big red letters on the back. Sheer panic engulfed her mind and body. She wanted to scream and scream till her vocal chords ripped to shreds. But only a low moan escaped her lips. She hugged her body with her arms and rocked back and forth. *I will not go back. I will never go back.*

Kat found her like this when she came to take her for breakfast. She put her arms around her, and asked her what had happened. Then she saw the photo in her hand and prised her fingers away so she could take it from her. "This is you, with your sister, isn't it?" she asked.

"Yes, Seema and her husband Bittu on their wedding day," said Moti.

"And this man?"

"Balwan, the guy who tried to rape me. I don't know how this picture got here. It was lying just inside the door when I woke up this morning. And there's a warning on the back."

Kat turned the picture over but couldn't read Hindi to decipher the message. "What does it say?" she asked.

"I'm coming to get you bitch!" Moti translated, tears running down her cheeks.

Kat was horrified. "Are you saying Balwan came to your room without anyone seeing him? More likely he has someone inside to act as his go-between."

"He doesn't know anyone here, can't speak English or Tamil. Who would help him?"

Kat's cell phone rang. It was Deepika. "Where are you? Lolita and I are waiting in the canteen," she said.

"We're coming," said Kat and then, to Moti: "If we don't go, the Gossip Queen will start prying."

"You go, I'm not hungry," said Moti. "Tell her I'm on one of my diets."

Kat told her she'd be back soon and checked Minx's room. There was a 'Do Not Disturb' sign hanging on the door. She must have been studying late as her grades were slipping. She decided not to wake her up and walked down to the canteen and into the middle of another drama. Lolita had just picked up a plate and was moving to the food counter when someone grabbed her waist from behind. She dropped the plate to the ground with a loud clang and wrenched herself away with a shriek.

Turning around quickly, she saw an ugly man in a floral shirt grinning at her. "Bastard!" she screamed. "What are you thinking?"

A bunch of thugs sprinted towards her, shouting threats. The man stuck his arm out and waved them back. "Not seen movies?" he asked them. "Beautiful fair girl fight with rowdy black hero. Then sing duet in Sujjerland." He laughed. His goons laughed too, as if this was the greatest joke in the world. The others in the canteen backed away to a safe distance.

"You lunatic! Who the hell are you?" Lolita shouted.

The man gestured to one of his men who stepped forward with a big, rectangular parcel wrapped in shiny gold paper. He placed it reverently on the table before her.

"I am Jambu," said the man in the floral shirt. "This is my 'parisam'. You know meaning?"

"What? Are you crazy? You want to marry me?"

"No marriage. Already married. Two kids," he said, in a matter of fact tone. His eyes ran up and down her body, making her squirm. "Say 'yes' or someone throw acid on your beautiful face." He paused for the threat to sink in, then turned and swaggered out, with his gang one step behind him.

Lolita turned to her friends and saw that Deepika had already opened the parcel, eager to see what it contained.

"My God, what are you thinking? Throw it at his face," she said.

"He's left already," said Deepika, opening the box to reveal a brocade saree in deep red, embossed with zari. A necklace and bangles studded with gaudy red stones was laid out on top.

Kat spoke in a whisper. "He's the rowdy I told you about, Jambu. The one Vir fought with in order to rescue me and the freshers. I haven't seen him for a while now, but looks like he's hired a new set of goons with his father's money."

Lolita was not listening. "Are those jewels real? Wonder how much I'll get if I sell them," she said, half to herself. She was unable to sleep wondering if she would be expelled for not paying her fees.

Kat glared at her. She didn't seem to realise she could get into real trouble with her devil-may-care attitude. "What's wrong with you?" she snapped. "You don't mess with people like him. Got a death wish or something?"

How can you understand my struggle to survive each day? The way I have to grab at anything and everything, Lolita thought. But she couldn't tell her friend the truth. She shrugged, dropping the matter with a casual remark: "No big deal. I've handled worse scum in my life."

But she found soon that she had underestimated the threat. Jambu was not so easily dismissed. He wanted to get back at Kat who'd seen him humiliated by Vir. He had not been able to trace the man, or he would have taken an armed gang to chop him into pieces.

Jambu was obsessed by fair skin and longed to get his hands on Lolita. He began to stalk her, passing cheap comments and telling her what delights he had in store for her. And what he'd do to her if she did not fall in with his wishes. She soon realised she had to do something if she did not want to end up blinded and scarred from an acid attack. She didn't even consider going to the police. What would they do, except leer at her and suggest that she must have given the wrong signals to Jambu? Even worse, they would tell the goon about her complaint, making her situation even more dangerous.

Later that evening, when she was in the hideout with the girls, she asked them for help in handling him. Minx added to her worries by telling her that she'd seen the Asuras and Jambu smoking weed together in a dark corner of the car park.

"They were drooling over some new apps on Rakesh's smartphone, a gift from Jambu," she said. "Rakesh now has a virtual girlfriend who'll strip and talk dirty whenever he wants."

Moti came in then, looking wan and teary-eyed. She had been unable to sleep ever since she found out Balwan was in town. Kat hated the way she looked now, her hair in a mess, all her newfound confidence shattered. To make things worse,

Moti had encountered a new problem. Someone had set up a website in her name and posted trashy comments on several students and professors. Professor Annabelle had found out about it and summoned her to her room.

Deepika's eyes popped with curiosity. "Really? Can you give me the link to the website? What did you say about that nasty creature?"

"Shut up Deepika," said Kat. "You know Moti would never do something like that."

"Yeah," said Lolita, "especially as the only thing she's learnt till now is how to download viruses and share it with us."

No one laughed at the feeble joke, nor could they come up with any real suggestions to help tackle the bullies that were taking over their lives. The disheartened bunch plodded back to the hostel, unaware that hostile eyes were watching them through a pair of binoculars.

Ha. No giggling? You fools finally realised you are in danger? What did you expect with the kind of life you lead? No decency or morals. Exposing your bodies to trap men. But I'll make sure you get your punishment. And you won't see me coming.

23

Kat was in the Japanese rock garden next to the canteen, leaning against a tree, watching Minx pace up and down as she ranted. The college formed a gaudy mosaic of various architectural styles, guided by whatever caught the fancy of the founders, money and good taste not a concern.

Minx had grown increasingly volatile after her fight with Sushil. To give her credit, she had tried to apologise to Sushil for her rude crack about his mother. After all, she'd known them all her life and they had always treated her like family. But when he refused to take her calls, her mood had veered to the other extreme.

"Who is Sushil to look down his nose at me? Stupid mamma's boy," she said. "I'm not good enough for him anymore? Did I ask him for the car? Or beg him to marry me?" She paced some more before continuing her diatribe. "And my mother! Nag. Nag. Nag. Did she confront Pa about Lily? No, she cries like Nirupa Roy in an old Hindi movie."

"She only wants to see you happy Minx," said Kat.

"To see me become a slave like her. I told her I caught Sushil kissing a girl at a party, but she doesn't think it's important." Minx's voice rose. "I'll show them. I'll be rich, famous, successful."

"Of course you will. Once you finish your Master's, you can set up your own design studio as you planned."

"No, where will I go for the money? I can't ask Sushil now, can I? I've got to do something on my own." She walked up and down a few more times. "Yes!" she exclaimed. "I'll go meet Reggie."

"Who? The cinematographer who judged our fashion show?"

"Yes, he's one of India's best. He's shot Priyanka, Katrina, everyone. He said he'll do my portfolio and launch me."

"Modelling? Didn't you see Kangna in the movie 'Fashion'? We hear so many stories...."

"Grow up Kat. Don't believe everything you see in movies. If you're not careful, you'll turn into your mother."

"It's not just the movie. We all know about the drugs, the drinking, and people exploiting you. Even Reggie...."

"Don't worry, I heard he's not interested in girls," laughed Minx. "And stop talking. I've put on my moron filter." Kat saw her face set in stubborn lines and knew from past experience that it would be impossible to budge her now.

Minx made the call at once, introducing herself. Reggie said he'd fit her in the very next day. He knew someone who was looking desperately for a new bombshell. And he knew he'd get a few lucrative assignments himself, by helping out heroes and producers.

"Just bring your beautiful self," he told Minx. "We've got heaps of designer costumes that will fit you perfectly. I'll call my top stylist and make-up artist too. We're going to have a blast!"

****

When Minx went to his studio the next day, she saw that he'd pulled out all the stops for the shoot. The hair stylist ran an expert eye over her hair and got into fast mode. She teased

Minx's hair into several flattering styles: riotous curls, pinned into a sleek chignon, back-combed into a bouffant. Minx could hardly recognise herself after the transformation. The make-up artist worked her magic with glossy lip colours, glittery eye accents and sheer foundations that made her skin glow. She was then given exquisite outfits to wear: skirts and halter tops, Versace gowns and slinky sheaths, accessorised with Dior clutches, dizzy heels and sporty hats.

She preened in front of the arc lights in the studio and listened to Reggie croon as he clicked away. "Wonderful. Now pout your lips. Look at me as if you want to tear my clothes off." The patter flowed smoothly from his lips.

She was Kareena. She was Megan Fox. Her bruised ego fed on their 'Oohs' and 'Aahs' as she posed against different backdrops. She wondered for a minute if she was high on the colourful concoctions they plied her with.

A break at last. "You're doing great Minx," said Reggie. "You're a complete natural."

"You think so? Really?"

"Let's take some experimental shots now, shall we? Where you're not wearing so many clothes."

Did she want to do that? What would Sushil say? she thought. "Yes, let's go for it," she said.

Two hours and several glamorous shots later, the shoot was over. The praise had worn thin now and a niggling voice inside her was getting too loud to be ignored. They were going straight to a club where Reggie promised to introduce her to some celebrities, perhaps even some movie producers.

Lolita had joined her an hour into the shoot, rather peeved that she had not heard about it earlier. She insisted on going with

Minx to the club too. "It's good to know people in high places," she explained, her eyes glinting.

It was a high-end club in one of the city's five star hotels. A bartender with streaked hair and a goatee was making drinks. A young couple was making out on a sofa in a corner. A guy with dilated pupils popped a little white pill into his mouth. Minx's head throbbed from the loud music and the noisy crowd packing the dance floor.

"What will you drink?" Reggie had to shout to be heard over the noise. Minx asked for an orange juice while Lolita chose a mojito. They had taken just a few sips when Reggie came back to escort them to meet his friends.

"This is Santhaan!" he said as he introduced Minx to a thirty-something man seated like royalty on a sofa, with a gaggle of men standing around him. One particular giant of a man with a huge mass of hair stared at Minx as if he'd never seen a girl before.

"Hi, call me Shaitaan!" said the man. Minx thought he looked like King Kong in a Syed Bawkher suit, pretty bad looking even for a primate. Two washed-up girls clung to him tighter than their skimpy costumes to their excess flesh.

"Santhaan is the son of our finance minister, Minx. He's looking for a heroine for the movie he's producing," said Reggie.

"Producing and starring!" corrected Shaitaan.

What? You've got to be kidding, thought Minx. Doesn't he have a mirror in his house? And he looks as if he is at least two feet shorter than me.

"I'll send you the pictures we took today," said Reggie. "I'm sure you'll like her!"

"Yes, I like her already," leered Shaitaan, trying to put his arm around her. Over my dead body, thought Minx, taking two swift steps backward. Lolita, who had been hovering in the background, stepped up now to offer her hand. It was not every day she got to meet a minister's son.

"I'm Lolita," she introduced herself. Shaitaan enveloped her in a bear hug from which she had to prise herself loose. Minx felt like she was in a never-ending horror show. Her headache was killing her by now. She said her goodbyes swiftly and dragged Lolita off with her.

She dragged in deep breaths of fresh air as soon as she was outside and hurried to her car. Lolita was giggling as she followed her.

"What?" snapped Minx.

"Did you see Shaitaan's nose?" asked Lolita. "So straight and classic? It didn't fit in with the rest of his face. Do you think he's had a nose job?" She giggled again.

The man who'd been watching them in the club walked out right behind them. But they didn't spot him or suspect anything. He had made sure of that.

24

The next day, Moti's past washed up at the hostel gates. Or more precisely, behind Appu's tea stall. Moti saw Appu go behind his stall to talk to someone. Must be one of his customers buying grass, she thought. But then she realised there was something familiar about the man in his dirty kurta pajamas. *God. It looks like Balwan. Yes, it's him.*

"That's Balwan behind the stall," she whispered to Kat.

"Let's clobber the bastard," her friend replied. "He has to understand that he's not in his village where he can do whatever he wants."

Moti hid behind her as they strode forward. She was shivering as she remembered her last encounter with him in the village. But the man loped off towards the gates before they were able to confront him.

Kat saw this and took out her anger on Appu. "Who was that?" she asked him. "Why is he running away? Were you selling him grass?"

"No madam. Friend. Just talking," stuttered Appu, his face bleached white. "I don't sell grass. Who told you?"

"Everyone knows. The principal and police will also know if you don't stop lying," she snapped. "Tell me the truth. Is that Balwan? How did you meet him?"

Appu took one look at her grim face and decided it was wiser to confess. "Yes," he said. "I met him in the arrack shop on the main road and we started talking. I know little Hindi."

"What does he want? Are you spying on Moti? Tell us, or we'll call the police."

Appu took a step back as if to ward off a blow. "He bought me a drink and told me to watch her. To tell him if she has any boyfriends."

"So it was you who slipped the photo under my door," said Moti, finding her voice at last.

He nodded, not raising his eyes to meet theirs.

"You bloody well stop this. Tell Balwan you can't spy for him and warn him to keep away," said Kat. "And tell us if you find out what he's planning to do." She pressed a hundred rupee note into his hand. She knew some people understood money better than anything else.

"Don't worry. What can Balwan do?" she consoled Moti as they walked away. "I'm here for you — you're not alone."

Moti had no time to dwell on this. She was already late for her meeting with Professor Annabelle, visiting professor from the US. Minx had been ranting about her. "What does she want to talk to you about? Killjoy! She told me not to wear my stilettos."

Lolita laughed. "She made me go to my room to change my skirt the other day. Said it was not long enough."

Kat was the only one who had given Moti some sensible advice. "Just tell her you did not create that website. You don't even know how to do something like that. She can't punish you for something you haven't done. The college has to investigate and find out who is behind this nonsense."

Moti took a deep breath to calm herself, knocked and entered the professor's room. Professor Annabelle was seated behind a big desk with papers stacked in piles. Her pens and pencils were lined up parallel to the sides of the desk. She looked up, removed her reading glasses, placed them in their case and closed it. She glared at the girl, enjoying the effect she had. Moti shifted from foot to foot, wondering if she could pull out a chair and sit down. The professor never asked the students to sit, part of her bullying tactics. She was a great one for making students learn lessons and 'advance to the next level', like they were a video game or something.

"So what do you have to say for yourself, Miss Motwani?" the professor asked, when she felt the silence had lasted long enough. "I hear you've been busy giving people nicknames. Don't you realise how hurtful that can be?" Her voice rose. "I'm told you call me AnnaBlah. How dare you?"

"I didn't... I wouldn't," stammered Moti, but so softly she couldn't hear her voice herself. She was so stressed out she couldn't remember the explanations she had rehearsed. In fact, she seemed to have forgotten all the English she had learnt so laboriously over the past year.

"So I'll take your silence as an admission of guilt," said the professor. Moti's eyes filled with tears. She had tried so hard to be a model student, to impress all the lecturers.

"You will perform 25 hours of community service at our college hospital. That will help you acquire a sense of responsibility that you so sorely lack. Meet Dr. Gaurav — he will take you in hand," said the professor.

Community service? What's that? I don't want to ask her. Let me get out of here first before I break down and disgrace myself. Moti bobbed her head and exited the room.

Deepika was waiting for her at the end of the corridor, eager to listen to every juicy detail.

"Community service? Cool," she said. "So now you are in a celebrity league along with Lindsay Lohan and Naomi Campbell."

Moti looked blankly at her. Hollywood stars and gossip magazines were not the staple in her village. Deepika rushed away to spread the news, her high heels tapping a staccato rhythm on the floor. Moti continued on her way past the office when an office assistant intercepted her. "Someone from your hometown called asking for your mobile number," she told her. "Some emergency."

Moti's legs trembled on hearing this. *Had her mother been admitted in hospital after a beating? Or was it her sister?* Her phone rang.

"You bitch! You think you can cut me off by threatening Appu?" It was Balwan, sounding like he had had a drink too many. Moti shot a scared look around. There was no one near her.

"What do you want?" she whispered.

"I've come to drag you back. Make sure you go to jail for trying to kill me. You think you get away? I can't find you? The police also looking for you, pyaari." His mocking laugh made her shiver.

"I can't talk now. Someone may hear. I'll call you later," she said.

"No pyaari, now. You will come now. I'm waiting near gate. You don't come, I come. I tell all your friends about you." He hung up.

She stood stock-still, her heart pounding as she imagined the scene if he were to reveal himself in front of all the students. How they would snigger when they saw the fat, country bumpkin with her lout of a fiancé. But was there anything she could do to stop him? He had warned her that he'd already filed a case against her, so she couldn't call the cops. The scar on his forehead would be enough proof of her assault. She could only hope she'd be able to pacify him and send him away so she could complete her studies. She dragged her feet as she walked slowly to the gates.

Balwan was standing just outside, with his arms on his hips. His kurta was dirty, his hair was matted. He looked like he had not bathed in days. The wound on his forehead was an ugly red and his eyes blazed with hate as soon as he saw her.

"What you are thinking?" he pounced as soon as he saw her. "You want to go to jail for the rest of your life? Or you want to come back with me? Be a good wife and servant?"

"Please let me go. I beg you. You know I was not trying to kill you, just defending myself."

"Everyone laughed at me when they found out," he said, moving threateningly towards her. "Called me *hijra* who cannot control his woman. They said *you* were a man, not me. How I can take this?" He grabbed her shoulders and shook her till her teeth rattled. She reeled away from the fumes of liquor on his breath.

"I'm sorry. I promise I'll never come to the village again. You go back and tell them you hit me, killed me. Whatever you like."

He wasn't listening. He looked like a maniac. "That's what I do. Break your legs. Gouge out your eyes. Make you blind beggar wandering on road."

She started weeping, her fears rising up again to paralyse her.

"You better do what I say now, bitch. I give you two days to finish things here. Remember, no tricks. I know where your mother is and your sister. I and Bittu will make them pay. A good beating, then a kitchen fire. Accidents happen, no? There are so many ways to kill a woman." He turned and walked away.

25

Things were not going too well at HATCHET. Bishnu was pacing up and down in his room and swearing: "He's a banana-eating fool. A dinosaur that should be extinct by now, or put down."

Vir sat watching him call Reddy names. He was tempted to add several expletives too, all of them unprintable.

"The idiot knows nothing but will not take our help either," said Bishnu. "I wasted two hours taking him through our algorithm, telling him why we thought the killer would surface in the campuses we pinpointed. I asked him to increase security there and station a few plain-clothes men. But the ass won't listen. Says there are several VIP visitors to the city in the next few days and he can't spare his men. Also, that there are too many colleges on that road and we need to be more precise, provide actual evidence. As if the killer will send us his itinerary. And he had this smirk on his face throughout as if he was humouring a madman."

"Yeah, I've seen the look on several faces since I came," said Vir. "They think I don't realise things are different here. Reddy feels he knows best and we should take a back seat. Nothing unusual about that. It's the way police agencies anywhere in the world function. They don't trust outsiders, and don't want to let us in. They're afraid we'll take over. We can only hope that they'll accept us in time."

"He's got a colossal ego, as big as his brain is small," said Bishnu. "And he loves flaunting it."

"I get what you feel," said Vir. "We need to get a break soon, or we'll never catch the killer. Even dumb luck can change the equation, like the cops catching Ted Bundy when he sped through red lights."

"Yeah, right. Maybe we should start praying for luck," said Bishnu, dropping into his chair.

"We have to keep going, you know," said Vir. "Use our expertise and resources to catch the killer. We owe it to the victims and their families." *And I owe it to Rima.*

In the days following Rima's death, Vir had often lain awake, wondering if he could have done anything to prevent the tragedy from happening. Maybe he could have persuaded her not to go, or taken her himself instead of letting her take the bus. What would have happened if she had taken the next bus or the previous one? Would she have escaped her fate? So many questions... and no answers. He had read several books on reincarnation, and books by Dr. Brian Weiss, looking for a window into the other world. Refusing to accept that he would never see her again.

Bishnu broke the silence that had fallen. "Okay, let's see where we are now. We sent our own team members to interview the slum dwellers in Olcott Kuppam," he said. "The killer would have had to drive slowly through the slum to get to Broken Bridge. But they say they saw nothing."

"I saw the transcript of Ponni's interview. She says that the road is so bad during the rainy season it's difficult for anyone to drive a car to reach the bridge. And we'd inferred that the killer did dump the bodies during the rains, when the river was in flood."

"Let's go take a look again, shall we?" said Bishnu. "Why do we assume that the bodies were dumped from the bridge just because they washed up near it? Maybe it was further upstream, or from across the river."

"From the MRC Nagar side?" asked Vir. "It's pretty well-developed now. Wouldn't someone have seen something? No harm in taking another look though."

They were soon in Bishnu's car, driving through Cathedral Road and onto Beach Road. As it was quite late at night, traffic was relatively light. "How come Cathedral Road still has its old name?" asked Vir. "I often feel I've come from an alternate universe as familiar roads have unfamiliar names. Edward Elliotts Road has become RK Salai. Mount Road's become Anna Salai."

"You'll get used to it soon enough," said Bishnu as he turned left into MRC Nagar. "This place has developed really fast in the last few years. So many multi-storey buildings. The killer would have been afraid he'd be seen if he tried to dump the bodies anywhere here. And he would have had to make several trips, unless he's got an industrial freezer where he stacks his corpses."

"What about this construction site? Or this old Electricity Board building? Probably deserted late in the night," said Vir as they drove slowly down the road. "And there's this dirt track leading to the river, with no lights to speak of. On a dark, rainy night I'd think it's a definite possibility."

"He would have had to make a few recce trips as well. Maybe someone saw something. Let's ask this guy," said Bishnu. He stopped the car and they got out to intercept a cyclist with an aluminium can fixed to his carrier. A *chai wallah,* selling tea in disposable cups.

But when they asked the man, he directed them to a 'petty shop' by the roadside. "Everyone knows Murugesan and he knows everyone," he said. "I think he's been here for more than 30 years."

Murugesan was a wiry old man with straggly white hair. His shop displayed the usual glass jars on the counters, bananas and chips packets suspended from strings over his head. He got up from his seat behind the counter to spit out a gob of tobacco when they asked to speak to him.

"Hasn't he heard of oral cancer? And why is he spitting on the road?" Vir muttered, drawing back in distaste.

Bishnu rolled his eyes at him and spoke to the old man, telling him they were looking into the dumping of the bodies in the Adyar River. "Could someone have dumped them from this side of the river?" he asked.

"Lots of traffic nowadays. Buildings also," said Murugesan. "And all the tall buildings have security guards. How he can dump bodies without getting caught?"

"What about the construction site? How long has the work been going on?"

"They started work some eight or nine months back, then stopped."

"Why, what's the problem?" asked Bishnu.

"The watchman said there's some case in court. Fight between two brothers who own the land."

"Okay. Now tell me, do you have floods in the river? How about the monsoon six months back?"

"It was very bad," said Murugesan. "They opened the gates at Chembarambakkam Lake because it became full. We had terrible floods. People went to safety to Corporation schools. The government gave food packets. Lime rice. They didn't like it. They wanted biriyani." The man was happy to talk to someone after hours of sitting alone behind his counter.

"Thank you," said Bishnu. "You have been very helpful. We'll come back if we need anything further." He passed Murugesan a hundred rupee note which he tucked into the folds of his *dhoti* at the waist.

The friends moved away, discussing the information they had just received. "If the river was in flood," said Vir, "the killer could have very well thought the bodies would be carried into the ocean and never be found. Or wash up on a shore far away."

They walked up to the gates of the construction site. A man was seated in front of the security hut, reading a Tamil newspaper. He looked up at them and asked them what they wanted. Bishnu showed him the police ID he carried for such occasions and asked him if anyone could have driven to the back of the building and accessed the river.

"Not since I started here," said the watchman. "No one enters except the owners, and even they don't come very often these days as nothing's going on here. And I lock the gates if I go somewhere."

The two friends looked at each other, disappointed. Then Vir picked up on something. "You spoke of starting here. When was that?" he asked.

"Two months back. The fellow before me was a drunkard. Always at the arrack shop in the slum across the river. The owners kicked him out because they lost a lot of cement bags."

"We're coming in to take a look," said Bishnu. They skirted the piles of gravel and stacks of bricks. The walls of the building had risen up to the second floor and a broad gravel path led to the back. They walked down the path and came to the end from where they could see the river waters.

"Not much of a current now, but it must have been a torrent during the floods," said Bishnu.

"Definitely a possibility," said Vir, looking up to see how many buildings had a view of this particular spot. "And it would be difficult for anyone to see us from any of the buildings around, especially on a dark rainy night."

"We know now why he switched his dump site from here two months back. He could no longer drive in like he used to," said Bishnu. He felt upbeat about the progress they had made in the investigation.

But not for long.

26

Minx was in trouble. She quickened her steps on the dusty dark road leading to the hostel gates. The stupid auto driver had dropped her off on the main road. She should not have gone out today without her car, especially when Kat had told her about Vir's warning that their college was on the killer's list.

She looked back. The man was still following her. She caught a glimpse of his face under the solitary road light. It was the giant with the huge mass of hair who'd stood next to Shaitaan at the club. Was he bringing a final warning from his boss? She started running. Just a few minutes to the gate and the watchman — unless he was too drunk to help. She did not want to be caught on the road by this thug. She tumbled down on the dirt road, tripped by a huge root, and felt a searing pain in her knees. *I have to get up and run!*

"What is it Minx? Why are you screaming? Wake up, wake up!"

Minx sat up with a start, extricating her legs from the sheet they were tangled in. *It's only a nightmare. Or maybe it's my mind sending me a warning of things to come.*

"What's happening, Minx? What are you hiding from me?" asked Kat. She could not bear to watch her friend pretending that everything was fine when it was obvious something was wrong.

"It's Shaitaan," said Minx, deciding to come clean. "You know, the minister's son?"

"Who? That lecher?" asked Kat.

"What do you know about him?"

"There are so many stories about him in the local magazines. He kidnapped an 18-year-old TV actress and raped her. But the police refused to register a case and threatened her into silence."

"Then how did the magazine print the story?" asked Minx.

"They didn't print his name but people could guess from the hints they gave. If they take him on directly, his goons will burn their press down. It's happened before, you know."

Minx's eyes filled up as she told Kat about her modelling fiasco. She showed her the racy pictures that Reggie had emailed her and told her she had been too ashamed to reveal this earlier. Shaitaan had been hounding her, asking her to come meet him and promising to make her a star.

"You didn't agree, did you?" Kat asked quickly.

"No, I hated the sight of him and told Reggie too. But Reggie is pressurising me, saying Shaitaan has tons of black money. That he will shower me with gifts and spend a fortune on publicity. I told Reggie there was no way I was going ahead and warned him to delete my pics so no one else could see them."

"You did a smart thing there. So why are you so worried now?" asked Kat.

"Read this," said Minx, showing Kat the email she'd received: WE KNOW WHAT YOU DID!

"How do you know this is about the photos? It could be just some pervert trying to frighten you."

Minx showed her the next email: PHOTOS DON'T LIE! "This definitely shows that someone has the photos and is blackmailing me," she said.

"Maybe we can trace this," said Kat. "But don't think of going to the cops. They're too scared of Shaitaan and will inform him about the complaint. Or they'll leak the pictures themselves to the local magazines." She paused, trying to think of a solution. "Maybe Sushil can help," she said. "After all, he's a big shot in the media."

"No, no. I don't want him to know. He's not even in touch with me these days." Minx grew agitated as she thought of how Sushil would react if he found out.

Kat looked at the date of the second email. It had been sent just the previous night. Probably the reason for Minx's nightmare. "Don't worry," she said. "We'll figure something out tomorrow."

But the matter had escalated to a new level the next day. Minx's bold pictures had hit the tabloids and were plastered on walls all around town. She looked gorgeous, with smoky eyes, a sexy pout and a totally bare back. Shaitaan's interview accompanied the pictures and he had waxed eloquent about this 'hot new sex symbol'.

"What does the creep think? That I'll change my mind once I see all the publicity?" Minx screamed. "Did Reggie give him the pictures when I explicitly told him not to? The bastard's phone is switched off or I'd give him a piece of my mind."

"Could it be someone else?" said Kat. "Maybe the Asuras? They always know stuff about everyone and may have hacked into our computers. You know Rakesh is obsessed with you."

Minx sprang up. "Let's go to his room now and slap the truth out of him. Someone should have stepped on him as soon as he crawled out from under a rock."

"Wait," said Kat. "He won't be in his room. Today's the inter-collegiate final. He and all the boys are probably at the cricket grounds."

"All the better!" said Minx. "Are you coming or not?"

That's the problem with her, thought Kat as she sprinted to follow her out of their hostel and towards the boys' hostel. Minx was impulsive and headstrong, plunging headlong into trouble through her rash actions. How was she planning to get into the room if it was locked? Did she want to break it open? She called Moti to tell her what they were up to and to keep an eye out for the boys' return.

As Kat had expected, the hostels were empty, as even the girls had gone to the stadium to support their team. But it was still a scary expedition. What if someone saw them and reported them to the Principal? Going to the boys' hostel was a strict no-no and they could be expelled. Her heartbeat speeded to a gallop.

She was relieved when they made it to Rakesh's room without being spotted. The door was just bolted and not locked, so they did not have to break in. Minx pushed open the door and closed it behind them.

"Filthy pig!" she spat, as she saw the magazines, papers, dirty clothes and grime covering all the surfaces.

"So what are we looking for?" asked Kat.

"Dirty books, binoculars, sleazy pictures — I don't know! You're the one who watches all the detective serials," snapped Minx. "Anything that can get him into trouble so we can put him out of commission."

As expected, there were several porn magazines and CDs strewn on the bed. Minx rummaged through them while Kat opened the wall cupboard and gasped. The inside walls and doors were covered with photos: Kat, Minx and the other girls lolling at Appu's; Moti chasing Kat with a bucket of water; Minx dressing for the fashion show; even a picture of Lolita sneaking a smoke behind some trees.

"The creep!" hissed Minx. "He's been stalking us."

"Can you see any of the pictures that Reggie took of you?"

"Not here. Probably on his computer," said Minx. "I tried to open his mail box, but we need his password."

"Well, let's try his name," said Kat as she keyed it in. "Nope. 'Viscom', maybe? No, that's not it either. We don't know his date of birth, his pet's name, all the usual stuff people use." She thought some more. "What does this guy really like?"

"Try the names of the porn stars. You'll probably hit the jackpot."

"Hmmm... let's try 'Minx'. Nope. Or maybe your full name, Minaxi. Rakesh thinks it's a lovely name and hates the fact that you shortened it."

Minx ground her teeth in rage.

"No luck," said Kat. "I'll have to use the password cracker."

"What?"

"Software to crack passwords. I saw it on a detective show and did some research."

"Who are you planning to hack?" asked Minx.

"For my script, you know? I had to find out how much time it takes, whether it works. Sshh. Let's see if I can pull it off. Ah... here it is. Download... install... run... come on, move it. It's taking too long."

"Hurry, they might return any time," said Minx, finally realising what a big risk they were taking. She shifted from foot to foot, and peered at the screen.

Kat seemed to be on a high, happy that it was working: "Yeah! I'm in. I've got a career as a hacker. Look who he's got on his mailing list. Jambu, Shaitaan. And isn't this the reporter who interviewed Shaitaan? I think we've found the source of the photos and our blackmailer."

"Open the mail to Shaitaan. Let's see what he says," Minx said.

Too late. Voices outside the hostel. Footsteps approaching the steps at one end of the building. Rakesh's distinctive bray. They couldn't leave the room now without being seen, but maybe they should try anyway. Even as the girls looked at each other in fear, the voices came nearer still. Probably on this floor already. Kat looked around frantically. It was a small room with just one door and a window with bars. There was nowhere to hide. No wardrobes. And if they hid under the bed, they would be seen as soon as Rakesh opened the door.

They were trapped. Kat flinched as she imagined the look on the boys' faces when they opened the door and saw them. They would call them sex-crazed, lurking in their room in order to get some action. They would snigger and scoff, tell their friends that the girls were nymphomaniacs. And then they would take them to the principal, making them the laughing stock of the college. The office would call their parents and they would be suspended. Kat wanted to bang her head against the wall. What a fool she had been to spend so much time in the room without realising she could be caught and disgraced.

She looked around desperately again. Maybe they could flatten themselves against the wall next to the door and hit the boys on the head when they entered. They did it in movies, didn't they? But this was no movie. They couldn't knock out three of them, and the boys would immediately recognise them. Could she create a diversion perhaps? Say that she'd seen a thief enter the room or that she had seen some smoke? No way would they believe her. Who was she kidding?

It was over. It was all over.

27

Kat's cell phone was pulsing in silent mode. "Why did it take you so long to pick up?" asked Moti who had been watching out near the boys' hostel. "You have to get out. The Asuras are here."

"I can hear them," whispered Kat. She and Minx stood transfixed as they heard Rakesh at the door.

"I got some mind-blowing pics of the cheerleaders from the other college, guys," he was saying. "Wait till I show you."

The knob turned. Kat closed her eyes and prayed. Minx reached out to clutch her hand. They were trapped in Creep House. Sweat poured down their faces. They crouched low as if to evade notice by making themselves smaller; waiting for the door to crash open and for the boys to discover them. Kat could imagine their shock, and then their joy that their wildest fantasies had come true. Then they would batter them with innuendo and slimy jokes; perhaps try to blackmail them into doing whatever they wanted.

And for what? thought Kat. What had they really found out? Just that Rakesh was in touch with other creeps of the world. Surprise!

A phone rang, outside the door. Kat opened her eyes, hardly daring to hope.

"Yes, yes. We'll come at once," she heard Rakesh saying. And then, "BB wants to see us at the office. Let's go."

Was he... would he? She waited with bated breath. The footsteps retreated down the corridor.

"Shall we run out?" Kat whispered.

"Let's wait. Moti will tell us when it's safe," said Minx.

The boys went down the hostel steps and saw Moti coming towards them on the paved path leading from the office.

"Coming for a kiss? Sorry, we've got to meet BB now," sniggered Subu.

"Where's your crown, Piggy Biggy? Got my messages congratulating you?" Rakesh asked.

"Yeah, they're all here," said Moti, tapping the cell phone in her hand. She waited for them to move on before making her call to Kat. The girls came charging down the stairs, still trembling from their close shave.

"How lucky BB called them just in time," said Kat.

"Yes, real lucky," said Moti, in BB's deep voice. Kat started laughing as she caught on.

"I wish we could see their faces when they find out," said Minx.

Kat was getting a call. Vir. He was on his way to pick them up for their self-defence sessions. He wanted to make sure they were as prepared as realistically possible to handle any attack. Kat called Lolita who came with them to the gates to wait for Vir. Deepika said she'd join them at the gym as she was already in the city to do some shopping.

"Bishnu will meet us at the gym," Vir told Kat when she got into the front seat. She introduced her friends to him and he quickly assessed them with some pointed questions. He's really good at this stuff, thought Kat. She could see that her friends thought he was a real charmer and was happy that she had seen him first.

Vir pulled into the parking lot of a leading gym in Nungambakkam. Some major renovation work was going on and sheets of tarpaulin were stretched across the glass front. Poles criss-crossed the building to form perches for the workmen to stand on.

"The owner is Bishnu's friend," said Vir as he unlocked the front door. "He's upgrading the gym with ultramodern facilities. They have strength training, free weights and cardio on the first and second floors. We'll be having our session in the basement."

They walked through large rooms with new-age gym equipment and followed Vir down a flight of steps to the basement below. He turned on the lights. It was a spacious hall with a wooden floor. One wall was entirely mirrored.

They heard a loud "Hi" and looked up the stairs. Kat recognised Bishnu, who clattered down the steps to join them. Vir made the introductions.

"So what's happening at the shooting?" he asked Bishnu. And then to the girls, "The dude's been trying to get a role in a Hollywood movie they're shooting on Island Grounds."

"Well, they offered me the role of an Indian prince," said Bishnu, with a grin.

"What an original idea! Where have you parked your elephant?" asked Vir.

"The head honchos won't give permission. Anyway I'd need a princess. Interested?" He cocked an eyebrow at Lolita.

"What kind of girl are you looking for?" she asked, with a flirtatious smile.

"Someone who will love my cute face and body."

"Who says you have a cute face and body?" Lolita shot back. "Why don't you ask Kat?"

"I'm looking for true love, not a smashed nose," said Bishnu, throwing a droll glance at Vir.

"You would never guess, but I've got to tell you," said Vir. "This goofball is in law enforcement."

After a few more minutes of banter, Vir got down to business. "Bishnu's our dummy," he said. "Feel free to kick, punch and gouge as required."

"Hey come on," said Bishnu. "Don't I get a protective body suit?"

"Don't be a wuss," said Vir, handing him some protective gloves which he could use to ward off blows. And then to the girls, "You're going to learn Krav Maga, first designed for the Mossad, the Israeli intelligence agency. It's one of the most effective self-defence disciplines in the world where you focus on attacking the body's most vulnerable points — eyes, ears, chin, throat, solar plexus, groin and knees."

Kat went first after he demonstrated some moves, but her tentative jabs did not pass muster. "Go at him wholeheartedly," said Vir. "You don't get a second chance. The trick is to hit hard and run to safety. Some other rules you should never forget: Always park under the lights. Never get into the car of a stranger. Keep an eye on your drink to make sure it's not spiked."

He moved on to demonstrate how to neutralise an attacker with a gun, in just three steps: "One, shove the gun away from you with your right hand. Two, punch his nose with your left. Three, grab his pistol away, again with your right."

They practised for a while before the session degenerated into a free-for-all. Lolita charged at Bishnu with a yell, knocked him down and landed on top of him. He hammed, pretending he was in mortal terror.

"Tell me you don't have an ugly six footer with cauliflower ears in your life," he whispered in her ear.

"I'm not telling you anything," she replied.

"I've got ways to make you talk, lady," he growled.

Vir put on some music and told them to do some limbering exercises as they needed to improve their flexibility.

An uninvited guest was staring down at them from the shadows on the floor above. *You sluts. Think these guys are very smart? They're just amateurs, using any excuse to get their hands on your bodies. And you think it's all such fun. It's not going to be fun much longer. And I think I've decided who I'll take first.*

"Hey, what are you doing? Spying on my friends?" The watcher pivoted on his heels when he heard the voice behind him. *She's seen me. I can't let her tell the others. Thank God the music is loud.*

His hand whipped across her mouth to stifle her. He dragged her to the room farthest from the basement stairs, the room with the dumbbells.

28

It was the next day. Afternoon classes had been cancelled. Kat, Moti and Lolita planned an expedition to Santhome beach. They loved to frolic in the waves and nibble on corn on the cob and slices of mango dipped in spices and salt. Minx refused to come as she had just had an uncomfortable session with the head of the department about her poor grades. So the three girls were forced to take a train to Guindy and then an auto. But they had obviously chosen the wrong day for the trip, as they were held up for hours by an election procession. They were still some distance from the beach and it was too hot for them to try walking to their destination.

They sat waiting, cursing as the noisy show wended its way along. Drumbeats. Dancers. Men in tiger costumes. Slogans raised in support of Charan Raj, leader of the Opposition and head of the local wing of the People of India Party. Men wearing the red and blue party colours, distributing leaflets listing his campaign promises: free rice, free goats, free grinders, free cell phones. It seemed to be an outpouring of love for humanity. Then came the man himself, standing in an open jeep with folded hands, seeking their support in electing him Chief Minister.

"This is a travelling freak show. How does this guy expect us to vote for him after making us wait on the road for hours?" muttered Lolita.

"He's supposed to be a good man who keeps his promises," said Kat. "And anyway, he'll be an improvement on Shaitaan's party which is just a bunch of criminals. No wonder we're living in mortal fear of a serial killer, with the cops chasing their own tails."

Lolita did not agree with Kat's views. "So you think Charan Raj should be our next Chief Minister?" she asked. "That man is as fake as his smile, but everyone thinks he's a Gandhi who will change the world."

Kat was surprised at her vehemence. "Hey cool down," she said. "Why is he making you so angry?"

Lolita scowled and refused to answer. The temperature seemed to shoot up further in the cramped auto.

Moti changed the topic. "Did you hear anything from Deepika?" she asked, wiping the sweat from her forehead.

"Nothing further after that sms where she said she was rushing to see her father who had had a heart attack," said Kat.

"No updates on Facebook either," said Moti. "I really hope he's better now."

"I hope so too," said Kat. "I called a few times but her mobile's switched off. Must be spending all her time at the hospital."

The tail end of the procession finally dragged past and traffic started moving. Tempers flared, horns blared. Everyone wanted to go first with the result that they were gridlocked for another half hour. They finally reached the beach and tumbled out of the auto, happy to feel the breeze on their faces. But not before a fierce argument with the auto driver who wanted to be paid two hundred rupees extra for the long wait.

They were near the lighthouse, their favourite spot. Here they were far from the crowds that thronged Marina beach. They bought some corn on the cob and strolled to the shore line.

Then they hiked up their pant legs and stood in the crashing waves, feeling like they were little children once again. After half an hour, they reluctantly pulled out their wet feet and plonked down onto the sands.

As they sat chatting, there was a ping on Lolita's mobile. "Smile at Jambu and your hostel fees will be taken care of," said the message. She looked around, startled. Jambu had been following them as usual. In fact, he had walked up to their auto when they were waiting for the procession to pass, offering to give them a lift in his air-conditioned SUV. Now he was sitting on a stool a few feet away, stuffing his face with *bajjis* from the vendor on the sands.

How does he know about my hostel fees being due and that I need money? Or is it someone trying to create trouble for me? Lolita was puzzled. *Kat keeps warning me about him, but she doesn't realise how desperate I am for money to pay my fees.*

She turned in Jambu's direction and smiled at him. His mouth fell open, bits of bajji scattered around.

Ewww! A crocodile with a slobbering mouth, she thought.

"Did you just smile at Jambu?" asked Kat. "What's wrong with you?" She wanted to slap Lolita and make her understand what a fool she had been.

As Kat kept jabbering away, Lolita was looking at a message she'd just got from her bank. A big sum had been deposited in her account. Jambu must be having an accomplice at the bank to deposit the money, she thought. Or maybe it was the Asuras, for this plan seemed too devious to be Jambu's handiwork. Rakesh was here at the beach, but not the other two.

Another ping: "Good girl. Now talk to him and stop worrying about your tuition fees."

Why not? He kept his word last time. Once this semester's tuition is paid up, I need worry only about the last one. Then I'm off to take up a job in the company I interned with.

She got up, ignoring the gasps from her friends and strolled over to Jambu to stand next to him. He looked up, turning red in excitement. "Hello, good evening, how are you?" he stammered.

"I'm fine," said Lolita, looking down her nose at him.

"Please, please to sit!" Jambu pushed one of his henchmen off his stool to make place for her. She sat down, turning her back on her angry friends.

"What's wrong with her? I told her all about Jambu's criminal record," Kat was saying to Moti.

"Very happy you talk to me. Having some snacks?" Jambu offered Lolita his plate.

Sick! She almost threw up at the thought. *This should be enough. I talked to him, didn't I?* She stood up and walked away without a backward look.

Ping. Another sms. Another deposit. That had been easy, she thought — almost too easy. It was just another stupid guy who was paying to see her smile.

The man watching from some distance away was enraged. *Shameless whore. She should be locked up and tortured till she repents. And her friends are just as depraved as she is. They are to blame for everything that's going to happen.*

29

The stalker was angry. That girl in the gym was not one of his chosen. He would have left her alone if she hadn't challenged him. She should have turned and run away or pretended not to have seen him. But she had seen his face and questioned him. He had no other option but to silence her.

He had dragged her into the room with benches, barbells and dumbbells, then locked the door behind them. He clamped his arm around her waist and crushed her mouth with his hand to prevent her from raising an alarm. She still made whimpering noises and used both hands to try to wrench his hand away. Then she tried to bite, but his hand had pressed down harder, making her lips bleed. She'd scratched the arm holding her round the waist, dug in with her nails and twisted frantically in an effort to get away.

He held firm, seeming to feel no pain from her attacks. He let go of her waist for a second in order to snatch the heavy dumbbell from the stand in front of him. He brought it down on her head with a sickening crunch. And then again, and again. He smashed her head and face into pulp, making sure that not a single cry escaped her mouth. He stopped to listen for raised voices or running footsteps. Nothing. He was safe.

He pulled her body to the corner farthest from the door, then bent down with a knife. He straightened up after a minute, pocketed the knife and placed something carefully in an inside pouch. He then pulled the dust cover off the leg press and used it to cover the body. He picked up a dirty piece of cloth lying in the corner of the room and wiped the dumbbell clean, then mopped up a bloody smear on the floor.

A swift look around and he was ready to go. He listened at the door, then opened it and slipped out. He walked with soft steps to the exit and disappeared outside. He was satisfied that no one had seen him. He was safe.

****

Lolita was in her own hell, looking behind her constantly in fear. And the worst thing was that she had no one to blame except herself. Maybe she could blame her father, but that wasn't going to help her here. *Why did I think it was such fun to speak to Jambu?* she thought now. *Getting my fees paid isn't worth all this.*

Jambu was relentlessly stalking her inside the college and outside, with staring eyes and the look of a carnivore circling its crippled prey. "I know where your mother live. I go talk to her?" he'd asked her this morning when she was on her way to class.

"Talk to her for what? To marry me? You're married and have kids, remember?" she spat back.

"My stupid wife in village? No worry, darling." He moved closer to her, crowding her till she was forced to take a step back. "I give you bungalow. Car. Diamond necklace."

"Who do you think you're talking to? I've got a complaint ready and will go to the police if you don't back off."

His tone changed, growing more threatening. "You think I don't know about your mother? She is pure woman like Kannagi in the old story? And who is your father? You can go to police station. My friends will wait for you there."

She ran away from him only to run into the Asuras who were blocking the corridor, harassing the girls as they went by. What kind of college is this, she wondered. Isn't there a single place where we are safe from thugs?

The Asuras were delighted to see her. After all, she was by far the prettiest girl in college. "You look a little wasted," said Subu. "Been doing something you shouldn't?"

"Busy night, I guess," Rakesh pitched in. "Who's the lucky man?"

The constant attack was making her physically sick. She could hardly concentrate in class and became the focus of Professor Lakshman's caustic remarks. And when she came out of class, Jambu was still waiting.

"Hello baby? Last chance. Or I tell to everyone. Tomorrow." He walked off after delivering the warning.

Lolita stood staring behind him. *What does he know? How? Damn him! If I allow him to blackmail me, he'll never let go.* Her cell phone rang. It was Aryan. She rejected the call. She had no time for distractions and had no intention of telling him about her problems.

Kat had left the class just behind her. "What's Jambu talking about?" she asked now. "Is it about that day in the beach? You never told me why you spoke to him."

Before Lolita could answer, her cell phone rang again. "My mother," she said to Kat, who nodded and continued on her way. Must be something urgent if she's gone to the post office to make the call, thought Lolita.

"Lalitha, some rowdies came to the convent yesterday. They said they know you." Her mother's voice quivered. "Why did you tell them where I lived, and about your father?"

I didn't. How did they find out?

"I said I was a widow so the nuns would take me in here,"

moaned her mother. "If they find out I lied, they'll throw me out. Where will I go in my old age? Haven't I been through enough? Please tell these men to leave me alone."

"Don't worry ma, I'll take care of it," Lolita said, spending the next few minutes trying to calm her down. But what could she do? Her mother had lied, and she had too. Now the world was going to find out. *I need help. I'm not becoming that creep's mistress or waiting for him to throw acid in my face. I'll have to ask my friends for help, telling them everything before they find out from someone else.*

She went looking for Kat and found her watching TV in her room with Moti. Moti was eating a gooey pastry off a red plate. "So, tell me. What's with this new plate you've been carrying around?" Kat was asking her.

"I read some research that says we eat 40 percent less when we use a red plate," said Moti. "Because it signals danger and makes us stop eating."

"That's crazy," said Kat laughing. She looked up, saw Lolita's face and stopped laughing. "What's the matter?" she asked her.

"I have a confession to make," said Lolita, her voice low. "I lied to you about my parents, saying they were rich and in the US." The words tumbled out in a rush as if she was eager to get it over with.

"What? Slow down. Here, have some chocolate. It'll help calm you down," said Kat, holding out a chocolate bar.

"No, I'm fine. Just listen," said Lolita. "I have to tell you everything before I lose my nerve. My mother and father were not married when I was born. In fact, they never got married." She paused, looking at their faces to assess their reaction.

"That's not a big deal, is it?" asked Kat. "Kamal Hassan married Sarika only after his daughters were born."

"Grow up Kat!" snapped Lolita. "We're not living on Page 3. And in their case, they could afford to be open about it. Not like my mother."

"I'm sorry. Tell us what happened." Kat decided to keep her mouth shut till she had heard the whole story.

"My father was the son of a rich landowner. He was studying in Chennai and used to visit our village during the holidays. That's when he saw my mother." She pulled out a faded black and white photograph from her handbag. "I was five years old when this picture was taken," she continued. "This is the only picture I have of our family."

They saw the pretty little girl sitting on her father's lap, looking up at him with adoring eyes.

"Your mother looks beautiful, like one of Ravi Varma's paintings," said Moti.

"She was just 16 when my father saw her. He spoke to my grandfather, gave him some money and set her up in a house in the village. No marriage, nothing."

"But didn't your grandfather protest?" Kat was appalled.

"He was a labourer working for the landowner — what could he say? Rich men call the shots, Kat. They can have ten mistresses if they want," said Lolita.

"Where's your father now?"

Lolita tapped her finger on her father's face in the picture. "Don't you recognise him? You see him on TV often enough."

The girls looked at the man with a big moustache and his hair parted in the centre, wondering why he looked familiar.

"Wait, I'll show you," said Lolita as she flipped through the news channels on the TV. "He's sure to be holding forth to a crowd somewhere. Talking of what a great man he is and how he's going to transform their lives."

Kat and Moti looked at each other, shocked at the bitterness in her voice. Who was this man and why was she so angry with him?

"Yes, here he is," said Lolita, slapping the photo next to the man occupying centre stage at a political meeting. A huge crowd was applauding him, pumping their fists in the air.

"Charan Raj, the CM candidate?" whispered Kat.

30

Kat could see the resemblance to the man in the picture, though he was much older now and better dressed. His moustache was more refined too, as befitting a respected *neta*.

"Yes, he's left his shady past far behind," said Lolita as she slumped back in her chair, feeling drained. "It's been 11 years since I saw him last. He married the daughter of the local leader of the party and became his successor when the father died. That's what he'd been gunning for — a rich wife and political power at one go."

"So he ditched you and your mother?"

"His new wife did not want to share him with a village girl," said Lolita. "She came to see us, called my mother names. Then she threw us out of our house and threatened to kill us if we contacted him again. My grandfather was dead by then and my mother had to find some work to support us." She stopped talking, unable to go on.

Kat looked at her and saw the little girl who'd seen her family shatter before her eyes. No wonder she's so desperate at times, she thought. Rebellious, angry, doing whatever she can to thumb her nose at the world. "But didn't your father try to find out how you were?" she asked.

"No, the coward was happy to let his wife do the dirty work," said Lolita. "It was like we didn't exist anymore. My mother got a cook's job at a convent in the next town and the nuns allowed me to study there for free."

A convent! That's why her English is so good, thought Kat. "Thank God for that! At least you had somewhere safe to stay," she told her.

"You've got to be kidding," snapped Lolita. "I was a charity case, the butt of ridicule. All the children had rich parents who sent them cookies and chocolates from Switzerland. And wind-up toys that clapped or laughed at the push of a button. The brats made fun of me and my clothes, which were faded cast-offs donated to the church."

Years of hurt came spilling out as she found sympathetic listeners, for the first time in her life. She could not stop now and continued her story in a low voice. "I had just one sweater, an old thin one. Jenny, a bully from the tenth standard, put her finger into the hole and pulled so hard it became huge and I couldn't wear it again. My mother slapped me and asked me if I thought money grew on trees." She began to cry. Kat held her close, thinking that she had never seen her cry before. How can kids be such monsters, she wondered.

"The boys were worse," said Lolita. "They took me to the school playground and asked me about my father. I told them what my mother had said. That he'd died when I was a baby. They laughed and said my mother was lying. Benny, the school bus driver had told them my father was alive but did not want me." Her voice broke. "The boys stood around me in a circle, clapping their hands. Chanting 'Ugly, dirty, stupid'. Over and over again, till I ran away and hid in the cemetery behind the church."

"Why didn't you tell us all this before?" asked Kat. "We could have helped you."

"I didn't tell anyone," said Lolita. "I was too embarrassed. And I didn't want you to run away too because you thought I was worthless." She felt exhausted, worn out by all her struggles.

But maybe there was some light ahead. Maybe she could move forward to a better life with the help of her friends.

****

Minx was struggling to catch up with her overdue course work, but felt so bored she wanted to scream. She saved the project file and opened her mailbox, only to wish she hadn't.

The picture she had been sent was lewd to the extreme. Her face had been morphed to fit a voluptuous nude body — someone else's. She felt as if she had been slapped hard in the face. Her insides liquefied in horror. "LET'S SHOW THE WORLD WHAT YOU GOT" read the message.

She sent an SOS to Kat and showed her the picture when she came rushing in. Kat's face turned white with shock. They sat in silence, unable to find words to describe the horror, feeling grossly violated as if they had really been photographed in the nude.

Minx's head was teeming with desperate questions. Who was the pervert? What did he want? What if this went viral and everyone thought it was her? No one would care to find out whether it was true or not. She would never be able to live it down.

"Is it Shaitaan?" Kat finally broke the silence. "Didn't you blast him when he called you the other day?"

"Yes, I did. He's a fucking weirdo. I told him I would kick him in the balls if he came anywhere near me," said Minx.

"Maybe you shouldn't have been so... direct," said Kat.

"What? You think I should live in fear? People like him can only understand one language."

"But why is he still chasing you? There are so many girls desperate for a role — even Lolita."

"Because he's a maniac and can't take 'No' for an answer. He's used to everyone licking his boots because his father's a minister."

"But do you think he has the skill to do all this morphing?" asked Kat.

"Maybe he hired someone, he's got enough money. What are we going to do to stop this? I'll die if anyone comes to know."

"I'll call Vir. He's the expert. And we can trust him to keep it quiet," said Kat.

Fortunately for them, he was relatively free at the moment and said he'd come down to meet them at an outdoor cafe nearby. Moti joined them as she wanted his help too — to track down the bully who had set up the website in her name and got her into trouble. Lolita came along, hoping to flirt with Bishnu if he accompanied his friend.

Vir took a look at their anxious faces and asked them to tell him about their problems. He listened carefully, thinking that their campus had several guys running around who belonged in jail. "Don't worry," he told them. "I know how we can take them down, and make sure they stay out of your lives."

"Where do we start?" asked Kat.

"I'm not clear about one thing though," he said. "Why aren't you reporting these issues to your college authorities or to the police? These are major crimes punishable by law."

"Yes, I could complain," said Minx. "And tomorrow I'll see everyone, including the cops, sniggering at me, looking at the pictures that will be freely available for any pervert to look at."

"And everyone will blame it on her morals, her night life, her clothes," said Lolita, sounding bitter. "Saying that she deserved what she got."

"Do you really think Shaitaan will let us get away with a complaint against him, even if we're able to convince the cops to file an FIR?" asked Kat. "You know it takes many years for a court to pronounce judgement. Who is to keep us safe from his goons till then?"

Vir realised that cynicism ran deep in the country. People believed that all systems were corrupt — politicians, police, all the authorities. They were certain that money power would win and it was useless to protest anymore. It would be better to struggle through their days, making the best of what came their way.

He took a deep breath and decided to help them in every way he could. "We need to trace the IP address from which these emails were sent," he said. "And identify the sender. If it's someone on your campus, your IT guys will have a record. Let me see your laptops."

They'd brought them along as he'd asked them to. He checked Minx's first. "Someone's installed spyware in your laptop," he said. "So he or she can read your emails, your chat conversations, find out your passwords, even see which websites you visited."

"My God — that's sick. It's like having an online Peeping Tom," said Minx.

"Who had access to your laptop?"

"I asked Rakesh to retrieve our files when our systems crashed," Kat confessed. "He said all our machines had the same virus and he would remove them."

Minx glared at her, her eyes promising that Kat would be hearing more on this later when they were alone. "Must be him then," she said now. "He could have taken the pics from my computer and morphed them. It's the kind of sleaze he enjoys."

"If he had access to all your machines, we need to check all of them," said Vir. "I'll get rid of the spyware on the machines here for now." After taking care of that, he went on to work on tracing the IP address of the cyber bully.

"Turns out both are from the same system," he said. "We're lucky he's not using a nym."

"What's that?" asked Kat.

"An anonymizer. If he's a smart hacker, he would have used one."

"He probably thought he's too clever and we are mere twits. So, does this mean we can find out the name of the culprit?"

"As I said, the IT guys in college will know who uses this IP address. But will they tell you?"

Minx turned to Kat. "How about that guy with the heavy crush on you? The one who came looking for you on his birthday with squishy *gulab jamuns*?"

Kat blushed. "Let me think. Suresh... yes, Suresh."

"Call the IT department and ask for him then."

Kat got Suresh on the line and exchanged pleasantries. When she told him she needed his help on something, he surprised her by the enthusiasm with which he agreed.

"I need to trace an IP address on our network. Some confidential matter... I know you'll understand," she said, laying it on thick.

"Of course, of course, give me the numbers," he said. He referred to his list and came back immediately with the name. "Anything else I can do?" he asked.

"Not at the moment. But thank you so much Suresh. I owe you one."

She looked at the others and blushed when she saw their expressions. "Just as we suspected, the culprit is Rakesh!" she said. "Now it's your turn Minx. Call Rakesh and ask him to come here. I'm sure he'll come running."

"Looks like I'm in the company of the most popular girls in college," Vir kidded, including Moti in his smile.

Minx made the call and asked Rakesh to meet her at the cafe. Alone. "The creep was in class, but said he'll be here in ten minutes," she said.

As they waited, Moti told Vir about Balwan, his background and the threats he'd been making. She asked him whether there was any way to stop him from terrorising her or taking out his frustrations on her mother and sister.

"Ask him to meet you in a public place where he cannot hurt you," said Vir. "Tell him outright that you have no intention of going back with him."

"What if he creates a scene? Beats me up? He's an illiterate thug and doesn't care who sees him."

"Just let him try. I'm coming with you," said Kat.

"Let me know when you fix up the meeting. I'll do what I can to help," said Vir.

Moti looked relieved, happy that there was some solution in sight to a problem that was looming larger by the day.

"Do you want to tell him about Jambu?" Kat asked Lolita in an undertone. But she shook her head, sure that she could take care of it herself.

They saw Rakesh charging up to their table, all puffed up that Minx had asked him to come alone to meet her, supremely confident that his charm had won her over. He had dressed up for the date, changing into one of his psychedelic shirts and gelling his hair into a turgid mass. He saw Vir and assumed that he was a friend of one of the other girls.

"So, a date with three beautiful girls?" he brayed, ignoring Moti. "Don't worry... I'll make you all happy."

"Stop the BS," snapped Minx. "We know what you did. So you can take that smirk off your face."

"How dare you do this? You thought we wouldn't find out?" Moti joined in.

Rakesh's face turned pale. "What are you talking about? What did I do?" he asked.

"You morphed my pictures, you freak," said Minx.

"You created a website in my name, getting me into so much trouble," said Moti.

"I don't know what you're talking about. Who told you this? Where's the proof?" He shot off the questions with a smug look on his face, confident that none of the girls had the smarts to finger him. Minx was so clueless she tried to open Excel files in Word and Kat's computer had a file listing everyone's passwords along with their names. The fools were simply asking to be hacked, he told himself. He could bluff his way out of this, then lie low for a while, keeping these fun exercises for his eyes only.

Vir saw the creep smile to himself and lost his cool. "How about this for proof? The morphed pictures were sent from your IP address. Would you prefer that we complain to your principal and the police?"

"Who are you? How is this any of your business?" Rakesh blustered.

"You answer my question first. I'm not the one in the dock."

"You obviously don't know who I am. I have friends in high places. You don't want to mess with me," said Rakesh.

"Really? Maybe all you scumbags can go to jail together. Tell me how many you are so I can book your room."

"Who is this guy? Who does he think he is?" Rakesh asked Kat. He was beginning to feel rattled by the stranger's air of confidence.

"He's a criminologist and an expert on cyber crime from the US. He's probably forgotten more stuff on these things than you've ever learnt," said Kat.

Vir hit him with all the proof he'd dug up, telling him it could put him behind bars for several years. The bully crumbled, as bullies do when someone faces them down.

"I'm sorry. It was just for fun. Let it go," he said.

"Why should we? People like you should be lynched and carted off to jail in handcuffs, with the whole world watching," said Kat.

"No, no. My father's already angry with me. I've been suspended for a week for hacking into the office computers. He'll kill me if I get into more trouble and the college expels me. I'm on my way to the railway station now to catch a train home and when I come back next week I promise I'll stay away from you all."

He looked at their faces. They were angry, unforgiving. Just like the face of the man spying on them from across the street. *One more man in your trap. Do you all know where this is going? Do you even care? But you will soon — when you see me. And that will be the last time you see anything.*

31

Lolita and Aryan were becoming an inseparable pair and spending all their free time together. Her friends were very happy for her.

"Aryan's cool!" said Kat. "Drool-worthy, but smart too. Why don't you ask him to help with your Jambu problem when you see him this evening?"

"No way am I telling him," said Lolita. "He's from a respectable family with a prim banker father and all. He'll dump me if he hears about my family and the whole mess."

"Oh, you still haven't told me why you spoke to Jambu on the beach that day."

Lolita told her everything, happy that she finally had someone with whom she could share all her problems, even things that she could not share with Aryan.

Aryan too was in a good mood when she met him later that evening. "I'm spending so much time with you I'm afraid they'll kick me out of my job," he joked. "I keep making excuses about meeting suppliers so I can come and see you."

But within a few minutes she noticed that he had fallen silent, keeping a constant eye on his car's rear-view mirror. When she asked him about it, he told her a vehicle had been following them from the time he had picked her up. Maybe one of her many enemies, thought Lolita as she craned her neck to look behind. But she couldn't make out anything in the dark except bright headlamps keeping pace with them.

Aryan turned into the parking lot of Pastry Paradise. They remained seated for a couple of minutes but the vehicle did not follow them in. Maybe they had been mistaken. They entered the cake shop and she ordered a luscious Black Forest slice, topped with whipped cream. As she scooped up the cake and let it melt on her tongue, his salad remained untouched. He was looking into her eyes with an intensity that made her blush.

"Do you know how much time I spend thinking about you? Longing to see you again?" he asked. She waited in silence for him to continue, wanting desperately to believe that she had found a man she could trust. Someone who would not desert her like her father had. He saw the glow in her eyes and was encouraged to continue.

"Will you marry me? I know we've not been together very long but why wait? Why not have a quick marriage, unless you've set your mind on a grand affair?" He reached out to clasp her hand.

She loved the idea. No one was going to organise a big wedding for her with a host of friends and relatives. She had no proud father either to perform the *kanyadaan*. Should she say 'yes'? Or was it too soon? She could not afford to make any mistakes. As she tried to marshal her thoughts, there was a screech of brakes and a vehicle turned into the parking lot. Jambu and his goons tumbled out of the SUV and stood glaring at them through the glass front of the cake shop.

Aryan turned to look at them and then at her. "I don't know these guys. Do you?"

"Yes," she whispered. "That's Jambu from our college. He's been chasing me for some time now."

"What the hell! I'll call the cops to handle this," he barked. "Why didn't you tell me about this earlier?"

"The cops won't help," she said. "His father is the owner of Jambu Distilleries and half the cops are on their payroll. He's also close to a minister."

"I have friends in high places too," he said, looking furious.

"Please don't make him angry. He's already been threatening me. Saying he'll expose me."

"Expose what? What do you have to hide?"

She should have kept her mouth shut. What could she say? And then it was too late to say anything. Jambu was at the door. She froze as she saw him striding towards their table. His eyes were bloodshot, malevolent. He seemed ready to throttle her and Aryan with his bare hands. The two young waiters looked terrified. Jambu glared at Aryan, not her. Maybe it was a male thing, she thought. Marking one's territory.

"Who are you, man? What you are doing with my woman?" Jambu attacked. "Take your hand off or I will cut it. Chop, chop."

"Are you drunk? How dare you talk to me like this?" Aryan stood up, squaring up to him.

"Please Aryan, let's go. I don't want a scene," she pleaded, reaching out to restrain him.

He shrugged her hand off without taking his eyes from Jambu. "Back off now before I call the police," he said.

"Call them, see if they touch me!"

"Better still, I'll beat you up myself. I'm not frightened of you and your thugs."

Jambu turned to his sidekicks and scoffed "Look at hero. Like Rajnikanth." They laughed. He turned to Aryan again. "Before you fight, ask if she is heroine! Or a slut like her mother. Ask her who is her father."

Before he could say more, a raucous film song blared out. He pulled his cell phone out with a curse and looked to see who was calling. His manner changed and became servile.

"Yes, yes, Shaitaan. I'm coming, coming," he said and rushed off with a final barb thrown at Aryan. "Ask her. See what she says. Then see if you want her."

A moment later, his SUV tore out of the parking lot with squealing tyres. There was absolute silence now, except for Lolita's sobbing. Aryan threw some money on the table, grabbed her hand and took her to his car. They drove in silence for a few minutes till he found a quiet side road to park.

"What was that about? Are you going to tell me or do I have to beat it out of Jambu?" he asked.

She cleared her throat, deciding to make a clean breast of it. And when she finished she sat watching his face, unable to make out anything from his expression. He remained silent, offered her a drink of water and turned the car to take her back. What was he thinking? Was he shocked? Disgusted? She was too scared to ask. He stopped just ahead of the college gates and bent to press a hard kiss on her lips. He walked round to her door and opened it for her. A wave of his hand, and he was off.

This may be the last time I see him, thought Lolita, as tears flooded her eyes. As she entered her room, she got his message. "Have to rush to Mumbai to see my parents," it said. Nothing further.

He had said nothing about a trip when they were in the cake shop, thought Lolita. Maybe it was just a lie to ditch her. He would probably never call again and she had lost her one chance at happiness.

Kat was horrified at the state she was in. "But he did kiss you, right? Why would he do that if he didn't care for you?" she asked.

"Probably a goodbye kiss. He realised he's made a mistake in saying he loved me. He must be thinking I'm just like my mother. A slut."

The skies were grey the next day to match her mood. When she dragged herself to college, an eerie silence fell. And after she walked past, the whispering started. She clung to Kat and asked her if she knew what was happening, but she didn't know either. When they walked into the canteen, they saw the posters. A picture of Lolita and below it a single line: ASK HER IF SHE KNOWS WHO HER FATHER IS.

Lolita was shocked but tried to put on a brave face. "Okay, so now everyone knows there was no Immaculate Conception. Big deal," she said.

"Then why are you so angry?" asked Kat. "Are you afraid they'll find out Charan Raj is your father?"

"Why should I be afraid of that? My father's the one who has to worry."

"Yes," said Kat. "He can't afford to mess up his image now. Maybe you can use his name to threaten Jambu."

"No way," said Lolita. "I can handle this creep myself."

32

Moti had received another call from Balwan, threatening to murder her in her bed. He said he did not care even if he were to be hanged for the crime; that it was a question of *izzat*. She realised she could not run away any longer. It was time to confront him and take a firm stand as Vir had suggested.

She called him and arranged to meet him on the beach near the lighthouse. Kat had come with her and they sat on a bench to wait. The sun was just going down. There were just a few families with children playing on the sands near the waves.

"I thought Vir would come too. What did he say when you told him we'd set up the meeting?" asked Moti.

"He doesn't talk about his plans," said Kat. "Maybe he's an old-fashioned guy who thinks women aren't equal to men."

"I don't think that's right," said Moti. "He's helped us so much already. Maybe something else came up."

"Isn't that Balwan?" whispered Kat, staring past her at the figure in pajama kurta that was nearing them. The man's eyes were even more frightening than they had been in the photo. Flat, dead, like a viper's.

Moti gasped as she turned to look at him. Her heartbeat accelerated, prompting her to flee from the threat. She looked around to see if there was anyone who could help tackle him as she knew how violent he could get. There was just one man sitting with his back to them, two benches away. They'd have to fend for themselves.

Her eyes focused on the face of the man who had been terrorising her. A feeling of impending doom made her dizzy. She clutched Kat's hand and told herself: *I'm not afraid. I will not run.*

"You are here at last," he spat at Moti. "Why so long to meet me, bitch?"

"What do you want? Why are you chasing me?"

"Why? Why? You are asking questions? Shut up and come now. We go straight to station and catch train. Then see what I do to you. How I beat you in front of the whole village." He dropped his shabby airbag on the sand and came forward to grab her shoulder.

"Back off," said Kat. "You're not in your village now. I'll call the police."

"Who are you, bitch? Want to come also? I like two girls in my bed."

Kat realised the situation was getting out of hand. They could not handle him after just one session on self-defence. Where was that stupid Vir? It would be too late to rescue Moti even if she called him now. Balwan put his arm around Moti's waist and started dragging her to the road, picking his airbag up on the way. Moti clawed at his face but he smashed his fist into her jaw, making her cry out in pain.

"Shut up and come with me. Or I'll carry you in a sack."

Kat ran behind him, trying to remember what Vir had taught them. Should she hit him or scream for help? She leaped forward, kicking him as hard as she could. He staggered when the blow caught him on his back. He turned with his arm around Moti's neck, immobilising her. He pulled out a wicked-looking knife from his waist and held it near Moti's eyes.

"Want me to cut out her eyes? Or slash her neck? Don't come near me."

Kat froze. He looked mad, fully capable of carrying out the threat. Tears were streaming down Moti's cheeks. She looked like a lamb waiting for the killing blow. Kat realised they had made a mistake. A big mistake.

The sound of a siren broke the silence and grew louder and louder. A police car was speeding down the inner beach road.

I'll run and intercept them, thought Kat. *Stand in the middle of the road, shout like a maniac. Whatever it takes to make them stop and come to our rescue.* And then another thought kicked in. *But what if he slashes Moti and runs away before they come? What if she gets killed because of me?*

Balwan turned too and stared at the police car. It screeched to a halt and four cops spilled out. He dropped his arm from Moti's neck and took a step back.

"Drop the knife, drop the knife," shouted a cop as he rushed towards him. Two cops circled him to come from behind. One pulled out a gun and jabbed it into the side of his head. Balwan dropped the knife, looking scared. He understood some of the words they were throwing at him, like 'murder', 'rape' and 'bank'. The cop in front of him looked at a photo in his hand and nodded to his colleague. "Yes it's him." The cop holding the gun on him pulled his arms back and slapped on the handcuffs.

"What? What?" screamed Balwan.

One of the cops spoke in broken Hindi to explain that he was being arrested for a bank robbery and the murder of the security guard. He was also wanted for rape by the police in his state.

"No, no. No murder, no rob," he protested to the senior cop, trying to pull himself loose and run away. The cop holding him let fly with his fist, knocking out a few front teeth. Another kicked him in his ribs. Balwan moaned and turned to Moti, as if seeking her help. The girls stared back in shock, unable to comprehend the sudden turn of events.

"He will not trouble you anymore," said the cop in charge. "We'll take care of him at the station. Break his legs if need be and send him home with an armed escort. He'll realise he won't go back alive the next time."

He saluted someone behind them and Kat turned around to see him going towards the man who had been seated on the bench. When the man came forward to meet the cop she realised it was Vir. The cop exchanged a few words and then drove away in the police car. Vir came up to them.

"So you were here all the while and arranged the arrest?" asked Moti, relief written all over her face.

"Yes," said Vir. "I'm sorry the cops were a little slow in arriving after I called them. But I wanted them to see with their own eyes that he is armed and dangerous. They'll warn their counterparts in Nagpur too. So he'll keep away from your mother and sister."

Kat pounced on him. "You didn't think you should tell us about it? I was terrified thinking he was going to cut out her eyes. Or kill her right here."

"He could see the open fear on your faces and that's what convinced him this was not a trap. If he'd run away we would have had to start all over again, wouldn't we?"

"Thank you. Thank you so much," said Moti. "I can now get on with my life and stop being afraid every minute of the day."

"Change your cell phone number," said Vir. "Don't give the new number even to your mother. And let's plan a few more sessions of Krav Maga, in case I'm not around the next time you need help." He turned to Kat and asked her, "Did you hear anything further from Deepika?" Kat had called Vir and shared her worries about the girl's uncharacteristic silence.

"Not a word," Kat replied. "Someone from the college office was also asking us yesterday."

"I got her mother's phone number and spoke to her after your call," said Vir. "When I asked her about her husband's heart attack, she was shocked and handed the phone to him. He told me he was fine, absolutely healthy. So the sms you got from her was false. Either she went off with a boyfriend after sending the sms or someone else sent it from her phone."

Kat was shocked. She considered what he had said and then said, "Deepika is a blabber-mouth and would have told us if she had a boyfriend she was serious about. Maybe... do you think she has been kidnapped?" Moti listened aghast, looking as if she would faint any moment.

"We don't know anything for certain," said Vir. "Her parents have come to Chennai and filed a police complaint. They feel terrible that they didn't know something was wrong. They kept getting messages which said she was too busy with her exams to call them. I need you and your friends to be alert and let me know if you hear anything," he said.

His cell phone rang just then. His face darkened as he listened. "Right now?" he asked. "Okay, I'll be there."

33

That's odd, thought Vir. A call from Bishnu that doesn't start with a joke. And he sounds so subdued. He left the girls with a hurried goodbye.

The package had arrived at the CBI headquarters just an hour back. There was no sender's address. The front office followed the strict protocol laid down for handling suspicious letters or parcels. It had to be checked for explosives and chemicals like anthrax that were being increasingly used by terrorists these days. A team of experts with their paraphernalia gave the parcel a thorough going-over. When they gave the all-clear, the receptionist opened the box. And screamed. Her high voice brought people running. She collapsed in a heap, her head missing the edge of her desk by a millimetre. A trainee who peered into the box started crying. Huge, hiccupping sobs.

Keegan, who was there on business, called Bishnu. The hotline from Delhi buzzed with instructions and Keegan carried off the parcel with him, despite Reddy's protests. When Vir came into the HATCHET office ten minutes later, the first person he saw was an ashen-faced Rom who escorted him to Bishnu's room. Bishnu nodded to him and indicated the parcel that lay open in the middle of his desk.

Vir looked inside and saw what seemed like a brass paperweight. Four fingers were folded into the palm and the middle finger was sticking out. And then he saw the detail that had set off the panic. The middle finger was bloody, human. It looked like it had been chopped off a woman's hand.

"Here's the card that came with it," said Rom. It was a plain card with a red rose and 'Best wishes' printed on it. The standard card that all gift shops offered.

"The killer is flipping us one," said Vir. "Issuing a challenge. Any fingerprints? Any idea where the brass paperweight came from?"

"No prints. He could have bought the paperweight from any curio shop and done the rest himself," said Bishnu.

"I hope the press is not aware of this. Have you warned Reddy to keep this quiet?"

"My boss spoke to the top cops here. He'll watch his step — for a while at least."

"Cut him off completely. It's getting too dangerous to have a loose mouth tipping off the killer," said Vir.

"He's not going to like it," said Bishnu. "He's mortified that he had to hand this package over."

"The finger does look like it's a woman's. How likely is it that it is Deepika's?"

"Your algorithm already predicted that her college was likely to be one of the killer's next targets. And Deepika is a young college girl, just like the other victims. Fortunately, I'd already taken blood samples from Deepika's parents for just such an eventuality. I'm having the finger checked against their DNA."

"Whoever the victim is, there's a hope that she's still alive, stashed away in a dark hole somewhere," said Vir, his brow furrowed. "But if this is the handiwork of the serial killer, why were there no mutilations in the previous killings?"

"Maybe, like Jeffrey Dahmer, he craves more and more stimulation and is not satisfied with just killing his victim anymore. He needs to torture and mutilate," said Bishnu.

"So, how sure are you that there are no missing fingers or body parts in the earlier cases? Did you see the bodies yourself?"

"We did ask to do the post-mortem with our own doctors. But Reddy claimed jurisdiction and we didn't want a fuss in front of the media. We only have the post-mortem reports. The bodies have been cremated by the families. And even if some were buried, an exhumation will provoke a huge hue and cry."

Vir turned the pages of the autopsy reports on the desk. "So these are from Reddy. They seem pretty sketchy, but no doctor worth his salt would miss such a significant detail."

There was silence in the room for a minute and then Bishnu exploded. "You're right. No doctor would miss something like this. But I did not speak to the doctor, only to that SOB. He wouldn't dare, would he?" He picked up the phone on his desk.

Vir raised an eyebrow and waited. He didn't envy the person he was calling.

"Good morning Mr. Reddy," Bishnu said. Very polite, very restrained. "I wanted a clarification from you on the serial killer case. Any chance you forgot to mention missing fingers or body parts?"

He listened to the rambling at the other end and then cut in. "Please answer my question, Mr. Reddy." And then he repeated what he heard at the other end, "So there were missing toes, the ones next to the big toe, on all the bodies. Can you explain how this important detail went missing from the autopsy report?"

Some more blustering from the cop. And then a scathing retort from Bishnu: "This is totally unacceptable. You have withheld a crucial piece of information that could derail our investigation. You can be sure I'll be taking this up with your superiors, and mine." He flung the phone down on the table, saying, "Reddy's fucked up big time. When the next body bobs up in a river, the blood will be on his hands... I'm going to get him. Make sure he's transferred to the most god-awful place I can think of."

He paced back and forth, back and forth. Then he dropped into his chair and took deep breaths to try and calm down. He looked up at the others with a wry smile. "I should have figured. I knew he resented us and thought we were intruding on his turf. But I didn't know he would go to this extent."

"Leave it for now," said Vir. "Don't let your anger cloud your mind. Think about what we know, and where we can go with it. We'll get back to Reddy when this is done and kick his ass so hard he'll never stand up again."

"Besides, look at the bright side to this," said Rom. "If Reddy didn't tell us about the missing toes, he's not told the press either. So that will help us weed out all the phoneys who call in, claiming to be the killer."

"Get many of those?" asked Vir.

"Just yesterday a woman called, claiming she had killed and drunk the blood of the virgins in order to appease Ayyanar, the guardian deity in her village," said Rom.

"Round-the-clock media coverage does tend to bring out all the loonies," nodded Vir. "Shall we get started on the new information we've got?"

"Yes, the missing toes," said Bishnu. "And just the ones next to the big toe. That's the killer's calling card."

"Probably an intrinsic part of the ritual he enacts at every killing," said Vir. "Rom, please check if there are any other cases in the country where the body had missing toes."

"But why this particular toe and not any others?" asked Bishnu. "This is not a random mutilation then and must have some significance, at least in his mind. We need to find out what that is so we can anticipate his next move."

They had lost a lot of time because of Reddy's unprofessional behaviour. Rom began cross-referencing the new information with that in their database. "There are several myths on what it means if the second toe is longer than the big toe," he said. "The person will dominate over his family or he could be a descendant of a royal line. And look at this, there's even a celebrity who displays this anomaly."

"The Statue of Liberty?" asked Bishnu. "I remember reading about it."

"Yes," said Rom. "Then there's podomancy, or fortune telling based on the toes. A fat second toe indicates pots of money after 20 years. Not useful info for us though, unless the killer hates people who are destined to become rich!"

"Anything about the cutting of the second toe?" asked Vir.

"Just that amputations of the second toe are usually carried out when a person suffers from hammer toe."

"How about foot fetishes?" asked Vir. "Several famous people had these: Casanova, Elvis Presley, Ted Bundy."

"Running with it," said Rom, his fingers flying on the keyboard. "These fetishes include an attraction to jewellery like toe rings and ankle bracelets."

"That's it," exclaimed Bishnu. "Married women."

"What?" asked Vir.

"Hindu married women wear a ring on the second toe," said Bishnu.

"Yes. A warning for guys like me to keep off," said Rom.

"That's a good lead," said Vir. "I'd forgotten the custom.... But these girls weren't married. They wouldn't have worn toe rings."

"And they're not going to wear them after he kills them either. So what's his deal?" asked Rom.

"That's it," Vir exclaimed. "They are not fit to be married, now or in any future life. He's saying they're not pure enough. And that's why they had to die."

34

"So that fits right in with the belief of many serial killers," said Bishnu. "They think their victims are worthless, and they're cleansing the streets of human trash."

"But our theory is that our man chooses victims who resemble his ideal lover," said Rom.

"A psychopath starts with 'I must have' and ends with 'It was not worth having'," said Vir. "He looks for idealised victims in order to degrade and destroy them. He's trying to eliminate the enemy within his own mind and thinks he can save himself by killing them."

"So he's totally out of touch with reality," said Rom. "Is he mutilating them before or after he kills them?"

"Probably after," said Vir. "When he has complete control over the victim and the woman cannot reject him. These mutilations excite him, trigger his sexual fantasy."

There was a knock on the door and Umang came in. "We compared the DNA of the finger with that of Deepika's parents," he said. "It's a match."

"That's fast work," said Vir. "It takes much longer in the US."

"High speed analyser," said Umang. "A breakthrough from our own guys — and we have exclusive access."

"So we know now," said Bishnu. "Deepika's been kidnapped, most probably by the killer."

****

Lolita had received an MMS on her cell phone. It was a video of her knocking on Professor Lakshman's door and entering his quarters at night. It showed her standing close to him, flaunting her body in a tight T-shirt carrying a provocative slogan. The video was followed by a message which said: IF YOU DON'T WANT BB TO SEE THIS, COME TO ME.

She showed the video to Kat. "I'll be expelled if this comes out," she said. "No one will believe me if I say nothing happened."

"Who could be hounding you like this?" asked Kat. "You've made so many enemies — Jambu, the Asuras, Shaitaan. It's even possible they've teamed up to bring you down. It's high time you asked your father for help."

"You're talking as if he's dying to hear from me and to protect me. I don't even know how to contact him. I can't tell his secretary that his daughter is calling. And he's always surrounded by a crowd."

"You need his cell number. He probably answers it himself."

"Okay, so do you happen to have the number lying around somewhere?" Lolita mocked.

"I know Vir has it," said Kat. "And you can trust him."

"Why should he help? After all, he's friendly with my father."

"Let's try. Or maybe we can peek at his contact list and you won't have to ask him outright."

Kat called Vir right away and was invited along with Lolita to his suite at the Taj. They were quite thrilled to peek into his penthouse suite and enjoy the breathtaking view from his private terrace. He ordered fresh juice for them and asked them how they were coping with the tension of having a killer on the prowl.

"This year has been a rude shock," said Kat. "We were having such fun, away from home and parents the whole of last year. But the monsters from our worst nightmares have come to life now."

"And every day we're afraid that we'll get some bad news about Deepika," said Lolita.

"About that...," he said, "I'm afraid it's already happened. We just discovered that she's been kidnapped."

They were appalled, more so as they felt guilty about the way they'd bitched about the Gossip Queen. With the thoughtlessness of youth, they had somehow thought they were immune to danger and death. But now their minds were conjuring up horrible visions of the chirpy girl at the mercy of a sick mind.

"Maybe the killer is someone we know and have seen on campus without realising it was him," said Kat. Lolita shivered at the thought.

"It's probably on the news by now," said Vir, turning on the TV.

"Here's an appeal from the mother of Deepika, the kidnap victim," said Pia, the TV1 reporter.

Deepika's mother was fair, plump and had a bewildered look on her face. She wore a big red *bindi* and *sindoor* in the parting of her hair. "I appeal to whoever has taken my daughter Deepika to let her go," she said. "She's a warm, friendly girl, our only child. So happy, so loving." Colour pictures of Deepika flashed on the screen: riding a cycle, wearing her graduation cap, eating ice cream.

"She does not deserve this," continued her mother. "We don't deserve this. We have done no one any harm. We're simple people leading ordinary lives. I appeal to you, whoever you are, to the goodness in your heart. We will be eternally grateful if you set Deepika free. We will not ask any questions or try to find you. Just let her go. Show the world you are not the monster they imagine. Please, please let my daughter Deepika go." The camera moved closer to focus on the tears that flowed down her cheeks.

Vir switched off the TV and they sat in silence. *It's like we're observing a moment of silence in Deepika's memory*, thought Kat. *Will the appeal soften the killer's heart and will we see her alive again? I promise you God I'll never say one nasty word about her again, if you'll just bring her back safely to her parents.*

"Bishnu's coached the mother well," Vir was saying. "She repeated her daughter's name several times and emphasised how innocent she was. Hopefully, it will make the killer see Deepika as a person and not as an object to be destroyed."

"Do you think it will work? That he'll release her unharmed?" asked Kat.

"We can always hope," he said. "But killers like these are normally beyond such appeals. They feel as much remorse as you would feel when you squash a bug. They are the closest to evil that I have ever come across."

A minute or two passed and then Vir changed the subject. He knew that wallowing in fear wouldn't help anyone. "You said you wanted to talk to me about something?" he asked. "Tell me how I can help you."

Kat had no energy for subterfuge. She could not think of any way they could see his contact list without his knowledge. "We wanted Charan Raj's cell number and were hoping you could give it to us," she blurted out. "Lolita needs his help to tackle some thugs."

Vir looked puzzled. "I don't understand. What's his connection with Lolita and why would he help her?" he asked.

Kat looked at Lolita. This was not her secret to share. Lolita took a deep breath and decided to tell him the truth. She had no other options anyway.

Vir looked thoughtful when he had heard her story. "Normally, I'd refuse to share personal information like cell numbers," he said. "But I think I can make an exception in this case. However, please keep my name out of it."

Lolita took down Charan Raj's number, already rehearsing what she would say to him. They stood up to leave, for they had a long way to travel to get back to college. Vir took a pen drive from his jacket and gave it to Kat.

"What's this?" she asked.

"A poison pill to kill your cyber bullies," he said. "Just boot his computer with it and all his data will go poof — permanently. Plus, it has a virus that will corrupt his back-up files as well as the systems of others who have linked up with his machine."

"Yes!" said Kat, giving him a radiant smile. "We'll do it tonight." *This will send the bad guys running for cover,* she thought. *And hopefully things will go back to the way they were.*

35

When Kat returned to the campus with Lolita, it looked like the place had been tossed by a tornado. BB had called the students to the auditorium to read out a list of security guidelines that he said had become necessary after the kidnapping of Deepika. The students rejected these vehemently, calling them Gestapo tactics.

BB continued regardless. "Girls will no longer be allowed to leave their hostels after 11 pm," he said. "You will not go to certain unsafe areas on campus which will be notified. There will be new dress regulations. Girls must wear only sarees or salwar kameez with a v-shaped dupatta pinned on both sides. You will not talk to boys and will have separate seating and staircases. And then some rules that are common to both boys and girls. You can't go to any hostel other than your own. You can leave the campus only twice a month, after you produce a fax from your parents."

The students began to chant "Hitler, down, down."

"Is this a college or a jail?" asked Lolita, standing up and shouting to make herself heard above the uproar. "You can't cage us in the name of security."

"Many parents have called," said BB. "They're worried about their daughters. So we have no choice. What is your problem with these rules? Why do you want to talk to boys and roam around at night? Have you come here to study or for something else? You must think of your college as a temple or church, not as a place to indulge in immoral activities."

"Immoral activities? That's very insulting to all of us sir," said Kat, jumping up with a red face. "Is it immoral if we want to use the internet late in the night when it's available only in the library? How do we go about it?"

BB gave a superior smile. "You will be escorted by male students," he said. "Which of you boys is willing to volunteer?'

Many hands shot up, including that of Amar and Subu. They were thrilled at the prospect of having a girl all to themselves late in the night. Rakesh would no doubt join them as soon as he returned from his trip home.

"Great," said Lolita. "And what if the escorts themselves harass us?"

The boys howled in protest, making rude gestures at her.

"We'll give you whistles that you can use to call for help," said BB, looking very pleased with his visionary thinking. "And we'll install surveillance cameras in all corridors and class rooms to make sure that no one is breaking the rules. Of course you'll have to pay a special fee for all this."

He took off his reading glasses, folded the paper he had been reading from and strode out of the hall with some students still pursuing him, buzzing like angry bees whose hive had been torched.

"Is he serious?" asked Lolita as the principal passed them. He turned to glare at her before striding off.

"Looks like it," said Kat. "And there's nothing much we can do about it. We'll just have to put up with it till we complete our studies."

Lolita was still fuming and told Kat, "Let's go trash Rakesh's computer tonight then, before all the rules come into effect. I badly need to blow off some steam."

Kat set her alarm for 3 am, when even the night owls on campus would be fast asleep. She took the pen drive and a torch, then went to Lolita's room to shake her awake. "There seems to be a security patrol today. We'll wait for them to pass the hostels and then go," she said.

Lolita sprang up, grabbed what looked like a dentist's pick and a screwdriver and stuffed them in her pocket. "Well, how did you think we'd get into his room?" she asked Kat, who was watching her with wide eyes.

"But why do you have these tools, as if you're a criminal?"

"It's not just criminals who need skills," Lolita shot back. "You'll never understand what I've been through. I'm terrified of the dark and of closed spaces. And once the bullies in school locked me up in a dark cupboard, in a pantry which no one used." Her breath came in gasps as her mind filled with vivid images that she had pushed to the back of her mind.

"It's okay. Don't tell me if it upsets you so much," said Kat, feeling guilty about what she'd said.

But Lolita went on, as if she could no longer keep the horror bottled up, when it was eating her up from the inside. "I shouted and banged on the door for hours, but they had left me and gone — the monsters. I thought I heard rats scrabbling about, waiting to rip my flesh to shreds. I thought I was going to die there in the cramped cupboard. The stink was terrible and it was piled with pieces of junk that tore into my flesh."

"Then what happened? Did they come back and let you out?"

"No they didn't, the bastards. I stopped shouting when I couldn't shout anymore, realising I was on my own. There was no space to swing a stone or a tool, even if there was one at hand. I found a small piece of metal wire, inserted it in the lock and worked it in a frenzy, having no idea if it would help. But it did, after hours and hours of panic, and I tumbled out half crazed, with bloody fingers." She shook her head, as if to get rid of the horror that was still clinging to her. "Now I can open almost any lock, as long as I have these. No one's locking me in, ever again." She patted her pocket to reassure herself that she still had her tools and fell silent.

Kat held her hand in a warm clasp. They stood together watching from the corridor as the security guards and their torches moved out of sight. Then they came down the stairs and moved towards the boys' hostel, keeping to the shadows and being careful not to step on twigs.

The security guard's whistle shattered the silence. They jumped, hid behind a tree and wondered if they had been spotted. They knew it was risky to break into Rakesh's room today, almost insane. But for some reason they wanted to go ahead anyway. They moved on again, relieved to see that the lights were off in the boys' hostel. They climbed on soft feet up to Rakesh's room. Lolita inserted her tools into the padlock in the light of the torch that Kat held in trembling hands.

What if someone came out of their room to investigate, Kat worried. What would they say? "Hurry, will you?" she whispered to Lolita. The lock opened with a click that seemed very loud in the silence. But no heads popped out to check. They slipped into the room and shut it gently behind them.

A message was blinking on the computer which was still on. Perhaps Rakesh's friends had been using it when he was away at home. They peered at the monitor and saw a challenge from someone called 'The Butcher'. Kat clicked on the icon. It was an online game in which the Asuras held the first place with 6875 points. The Butcher was second with 6823 points and was inviting them to another bout. "The prize money is three lakh rupees," Kat's eyes glinted. "Shall I?"

Lolita nodded. Kat clicked on "Accept". Then they sat by watching as the Butcher battered the strangely dormant Asuras. He overtook their score and knocked them out of the game once and for all. Kat smiled and moved to the next step in the Demolition Derby. She booted the USB and ran the killer software. Figures danced across the screen at a rapid pace, then a message popped up: 'All data erased.'

"Hope the virus is in the network too. It'll spread to Subu and Amar's systems as they are all linked together," Kat whispered.

"It's done, time to go," said Lolita. "Before someone catches us." She opened the door, peered out and saw that there was no one around. They tiptoed out and shut the door. Relocking it was easy. She just had to press the U-shaped arm into the hole. They scurried back to their hostel hoping they would not be caught now and heaved a sigh of relief when they made it without incident.

"That was awesome," said Kat. "It feels good to get back at those bullies. I hope our good luck continues and Deepika turns up tomorrow."

36

Deepika's body was found by the construction supervisor the next day, stashed behind the machines in the gym. The man had gone into the room to check the completion of the interiors, and reeled back in shock when the stench hit his nostrils. It didn't take him long to find the dead body hidden under the dust cover. He had staggered out clutching his chest and called his assistant who was in the next room. The assistant had the presence of mind to lock the room and call the police control room. Soon police cars roared into the parking lot and the first few reporters were trying to worm their way into the building.

Minx brought Kat the news as soon as it hit the air waves. The whole college was in a furore. "She must have been dead all this time, from the day we went to the gym," said Minx. "When we didn't even realise she was missing."

"It's terrible," said Kat. "Who could imagine that Deepika would become the news story herself?" Lolita joined them as she switched on the TV to watch the news.

Kat was surprised to see that the reporter was Sushil. "When did he come to Chennai, Minx?" she asked.

"I don't know. He never called me," Minx said in a dejected tone. Kat saw that Lolita was looking uneasy and wondered what was up with her. Sushil's voice drew their eyes back to the TV.

"This is the twelfth body to have been found," he was saying. "We have Deputy Commissioner Reddy with us to tell us more."

"The victim has been identified as Deepika, second year Master's student of Viscom at SS Padmaja College, Chennai," Reddy read out from the paper he was holding. "Her handbag with her ID was found near her body, but her cell phone is missing. The probable cause of death is a heavy blow to the head. A dumbbell was found lying on the floor near her and we suspect that this is the murder weapon. It has been wiped clean of fingerprints but we hope forensics will be able to tell us more. We will give you further updates once her post-mortem has been completed."

"I understand the body was found in a gym which is currently under renovation sir," said Sushil.

"Yes," Reddy confirmed. "We have to find out what she was doing there and how she got in, as it has been closed for months now. We will question the workers on the site and find out who had the keys."

"Do you think this is the work of the serial killer, sir?"

"Yes, she's a college girl who fits the profile of all the earlier victims."

"What do you have to say about the criticism we hear every day, that the police are getting nowhere? And that Chennai has become the most dangerous city in the country?"

"No, no, that's not true. Our teams are making good progress. In fact, we have identified some patterns which will help us predict where the killer will strike next," said Reddy.

"That is good news sir. Please tell us more."

Reddy was happy to oblige. "As you know, my team has been working day and night to crack this case and I can share one bit of information with you. I found that the killer never goes back to a college that he has targeted before. This means that Padmaja College and the other colleges which lost one of their students can be taken off the list. We will increase security in the remaining colleges to catch him when he attacks next."

He stared straight into the camera and delivered a challenge: "We warn him to surrender before we shoot him down."

****

Vir, who was watching the broadcast in Bishnu's room, turned off the TV with a curse. "This guy's a clown," he said. "He's telling the killer where his cops will be stationed. Whom did he sleep with to make it to Deputy Commissioner?"

"Bishnu," said Rom.

Bishnu ignored him. "He's not an IPS recruit, but worked his way up the ranks by keeping on the good side of the politicians," he said. "I thought he had been warned sufficiently to keep his mouth shut."

"It's good he hasn't found out about my role in the investigation," said Vir. "Or I'd find my photo plastered at every street corner and every jackass with a mike tracking me."

"He didn't accept our algorithm or our inference about the killer not returning to the same college a second time," said Bishnu. "But now he's tossing it to the media as if it is his own brainwave."

"We might be able to catch the killer if he worked with us. Now one more girl has fallen victim and that too when on her way to meet us at the gym," said Vir. "I feel terrible about that."

"Do we have the phone records for Deepika's mobile? What can we find out about the killer's location?" asked Bishnu.

"It was switched on a few times after her death to send messages," said Rom, "but always from crowded, central areas of the city. It could be anyone, anywhere."

"I think Reddy's making a mistake in assuming the killer is done with Deepika's college," said Bishnu. "She wasn't taken from her campus like the others were."

"I agree," said Vir. "First, the MO is different. A blow to the head, not a strangling. Second, the others had marks on their wrists to show they had been tied up for some time. Third, he did not dump the body in a river as in previous cases, showing that this killing was not a planned one. It's a break from his pattern, perhaps because he had to kill unexpectedly when she stumbled onto him."

"So, if he was already there when she came to the gym, he must have been following one of the other girls," said Rom. "That means Kat, Lolita, Minx or Moti is his chosen victim."

Bishnu nodded with a grim face and said, "He's going to kill soon as he needs the rush he gets when he carries out his ritual. I'll have to warn Reddy." He made the call, putting the phone on speaker mode. "DC Reddy, this is Bishnu. I just saw you talking to the media about the killer. I thought we'd agreed to be careful and not tip him off?" He grimaced as they listened to Reddy blustering on the other end. "But sir, we can't assume that he's moving to another college. If you'll let me...."

Reddy cut him off. "I don't want to listen to your fancy theories, young man. Or to your telling me what to do. I have some questions for you myself. You need to answer them first."

"About what?"

"Deepika's classmates say they met you at the gym," said Reddy. "Because you told them you'd teach them self-defence. What was your real motive in taking them to a deserted place like that?"

Bishnu was thankful that he had warned the girls earlier not to mention Vir's name to anyone. Or he would be bombarded by questions from the police and the media. He now pushed back at the cop: "So are you saying that I lured them there and killed Deepika? That I am the serial killer?"

"I'm saying you should have known better than to take them there," said Reddy. "You should be thankful I'm not hauling you to the station to question you... and now, I've got to go. We *cops* have a lot to do." He hung up on him.

There was silence as Bishnu sat slumped in his chair. "You know, I hated telling Deepika's parents the news. They were so hopeful we'd rescue her," he said. "I couldn't even tell them we know the identity of the killer and will catch him soon."

He relived the moment when he had told the parents that Deepika had been killed. He would never be able to forget the way the mother's eyes had blanked out — as if she too was lying in the grave with her daughter. He had reached out to hold her hands and found them icy cold. A high keening sound had emerged from her lips. He heard the father saying something and turned towards him. "It was not her time, it was not her time," the father was muttering, over and over again.

Vir felt low too as he realised the killer had been at arm's distance from them. None of their skills or software had helped prevent this murder. He could not help worrying about Kat and getting angry with himself. *Why did I let myself get close to her? Why open myself to love and loss once more?*

He remembered the dream that had haunted him for many months after Rima's death, the same one every time. He was sitting by the poolside. She was walking towards him in a pretty summer dress. She spotted him and raced towards him, her face lighting up. His arms opened wide to wrap her in his arms... and then he woke up, sweating and cursing. He would look around the room for her and wish he could have stayed asleep a little longer till he held her close again.

The dream had returned. But this time it was Kat who was in danger while he stood by, waiting for tragedy to strike him down again. He must talk to Kat and repeat his warning to her and her friends, telling them not to go out anywhere on their own, especially at night. He would assure her that they were closing in on the killer, hoping that if he said it often enough he would believe it himself.

37

Kat felt as if they were besieged — by the killer, the cops and the Asuras. And it seemed as if the last two were more difficult to handle. Rakesh's computer crash had brought down Amar's and Subu's systems as well. They'd stayed up two nights trying to retrieve the lost files and software without success. They flunked their exams as they were unable to hack into the office computer to steal the question papers. And they were afraid to complain to the principal, as they did not know whether the hacker had made a copy of their illegal activities. They knew Minx and Moti were not savvy enough to do something like this. But it could have been Kat or Lolita, helped by the stranger who had confronted Rakesh. Their suspicions made them so aggressive that Kat feared that they would be physically attacked.

And then there were the cops, harassing everyone on campus. Police cars with sirens drove into the college through the day. The students were tense, talking in whispers, voicing theories and suspicions. Classes were suspended for the week. Imagination ran riot and even students she had never seen came up to Kat and her friends wanting all the juicy details about Deepika: "Who do you think killed her?" "Does she have a boyfriend?" "Was she raped?" One boy even asked Kat if she thought she was next on the killer's list.

Minx had had enough. "You're living proof that it's possible to live without a brain," she snapped at the boy. "Get lost!" The girls holed up in their room, switching channels and hoping to hear something positive for a change. Maybe the killer had been caught or killed. Maybe they could start living again. But they only saw endless reruns featuring Deepika's face and profile. They were caught in a nightmare from which they were unable to escape.

Fortunately the media had been kept out of the college or they would have hounded them too. But the reporters hung around near the gates, pouncing on anyone who went in or out. They saw poor Deepika's parents being badgered on TV, with questions on whether the body was mangled and where and when they were holding the funeral. Minx's mother called, of course. "Come back home beti. I'm worried you'll be on the news next," she had moaned. And then she had gone on to ramble about Minx's father. "I heard him tell Lily he loves the scrambled fish eggs she cooks," she whispered. "What will I do if he moves in with her?"

"Throw in Arpita as a free gift," Minx snorted. "Relax ma. Father is not leaving you and I'm not getting killed. You know, Sushil's here too and I can call him for help. So stop worrying." *Not that he's bothered to call me. But she doesn't have to know.*

They were all summoned in due course to meet Reddy, who had set up his interrogation centre at the college library. His boorish questions soon set their backs up. "So you are Deepika's friends," he said with a curl of the lips. "The way you girls dress, the way you behave... I'm not surprised things happen to you." Kat's eyes widened at his tone.

"You go out alone in the night, drink and dance with boys. Think you can do anything and get away with it," he went on. "Then when something happens, you blame the police."

Is he saying we're responsible for whatever happens? If we are raped or murdered? thought Kat, opening her mouth to protest.

But Reddy was still talking, looking at them as if they should be behind bars. "Your principal tells me you went to a deserted gym to learn self-defence. Is that what you went for? Or to have some fun with that young man, five of you at the same time?"

"But isn't he with the police?" asked Kat. "He's also trying to find the killer. Are you saying we shouldn't trust him?"

"All these upstarts with no experience. They know everything. How? Because they studied in the US," Reddy muttered, half to himself. And then to the girls, "Now tell me everything you know about Deepika, her boyfriends, her lifestyle. Did she drink, go to parties, use drugs?"

They answered as best they could, trying not to antagonise him, but wondering all the while if the killer would ever be caught if this man was in charge. "Where is the other girl in your group?" he called after them when they were leaving after the inquisition was over. He read the name out from his list. "This girl Lalitha. Where did she go at a time like this? What kind of morals does she have? Tell her to come see me as soon as she returns."

38

Earlier that day when Lolita got out of bed, she had no idea what was going to happen, or she would have stayed in bed. She was only worried about the MMS and about how she could keep it from going viral. With the new regulations in place, evidence of her visit to the professor's room would certainly result in drastic action. Moreover, BB was angry with her for her defiance when he had laid out the new rules and would use the opportunity to expel her as a warning to other students.

Busy with her thoughts, she almost fell into Jambu's arms when she was coming out from the computer lab. He blocked her way with two goondas but chose to address them rather than her. Somehow that was more terrifying, as if she was not a person anymore but just an object he wanted to snatch.

"Take a good look at her," he was telling his men. "Tonight, she will come to me. Or you will bring her to me. Understood?" The men nodded, staring at her with bloodshot eyes that seared through her clothes, stripping her naked. They looked like they could hardly wait to maul her, dragging her to their den and laying her out for the sacrifice. Her blood froze. She ran to her room, took a deep breath and called the cell phone number Vir had given her. Charan Raj answered. How was she to introduce herself? As his daughter? As Banu's daughter? Her mouth dried up.

"Hello?" his voice repeated.

"This is Lalitha, Banu's daughter from Seeranur," she blurted out. There was silence for a full minute. Loud voices could be heard in the background. Lolita wondered if he would hang up. What would she do then? Keep calling till he sent his assistants to beat her up? She had no illusions about her father and would not have contacted him if she had any other choice.

"Who gave you this number? What do you want?" he said fiercely, keeping his voice low. She could hear the voices of his men fading. He must have moved away from them.

"There's someone in college here who seems to have found out that you are my father. I thought you wouldn't want this exposed," she said.

"Who did you tell?" he shot back.

"I told no one. His men went to our village and then to see ma."

"Who is he?" his voice rose.

"Jambu. His father owns Jambu Distilleries."

She heard the sound of vigorous clapping and slogans raised in his support.

"I can't talk now. I have to go on stage. Come to my farmhouse in Injambakkam tonight at eight," said Charan Raj, giving her quick directions. "And come alone."

She decided to leave at once as it would take her time to get to Injambakkam, located along the scenic East Coast Road leading to Mahabalipuram. Here the moneyed classes had huge bungalows with their own beach front and she would have to scout out the exact location of Charan Raj's farmhouse. She could not hire a cab or an auto as she was terribly short of money. She had to take a bus and then change to another in order to get there. Her thoughts were in a whirl as she wondered what her father would say when he saw her after so many years. Would he apologise for deserting them or accuse her of trying to blackmail him as she knew the elections were near? She had to convince him she wanted nothing from him, except to silence their common enemy.

After a hot, dusty journey she was finally walking in the fading light towards the farmhouse which was down a dusty lane. There was a big bungalow set far back from the gates among huge trees. A fence, a watchman and a vicious German Shepherd guarded access to the great man. She gave her name to the watchman; he checked his list and let her in. She trudged down the driveway and into a big room where several people were waiting. Some of them looked like party workers while others looked like they were the owners of the posh cars parked in front of the house.

There was an air of hushed expectation as everyone waited to pay obeisance at the new seat of power. Pre-election surveys had predicted a landslide win for Charan Raj and his People of India Party. All hail the new chief, thought Lolita. She was the odd person there, squirming as they looked her up and down. They probably thought she was his latest squeeze. She had heard several stories about his affairs with starlets.

A gleaming BMW pulled up at the portico and Charan Raj emerged, folding his hands in a respectful greeting. He was silver haired, erect, commanding; clad in a pure white dhoti and kurta. The waiting crowd stood up, forming a passage for him to go through. Two men came before him clearing his path while another two followed, carrying his files and briefcase.

A consummate politician, he smiled graciously at the waiting people, speaking in Hindi, Telugu or Tamil to his party leaders from different regions. He put a hand out to touch a shoulder here, shake a hand there. When he saw Lolita, his eyes narrowed and his smile froze for a second as his public mask cracked. He then pulled himself together, gestured her to wait and moved on down the line. The hall emptied out over the next hour as the waiting VIPs were ushered into his room one by one. He called her into his room after the last one had left. His assistant closed the door and left them alone.

The room was big, air-conditioned, with a thick Kashmir carpet and plush sofas set in a cosy grouping. A cloying rose fragrance hung heavily in the air, perhaps from all the garlands that his admirers had brought to greet him. The walls were plastered with photos taken on the campaign trail and with political leaders over the years.

He gestured to the sofa facing him and she sat down, wondering if she had made a mistake coming here. The hour-long wait had made her realise the kind of power he wielded; how easy it would be for him to get rid of her without even saying a word. She had no illusions about what he was capable of, and what was at stake for him. A long-lost daughter whom he had erased from his mind didn't stand a chance when weighed against a world of unlimited power and privileges.

She gazed at the face she had not seen for so many years. He was still handsome, with a magnetic aura that drew people to him in droves. Like lemmings committing mass suicide by throwing themselves off cliffs, she thought.

"So, what's the real story? Why now after so many years?" his harsh voice broke through her thoughts. "You think you'll get a lot of money by blackmailing me?"

"Definitely not," she shot back in anger. "If I had wanted money, I would have contacted you long ago."

"You think I'll pay you more now because the election is near and I can't afford a scandal. Drop your pretence."

"I don't want your money. I want you to stop Jambu from messing up my life and yours. That's the only reason I'm here."

"How did he find out if you didn't tell him?"

"He has a hired gang around him, some of whom have hacked into the college computers. Anyway, he found out my home address and went to the village in order to find out more about me. Anyone there could have told him about your connection to me. And now, he's threatening to reveal everything if I don't become his mistress."

"I know Jambu's father and can control his son. He knows his old friends will soon be out of power and he'll need my support to run his business." He paused, still looking unconvinced about her motive. "So that's all you want?"

"Yes," said Lolita. "But I do have a question for you. Something I've wanted to ask for the last eleven years."

"What?"

"Why did you desert us? What did we do to deserve that?" Her voice broke. "I waited so many months for you to come back and take us with you to the city."

He looked uneasy for the first time since she'd seen him. "My father-in-law made me his successor in the party on the condition that I left my past behind. That I never saw you or your mother again. Of course he's dead now, but...."

"You can't risk your public image by revealing your past," she completed his sentence for him. She had her answer and could see the real man behind the smile, when the fake warmth had been switched off. "You are a saint now, aren't you?" she asked. "Serving the people till your last breath? Don't worry. Just take care of Jambu for me and you'll never see me again." She stood up and turned to leave.

Her thoughts were chaotic. She wanted to cry but was determined not to. How could a loving father change into this cold, calculating machine? All she could hope for now was that he'd keep his promise and take care of Jambu, so she could finish her studies and leave all this behind. She knew her friends would be waiting anxiously for her call but did not feel like talking now. She was exhausted, feeling as if a loved one had died, leaving her all alone to face a callous world.

She took an auto back to the hostel, telling herself she could borrow money from her friends the next day. The auto dropped her off at the end of the lane leading to the college and she plodded along with her head down, past a car parked on the side.

She did not see the driver stepping out of the car as soon as she passed and taking a quick look around the deserted lane. But she felt the powerful blow on the back of her head. She staggered for a second from the impact before collapsing in a heap on the ground. A sinewy arm grabbed her round the waist before she could fall, then lifted her and dumped her in the trunk of the car, slamming it shut.

When she woke up she would find herself tied up, unable to see or speak. She would be helpless, counting the hours to her death.

39

Kat was worried as she had not heard from Lolita after the message she had sent saying she was on her way to Charan Raj's farmhouse. She was not back even at midnight and her cell phone had been switched off. Could she have gone off with Aryan without informing her? But why switch off her phone? With all that had been happening, Kat did not even know if Aryan was back from Mumbai and had got back with Lolita. She slept fitfully and tried calling her again in the morning, only to find that the phone was still off. She dug out Aryan's business card and called him.

Aryan greeted her warmly and told her he'd returned to Chennai a few days back but had been busy organising a sales workshop for his teams from all over India. "I wanted to talk to you all after hearing about Deepika. You must be shattered by the news. How is Lolita taking it?" he asked, sounding very much the eager lover.

Kat's heart nosedived. Lolita was not with him. She had been hoping against hope that somehow she was safe. "She did not come back last night after going to meet Charan Raj," she told him now.

"What? She's missing? My God, why did she go alone? I've been too busy to call but she could have asked me for help." He sounded distraught.

"Things have been very difficult for her in the last few days.

She needed her father's help and could not wait. In fact, I got a message from her only after she'd left for her father's farmhouse."

"This is terrible, terrible," he said. "I'll drive down immediately to meet you. Maybe I can file a police complaint so the cops start looking without wasting any time."

Moti joined Kat in her room soon afterwards, also worried about Lolita. "I checked Lolita's room just now. She's not back," she said.

"Aryan hasn't heard from her either," said Kat. "Do you think she even met her father or did Jambu kidnap her before that?" She was unable to think straight and felt guilty that Lolita had gone alone. "She should have waited for one of us, but she's always been rash."

Moti fell into a chair, her eyes wide as she had a vision of Lolita's body laid out on a platform for her funeral. She knew she would have nightmares that night.

They sat in a doleful silence till Aryan called to say he was at the gates. They met him in Appu's tea shop which was where students met visitors to the college. Several students had been called home by their worried parents and the place was deserted.

Aryan looked dishevelled, unlike his normal self. "Any news?" he asked as soon as he saw Kat. She shook her head and asked Appu for tea for all of them. None of them could eat anything under the circumstances. She told Aryan all the details, including her suspicion that Jambu had kidnapped Lolita.

"Do you think he's the serial killer then?" he asked, looking anxious.

"I don't know," said Kat. "But he's been threatening Lolita for a long time."

"Why couldn't it be Charan Raj?" he asked. "After all, he has a lot to lose now."

"Will a father kidnap his own daughter? What are you saying?" Kat asked.

"What if he keeps her stashed away till the elections? After that, he'll have the clout to suppress any story that comes out. He's not been the ideal father, has he? He shut her out of his life just so he could enjoy riches and power."

"You're right," said Moti. "I know my father will do anything to get rid of me, so why not a man who has so much at stake? We must work out a plan of action to find Lolita."

"I'm calling Vir," said Kat, picking up her phone. "He will definitely come to help us." But Vir was busy in a meeting and asked her to come into the city to meet him.

"I'll take the electric train," she told him. "I'll get there much faster than by road."

Aryan said he'd drop her at the train station on his way to make the police complaint while Moti decided to stay on campus in case Lolita turned up.

"Don't worry, we'll find her," said Aryan to Kat as he dropped her off. "I'll make damn sure of that." She made her way in, only to see that her train was just pulling out. While she waited for the next one, she received a call from Aryan.

"I'm at the police station and need her official name," he said.

"It's Lalitha Raj," she replied. "What are the cops saying?"

"They don't want to register an FIR and want us to wait at least

48 hours. I told them that would be too late and that they have to start looking right away. Don't worry. I'm not leaving here till they do something."

The platform was getting crowded even as she spoke on the phone. The train entered the station and people pushed their way to the front in order to get in first. And then, she heard shouting and saw a melee further down the platform. She was shocked to see a young boy falling onto the tracks in front of the speeding train. The driver blasted his horn and slammed on the brakes but it looked like the boy would be run over right in front of her eyes.

The train is not going to stop in time, thought Kat. The crowd screamed and a woman fainted. The boy, his eyes dilated with fear, rolled off the track and into the narrow gap near the platform. Just in time. The train passed him, missing him narrowly, and shuddered to a halt. Two young men reached down to help the boy climb back onto the platform. He was shaking, screaming that someone had pushed him in. His knees and hands were bleeding. Voices were raised, calling for the police. A Good Samaritan offered the boy a drink from her water bottle and asked him if there was someone with him to take him home.

The crowd milled around, exclaiming in horror, looking around for the man who had pushed him. No one had seen anything. Who was the killer? Kat looked around too. Was it the fat man who looked like a villain from a bad movie? Or the man with the big moustache? It could be anyone, maybe even the man standing next to her. She could not recognise a single face. Her legs trembled. Someone pushed her as the train pulled out and she moved back quickly from the edge of the platform. Where was the exit?

A hand tugged at her. She screamed and pushed it away, only to realise that it was a young girl who had just entered the station, asking her when the next train was expected. She apologised, said she didn't know and moved on. She was ashamed at how shaky she had become when faced with an emergency and tried to pull herself together. The buzzing of her cell phone drew her attention.

"It could be you next time," read the message. Her heart thudded. Her head swivelled around looking for anyone watching her. No one was paying her any attention. She ran out of the station, calling Vir on her speed dial. When he answered, she broke down. "There's a monster out here. I'm going back to college before he kills me too."

40

Lolita was learning to do the blind shuffle. A used bookstore copy of S.W. Erdnase's 'The Expert at the Card Table', a Christmas gift from Mother Superior, lay open in front of the little girl. She was eight years old, the daughter of Anna the cook at St. Agatha's Residential School in Ooty. Banu had changed her name to Anna when she sought asylum in the convent with her daughter.

The little girl found the trick quite difficult, especially the complex terminology: 'Under-cut about half deck, in-jog first card and shuffle off.' But she would figure it out in time. She was seated on the floor between the choir stalls in the church, her bare legs sticking out of her faded pink frock, knees tucked under her chin. Her two pigtails were tied up with bright blue ribbons. The threadbare sweater she wore barely protected her from the cold. But she was happy. She loved the church with its beautiful stained glass window of the Good Shepherd, its polished pews and the parquet floor.

Someone was slapping her face. Was it her mother? She tried to turn her head away, but couldn't. She tried to see who it was, but it was pitch dark. Was she awake or was she dreaming?

The man watched with enjoyment as the girl tried to move her hands and legs. But the rope was secure, as were her blindfold and the cloth stuffed into her mouth. He spoke in a low growl. "You are now in my control. Keep quiet and obey my instructions if you want to stay alive. Nod your head if you understand."

She heard the voice and struggled to make sense of the message. Then she nodded, ready to do anything to get out of the straitjacket she was in. The man removed the gag, held some juice to her mouth and asked her to drink.

"Please untie me, take off my blindfold," she croaked. "Who are you? What do you want? Please let me go."

"Now, now, just do what I say," he said. "Or you'll be sorry."

She screamed — a hoarse voice that she could hardly hear herself. Then she screamed louder: "Help, somebody help!"

He slapped her hard, again and again, flesh against flesh. The blows of a maniac. His fist smashed into her mouth to cut off a loud wail. The shock of the blows juddered through her body. He gagged her again and poked her arm with something sharp. Was it a needle, an injection to keep her drugged? No, no, she screamed in her head. She heard his voice faintly as the drug coursed through her system. It was chilling, taunting.

"You've been very bad. You didn't obey. Now you get nothing to eat or drink. You will be punished." He bent down and yanked off the ring she was wearing. It was a ram's head ring signifying Aries, her zodiac sign.

She began to float above the clouds. Her mouth was dry and she heard his voice fading away. And then a cacophony of sounds that made no sense....

41

The reporters were clamouring at the college gates, wanting to be let in. But the cops had strict instructions not to let them in till Reddy made his appearance. When he finally did arrive with sirens blaring, the gates were opened and there was a mad rush to the college auditorium where he was holding court.

"How did you people get the news so fast?" Reddy asked Pia, the TV1 reporter. "We are not even sure if this girl Lolita has been kidnapped by the serial killer," he said. "As I said earlier, his pattern is to take a girl from a different college each time."

"But sir, what is the safety you provide to girls when they are being kidnapped and killed at such alarming frequency?" asked Pia.

"What do you say to the Opposition demand that the case be handed over to the CBI?" asked another reporter.

Reddy's face turned red with anger. "I don't know what you people are saying. Do you know how many girls go missing in a day in Chennai? Seven. Most of them elope with their boyfriends. Then when the boys refuse to marry them, they file a case saying they were kidnapped."

My God, thought Kat as she listened to him. *He seems to be as hostile to women as the killer.*

He was not finished yet. "As for the safety of women, we are going to clamp a curfew on them so they cannot go out after 8 pm, unless accompanied by a male family member. They will have to dress decently and not talk to strangers...."

His voice was drowned by an uproar as the reporters and the students protested loudly. Slogans were raised against 'Taliban rule', 'victimisation' and 'dictatorship'. Reddy signalled to his men who evicted the press and the angry students. He refused to allow the media to talk to the students and the principal. He then vented his anger on Kat, Moti and Minx, bombarding them with questions about Lolita. When they mentioned Jambu and his threats, he was not very receptive, merely telling them he would look into all possibilities.

Jambu was probably speaking the truth about the cops being on his payroll, thought Kat. She told Reddy that Lolita had gone to see Charan Raj on some personal business on the night she disappeared. Reddy's eyes gleamed at this plum opportunity for him to introduce himself to the CM-in-waiting. "What personal business?" he asked, but she told him she did not know. She did not want to antagonise Charan Raj in case he was the one holding Lolita, or if they needed his help to save her.

She was worn out by the time the interrogation ended. She sat with her friends under the trees near the auditorium, wondering if her life would ever be normal again. Her phone buzzed. It was Vir, asking them to come to the mall nearby so they could brief him on the attack at the station and Lolita's disappearance. The friends headed out in Minx's car, realising with a pang that their numbers had been reduced to just three in the span of a few days. They sat silently, waiting for Vir at the outdoor cafe.

But when he arrived, they saw that he was livid. A vein throbbed in his temple as he tried to control his anger at the way in which they had flouted his warnings. He asked them how he could protect them if they were so irresponsible. One more girl had been taken by a killer running amuck. He could never forgive himself if another girl was killed. They hung their heads and listened in silence as he scolded them. There was no excuse they could offer for Lolita's actions.

"How could she do this?" he asked. "And how could you let her go alone after all that has happened?"

"She didn't tell us she was going. Or I would have gone with her," said Kat in a low voice. Moti looked like she was about to cry.

Vir took a few deep breaths. "Okay, let's get down to business. We can't afford to waste any time. First, tell me about the incident at the station," he told Kat. "Who did you tell about your plans? Was there anyone around who could have overheard you?"

"We were in Appu's shop," she said. "Moti and me. Appu brought us tea. Maybe he overheard and passed it on to someone like Jambu."

"Okay. Who else was there?"

"Aryan," said Kat. "He's manager at BigBen's and Lolita's boyfriend. He came to meet us as he was shattered to hear that Lolita was missing. He'd asked her to marry him and she was planning to say 'yes'."

"Tell me more," said Vir, taking notes.

"He was very much in love and showered her with gifts," said Moti. "A necklace, a cell phone, perfume...."

"If he was so much in love, how come he didn't go with her to meet Charan Raj?" asked Vir. He knew from experience that a boyfriend was often involved in the case of missing girls.

"He was conducting a sales conference at one of the resorts on East Coast Road," said Kat. "And she didn't tell him she was going either."

"Okay. So is there anyone you suspect, anyone hanging around her? Or someone with a grudge against her?" he asked.

"You know about Jambu," said Kat. "He's top on our list."

"Of course, the police are already talking to him on his movements last evening. Anyone else?"

"Aryan thinks it could be Charan Raj who has her locked up somewhere, till the elections are over. We don't know if she even left his farmhouse," said Kat.

"I doubt whether a man in the limelight like him would take such a huge risk," he said. "But we need to look at all angles."

"There's Shaitaan," said Minx. "Lolita said she'd met him a couple of times after Reggie introduced us at the club. She was trying to get the role I turned down. But Shaitaan told her she didn't look like an Indian village belle."

Vir looked confused. "Back up a little please," he said. "Who is Shaitaan? Doesn't that name mean 'devil'?" As the girls filled him in, he grew increasingly disturbed. "Quite a bunch of criminals you girls seem to know," he said. "Perhaps it's an indication of the kind of world we live in. Any more lovelies on your list?"

"The Asuras of course," said Kat. "You met Rakesh and then there are his friends Amar and Subu. They were furious after what we did to their computers, though they have no proof it was us."

"Unlikely that nerds like Rakesh would do something so physical," said Vir. "They could have helped set it up, though."

"Then there's Sushil," said Minx. Kat and Moti looked at her in surprise.

"What?" said Kat. "He met Lolita just once didn't he, when she came to see you after your accident?"

"That's what I thought too, till I saw them at the mall," said Minx. "He was paying for a whole stack of designer wear that she'd bought herself." She lapsed into silence, looking defeated. Vir waited for them to explain.

"Sushil is Minx's boyfriend," said Moti.

Minx corrected her: "Ex-boyfriend."

"You know the reporter who was covering Charan Raj's campaign in Tamil Nadu and is now covering the murders?" asked Kat.

"Yes, I've seen him," said Vir. "So he's dating Lolita, who is also dating Aryan?"

"I don't know if Sushil is dating her," said Minx, trying to be fair. "I blew my top when I saw them together and stopped talking to her. I don't know if they continued to see each other."

"You can't be serious," said Kat. "You've known Sushil all your life. How can you suspect him of being a killer?"

Vir intervened. "Killers don't wear a sign on their forehead, you know," he said. "They are often very popular and hide behind a 'mask of sanity'. Though if you dig into their past, you'll find they have a history of torturing animals, wrenching off the limbs of dolls — things like that."

"Minx is just being nasty, a dog in the manger," Kat insisted. "Sushil's not even based in Chennai, he's from Delhi."

"Well, killers change their location when a place gets too hot," said Vir. "We can't overlook anyone at this point of time. It should be easy enough to track him down for questioning as the TV channel will have a record of his movements."

"So go on, am I on your suspect list too?" snapped Kat, not too pleased at the way he had disregarded her opinion.

He ignored her outburst. "There's quite a lot to go on now," he said. "Keep me posted if there are any developments, or anything else you remember."

As he left, Kat stared at his back, annoyed by his abrupt departure. *So he won't tell us anything. Well, we'll make our own enquiries, and Aryan will help. He doesn't think girls are too stupid to be trusted.*

42

"Mother, please don't hit me," Lolita moaned, as she felt the hard slaps on her cheeks. The little girl liked Mr. James, the music teacher at the convent. He had long thin fingers with which he stroked her cheeks and gave her rich, creamy chocolates. He took her to his quarters and played some tinkling music on his recorder. It was called 'The Blue Danube' and was created by a famous musician, he said. Then he sat, pale and quiet, half in shadow, as he watched her dance to the music.

Her mother rushed in, shouting as usual. She should not go to the teachers' quarters. She should not trouble Mr. James. She would wallop her if she caught her here again. "Sorry Mr. James, please don't ask her to come here anymore. The sisters will be angry," she said as she dragged Lalitha away. She saw the chocolate her child was clutching in her hand, snatched it and slammed it on the table before Mr. James.

Lolita felt a sharp slash on her cheek and tried to get away from the pain. Oh God, she was still tied to the bed. It was not her mother, but the kidnapper. The drug was still clogging her system, confusing her mind. She heard him speak in a low growl. "I'm giving you another chance. I'll take off your gag. Don't say anything. Remember what happened last time." She nodded, moving her head as much as she could.

He slipped off the gag and held a glass to her mouth. She swallowed huge gulps of orange juice till there was no more. She was so hungry and her head wouldn't stop pounding. What was this maniac planning to do with her? "You are a fucking monster. They will lynch you when they catch you. Don't think you're getting away, you sadistic psychopath," she yelled. He punched her mouth hard. She felt the salty taste of blood trickling into her mouth. Then he put something round her neck and dragged it tight. She struggled to breathe, to stay alive. Drifted somewhere above and watched herself thrashing below.

Now she was in the cupboard, trying to get out. No, she was with Jenny who'd poured water on her bed and then told everyone she had wet herself. She was dying. All this was coming to an end.

His voice rose above her tortured breath. "Didn't I tell you to be quiet? Why should I keep you alive? Maybe I'll strangle you and dump you in the river. Or bury you. How would you like to be buried alive?" He giggled.

"No, no, don't. Don't bury me. You can't leave me in the dark. I'm afraid. I'll be good, I promise," she wailed.

He stuffed the rag back into her mouth and tied it. "I thought you were so pure, so perfect. But all of you are the same. Sex-crazed liars like my mother. But you can't cheat me, no one can. Everyone's afraid of me: the press, the police, the people." He giggled. A sharp prick on her arm as he drugged her again. Then he stood listening to the tinkle of her anklets as she struggled to break free.

He would soon take her to meet his mother. She was waiting, always waiting.

43

It was Aryan's insistence on registering an FIR about Lolita's disappearance that had set the media hotlines buzzing. As soon as he left the station, a sub-inspector leaked the news to the crime reporter of 'The Daily Sun'. The reporter told his counterpart in the group's TV channel and all hell broke loose. Reddy was besieged by baying newsmen.

When Aryan called Kat to ask her if there had been any news on Lolita, she asked him to join them at the mall. When he came to the cafe, Vir had already left. She told Aryan that the police were checking out Jambu, but Vir was not too sure that Charan Raj was a suspect.

"He'd say that of course," said Aryan. "Isn't he taking that man's help to establish himself here? We should check Charan Raj ourselves."

"I agree," said Kat. "He's got the money and the men to do anything. They could have picked her up as soon as she left his farmhouse. But how do we find out?"

"We can try and meet him and ask him what he knows," said Moti.

"Yeah. And he's going to confess all. Grow up Moti," said Kat. "How about his wife? From what Lolita said, she seems quite a shark herself. Maybe she's behind the kidnapping."

"It should be easier to see her," said Aryan. "But you'll need a good cover story."

Kat pondered for a while. "I'll say I'm inviting her to be the Chief Guest at our College Day function," she said. "She's going to be the CM's wife soon, isn't she?"

"That's a good idea," said Aryan. "I'll take you. I'll call in sick at work. I can't concentrate on anything other than Lolita now."

They found it easy to locate Charan Raj's house but it was not so easy to get in to see his wife. The guard at the security booth would not let Kat in without a prior appointment. When she insisted and showed him her student ID, he called the house and an assistant came on the line. When Kat made her request, he asked her several questions: her name, course and college. When she mentioned SS Padmaja College, he had more questions to ask: "Isn't that the college where the missing girl Lolita was studying? Do you know her?"

"Yes," she said. "Lolita is my classmate in Viscom."

"Do you have an authorisation letter from the Principal?"

"No."

"Whose idea was it to invite Madam then? What is the occasion?"

"We want her to be the Chief Guest on College Day."

There was a pause and then he turned her down. "Sorry, she doesn't attend any public functions as she keeps a very low profile. Please don't waste our time."

"Maybe I could just see her for a few minutes and explain in person?" Kat interrupted before he could put the phone down.

"No, sorry. You'd better leave now." He hung up on her. She exited the compound feeling dejected.

When she told Aryan what had happened, he pointed out that the assistant's behaviour had been very strange. "Why ask you so many questions if she never accepts such invitations?" he asked. "It's as if he was checking you out before sending you away. But don't worry, I'll find some way to get to his boss." He sounded very agitated and she reached out a hand in sympathy. "There's one more thing," he said. "Let's keep this between ourselves for now. I don't want Vir to find out we're looking into him and warn him." She nodded.

Much later that night, Aryan called her to tell her about some developments. "I've been waiting all evening on the road watching his gate," he said. "I finally got lucky and managed to talk to their cook Selvam who was leaving for the day."

"What did he say?"

"Seems Charan Raj's wife has been quite ill, ever since her father died. Some stomach bug they've not been able to cure. The cook was quite upset that this should happen despite all the care he takes. He says Charan Raj dotes on her, serves her with his own hands. He calls her his lucky charm without whom he'd never have made it so big."

"If she's so sick she couldn't have arranged the kidnapping, right?"

"All this makes me more suspicious of her husband, who is supposed to be quite a playboy. What if he's trying to get rid of the wife who knows all his secrets?"

"I've heard about poisons like thallium that are undetectable," she said. "But do these things happen in real life?"

"I'm bloody well going to find out," he said. "If he's got evil plans for Lolita, I have plans for him too."

Kat sat in her room for awhile, thinking about these developments. Then she left her room and went looking for Moti. The two went to the auditorium to see if the police had come up with anything new. They joined a group of students who stood watching as Jambu went in for questioning by Reddy. With him was a woman wearing too much lipstick and too few clothes. "That's his girlfriend," whispered the girl standing next to Kat. "He lives with her in an old house nearby."

The Asuras came charging up and tried to enter the auditorium. The cops stopped them however and they hung around, waiting for Jambu to come out. Kat heard them boasting about the wild parties they'd had at Jambu's place.

"Great fun, man," said Rakesh. "Scotch, grass, all those girls from Mumbai."

"Yes, Jambu knows how to take care of his guests," said Amar. "Hope he calls us to the party he's throwing for Shaitaan. He's planning to fly in belly dancers from some foreign country."

Jambu finished his interview and came swaggering out with an arm around his girlfriend. "No trouble, no trouble," he told the Asuras who rushed up to him. "They ask if I know where Lolita is. I tell them whole evening and night I was with Champa Darling. She also tell police."

Champa Darling smiled and looked around as if she expected the students to run up to her and ask for her autograph. The whole pack walked away towards the car park planning what they would do the rest of the day.

Moti was disappointed. "So it wasn't Jambu?" she asked. "I thought they could find Lolita by pressing him for answers."

"Not when he has Champa Darling to provide an alibi," said Kat. "Or when he's greased the palms of the cops so generously."

"Yes, maybe a few extra cases of Scotch will do the trick," said Moti. "We were fools to expect anything more."

Kat wanted to wail aloud. *Where are you Lolita? Will I ever see you alive again?*

44

"Pretty girls! Lock your doors, lock your windows. You don't want to be next." The tabloids were running riot, spreading panic about the Madras Mangler. The girls in the city were moving around in groups, like minnows fleeing a shark. Fundamentalists were crawling out from under rocks to ask girls to go back to their kitchens. The cops were running for cover. Even the garrulous Reddy was avoiding cameras. Vir and Bishnu were working round the clock with their team at the Ops Centre, running down leads and tracking tips that the public were calling in.

They were also taking a close look at people whom Reddy had cleared with suspicious speed, like Jambu. "Naturally, Jambu's girlfriend will say he was with her," said Vir. "She'll say whatever he wants her to say, as long as he's her meal ticket. We must check his movements independent of the police."

"Yes, and search his properties," said Bishnu. "Kat says they did not see him anywhere near Lolita the day she disappeared, nor did any of the students. I sent a few of my team members to the campus to interview them."

"I've seen Jambu and his men. None of the students is going to give him up or even want to be seen talking to the cops. How about placing a few locked boxes around campus, where they can drop information anonymously?"

"That'll work," said Bishnu. Keegan left the room to take care of it.

"I went to meet Lolita's mother," said Umang. "She identified two of Jambu's goons from the photos I'd taken, as the men who threatened her. But she has no other information to offer. She's very worried about her daughter, but too scared to venture out of the convent to come to the city."

"Can't blame her. The world's not been kind to her," said Bishnu.

"What news on the Charan Raj front?" asked Vir. "Has Reddy spoken to him?"

"Yes. Charan Raj told him he did meet Lolita for ten minutes but has no information beyond that. He was at a Party dinner immediately afterwards and his assistants confirm that. Reddy also promised to keep his name out of the press."

"That figures," said Vir. "Can't see Reddy pissing off the future CM by throwing him to the tabloids. The problem is that neither Jambu nor Charan Raj needs to be actually present at the scene of the crime. They have enough men to carry out their orders."

"We should talk to Charan Raj ourselves. But first, we'll meet Sushil as planned," said Bishnu.

It was only a short drive to Sushil's TV station and they found him very cooperative and open in his answers about Lolita. "Yes, I was attracted by her looks and took her out a couple of times," he said. "It was when I bought her some stuff at the mall that we ran into Minx." He paused, looking sheepish.

"Heard about that. Quite a scene, wasn't it?" said Bishnu.

"Yes. Minx told both of us off, after which I stopped seeing Lolita. I've been with Minx for too many years to break it off after a stupid quarrel."

"So where were you on the night Lolita disappeared?"

"In Trichy, covering the ruling party's mammoth rally. You can check the footage that aired on TV if you like," he said. He played the archived stories for them, proving he had been hundreds of miles away. "I'm staying in Chennai till the elections are done," he continued. "I'm also covering the Lolita story which has developed some political overtones. I suppose you know that Lolita had gone to see Charan Raj just before she disappeared? Shaitaan's party is going to town with this."

"Oh, it's out is it? Reddy was not able to keep a lid on it then," said Bishnu.

"A fat juicy story like this? No way," laughed Sushil. "Listen to what Chellamuthu, the ruling Party spokesman, has to say."

He played a clip of the man ranting at a meeting in Mylapore. "How many wives does Charan Raj have? How many girlfriends? Can you trust a man with no morals?"

"That's a nasty crack. Aren't there strict laws against slander of this kind?" asked Vir.

"If he files a case, he'll have to wait for years for the judgement, by which time political equations would have changed and witnesses turned hostile. The culprit ends up with just a slap on the wrist," said Sushil.

Chellamuthu was spraying spittle as he warmed up to the topic. "How can you trust a man who is ready to kidnap his own daughter so he can become CM?" he said.

Sushil turned down the TV to answer Bishnu's questions: "You spent several days with Charan Raj on the campaign trail. Did he say anything about all this?"

"No," said Sushil. "The circumstances do look fishy, though it may not affect the election results. Our voters are used to hearing much worse." He turned to Vir. "I was hoping I could interview you on TV, have you talk about DNA and all that stuff. How it helps the police to catch killers, establish paternity. It would have a lot of topical value."

"No, I don't think so," said Vir.

"Why don't you give it a shot?" asked Bishnu. "Maybe it will shake something loose or goad the kidnapper into making a mistake."

"Maybe if I'm not named and am off camera," said Vir, realising there was some merit in the suggestion.

"I can do that if that's the only way I can get you," said Sushil. After fixing up a time for the interview, the two friends left the TV station. Bishnu was returning to HATCHET while Vir was going to check in with Kat and meet Aryan.

He called Kat and asked her, "Are you free to meet at our usual place in the mall? Bring your friends and ask Aryan to join us as well. I need to speak to him in person."

"Sure," said Kat. "We'll be there, though Moti can't come. She's at the hospital for her stint of community service." Moti actually seemed to be enjoying her work there and was very keen on impressing Dr. Gaurav, her mentor. Kat suspected she had a crush on him and kept teasing her, asking her how old he was and whether he was married.

When Vir drove into the mall an hour later and walked towards the outdoor cafe, he saw Kat and Minx seated at a table with a good-looking guy. The man was clasping Kat's hand on the table and looking into her eyes as he spoke. Vir hated him on sight but put on a polite mask as he said his hellos and was introduced to Aryan.

"So you are the hotshot from the US," said Aryan in an aggressive tone. "Rich kid who studied abroad and all that." *Seems very insecure*, thought Vir. *Waiting to pick a fight.*

"Vir works with Interpol," said Kat.

"Ah, I can see that from the progress he's made rescuing Lolita," said Aryan, with a curl of his lip. Vir looked at him with a deadpan expression and refused to bite. *Could be that he is stressed out by Lolita's disappearance,* he thought. *Though he seems to have moved on to Kat soon enough. Maybe I should ask him if he knows the other victims.*

Aryan's tone changed, revealing how dejected he was feeling: "Why did she have to go alone? If she'd waited one more day, I could have taken her."

"I have a few questions for you," said Vir. "Can you give an account of your movements on the night in question?" *One third of women killed in the US are killed by their partners. Guess the numbers will be higher in India where men think they own women and can burn them for dowry or if they suspect her fidelity.*

Kat intervened. She thought Vir was being very rude when Aryan was so upset. "Aryan had gone to see his parents in Mumbai and then hosted a two-day conference on East Coast Road," she said.

"Which resort was that?" asked Vir, looking intently at Aryan.

"The 'Sun n Fun' resort," he replied.

"I told you he's the manager at BigBen's, the fashion store, didn't I?" said Kat.

"Oh, takes care of a shop then?" said Vir. *Guess he comes across a lot of girls there.*

"I was in military intelligence," said Aryan, rearing back in anger. "Graduated top of the class from MITS, the Military Intelligence Training School in Pune. Best in the country." *If that's true, it would be easy for you to kill these women and get away with it*, thought Vir.

Kat was uneasy and tried to soften the ugly turn the conversation was taking. "Aryan has been very helpful," she said. "He filed the police complaint and has done some investigation into Charan Raj. He found out the wife is suffering from some serious stomach problems. We think Charan Raj may be behind that too."

I wish Kat will stop defending him, thought Vir. *He seems to have no difficulty fooling women with his charm.*

"So you're saying he's poisoning his wife, is that right?" he asked Aryan. "Who did you speak to? Do you have proof?"

"I spoke to their cook Selvam. And no proof," said Aryan. "As of now."

"So, let's get back to your conference. Can anyone vouch for your presence at the resort?"

"DC Reddy has already questioned me. If you like, you can speak to my assistant, Dev," he replied. He scribbled a phone number on the back of his business card and gave it to Vir.

"So you were there throughout the day and night?"

"Yes, we all left the resort together the next morning by the company bus. We did not have our own cars." *Haven't you heard of cabs, my friend*, thought Vir. *You expect me to believe you couldn't have got away?*

He stood up and excused himself, saying he had to make a phone call. Kat watched him turn the corner and followed him after a couple of minutes. She couldn't see him anywhere and walked further on. She finally spotted him in the car park. What was he doing there? She walked up to him and blurted out the question that was on top of her mind: "Why are you being so rude to Aryan? Are you jealous or something? He's so upset and you seem to be questioning him like a suspect. Aren't we all going to work together to save Lolita? " He said nothing, merely giving her an impassive look before turning to lead the way back to the cafe.

The meeting broke up soon after, with Kat and Minx returning to the hostel in Aryan's car. "God knows what the kidnapper's doing to Lolita," said Aryan. "I feel so rotten, helpless." He struck his clenched hands on the steering wheel.

45

Lolita felt a light shining through her blindfold. The man was back and he was saying something. She was very hungry and hoped he'd brought her food. She realised she'd do anything just to stay alive. Why hadn't anyone come looking for her? Hadn't they realised she was missing?

"Do you think I'm evil?" the growly voice was asking. "But I'm not, you are." The voice rose. "You're making me do this, don't you see?" There was silence. Had he slipped away? She felt something sharp jab her face just below the blindfold. The voice started again, back to the growl. "Maybe I should cut your eyes out, so you can't stare at me and make me feel guilty. Or maybe I should carve my initials on your face so everyone will know I own you."

Her heart thudded faster. Would he really do that? She was tired of being helpless; waiting to see what he would do. Maybe the next time he pulled off her gag, she could shout at him, taunt him. Make him lose his temper and kill her. Anything to bring this torture to an end.

"Oh, I forget. Didn't you say you'd like to be buried?" Lolita gasped, wishing she had not told him she was afraid of closed spaces. "I'll put you deep in a hole, with your hands and legs tied, but your eyes and mouth open. So you can see the dirt and mud falling over you, covering your body, then your face. Falling into your mouth as you beg me to let you go. Then you'll scream and curse when I don't fall for your tricks. Till you begin to choke, run out of air and gasp for breath. Feel your insides burning up. Burning, burning...." He laughed his manic laugh.

Her body twisted as she reacted to the picture his words conjured up. He heard the anklets tinkle. His mouth split into a lurid grin that revealed his bared gums, like an animal preparing to attack.

"A slow and horrible death. Trust me. You will flail in terror as your organs shut down one by one. Not at all a good way to die, Lolita. Do you want to die like that?" He laughed again. "Oh, *you* don't have a choice do you? It's *me* who decides. Me. Do you want to beg now? Maybe I will let you go if you ask nicely enough. Or maybe I won't. You don't know, do you? Think about it. Maybe I'll just leave you here and go away on a trip. You can try to escape, but you'll fail. You'll try to shout, but you won't be able to. How much time will it take for you to die? You're so young and healthy, it could take forever."

Please, I'll beg. I'll do whatever you want, she screamed in her head. She swallowed and felt the gag move further into her throat. She choked and tried to expel it. Weak tears escaped her eyes and seeped down her cheeks past the blindfold. She was in a dark place again and she had to find a way to escape.

46

Jambu lived in an old house set in the middle of a large plot on a quiet, leafy street in the suburbs. He lived on the ground floor with Champa Darling, while the drunkard landlord lived on the first floor. Jambu kept him happy with regular supplies of cheap rum so he did not question the wild goings-on at his tenant's parties that went on till dawn.

Last night's party for Shaitaan and his men had been particularly successful. They were celebrating the murder of Punk Raja, one of the rowdies that the opposing party depended on to bribe and bully voters. Jambu had followed him late one night in his Sumo with six men armed with logs, knocked him down from his bike and beaten him to death. It had been particularly satisfying to Jambu as the man had been Champa Darling's previous boyfriend and had beaten her black and blue whenever he got drunk. She was under Jambu's protection now, and trying to wangle money from him for some breast implants that her rivals were flaunting.

The whisky had flowed generously at the party the previous night. The belly dancers flown in from Lebanon had gyrated to cheap Bollywood medleys. Isabella, the dark-haired dancer with the ripe curves, had been a big hit. Especially her grand finale when she flipped nine coins placed across her stomach, one by one, by just using her stomach muscles.

Getting up late the next morning, Jambu was sitting in his backyard, basking in the sunlight after his oil massage. His mother had told him never to skip the weekly massage if he wanted to stay in peak health. He was sprawled in a comfortable easy chair, pleasantly hung-over. Like a water buffalo chewing the cud, content with life. And like the buffalo, he was slow to anger, getting by on just the threat of his hulking presence. But he could be very dangerous when provoked.

The morning sun bathed him in its warmth as he drooled over the lush pictures of item girl Mona in the tabloid he was reading. Banana plants growing in the slush around the well waved their leaves gently in the breeze. Shaitaan called to thank him again for the great party and for smashing Punk Raja into pulp. Champa Darling had gone in to get his second cup of strong coffee....

And then he heard the rustling among the banana plants behind him. But before he could turn, the attacker was on him, hitting him viciously on the back of his head with a tire iron. *Whomp. Whomp. Whomp.* Again and again. He tried to stop the blows raining on him with an arm raised over his head, opening his mouth to scream. Too late. As his bloodied eyes were closing, he saw the face of the attacker peering at him. *I know him, I know him*, he thought before he collapsed.

That was how Champa Darling found him, lying sprawled on the cement platform round the well. His head was covered in blood, his mouth and nose were squelched. Her screams brought the landlord down from the first floor, and the police and ambulance in quick succession. And then the media arrived — always the media, hungry for more fodder to keep the TRPs rising.

****

Kat was watching Sushil on TV, interviewing an unnamed expert from Interpol, New York. Vir had told her about the interview.

"Thank you sir for speaking to us," said Sushil. "As you are aware, we are in the midst of one of the biggest hunts for a killer in the country, for the man who has been named the Madras Mangler. Could you tell us how modern technology can help us track him?"

"Thank you for inviting me to your show," Vir's voice replied, off camera. "It's no exaggeration to say that dead bodies can speak and tell us their story. The forensic pathologist interprets what they are saying so that we can get our hands on several clues. Like the time of death, the weapon used, the killer's fingerprints and DNA. We can isolate the killer's DNA from just a single strand of hair or microscopic bits of his skin under the victim's fingernails. We then cross-reference it with the DNA of our suspects or with that of criminals on our database."

"As you probably know," said Sushil, "such a database is not in place yet in India but we are working on it. Now tell me, how accurate are DNA matches when used to determine paternity?"

"The results are 99.9999 per cent accurate, meaning there is only a 0.0001 per cent chance of a mistake or mismatch," said Vir, going on to answer a few more questions on the topic. Finally Sushil thanked him and moved on to breaking news.

DC Reddy was on air again, reading out a statement to a gaggle of reporters: "GS Jambu, a student of SS Padmaja College, was attacked in the house where he was living with a friend. He was badly beaten up and is now in Sanjivi Hospital. The doctors say his condition is critical and that they are doing everything they can to save him. We are interviewing people in the neighbourhood to see if there were any witnesses to the crime so we can catch the attacker."

"Wasn't Jambu one of the suspects in Lolita's disappearance, sir?" asked a reporter.

"I have nothing further to say at the moment," said Reddy as he turned away. He had realised that media attention was a double-edged weapon and that he should be careful about what he said. His earlier decrees on how women should dress and behave and the 8 pm curfew he had prescribed had made him a hated figure. A woman's magazine had named him the foremost symbol of regressive thinking. His superiors had been displeased and threatened to transfer him to the refugees' camp at Mandapam, seen as a punishment posting. He had decided to keep a low profile till the furore died down.

The local tabloids and news magazines were free to speculate however. They wondered if Jambu's business or political rivals had orchestrated the attack on him, or if it was linked to Lolita's disappearance. Kat could not help wondering if Charan Raj was behind the attack. "The easiest way to silence Jambu is to kill him, don't you think?" she asked Minx.

"True," said Minx. "Do you think Jambu will tell us anything if we visit him in hospital? Maybe he feels guilty about what he did and will be more open with us than he was with the police."

"It can't hurt to try," said Kat, "especially as the cops are not getting anywhere. We'll tell the doctors we are his close friends, shed a few tears maybe."

But their attempt to see him proved futile. Jambu was under guard in a high-security room and no visitors were allowed. The cop stationed in front of the room would not budge despite their pleas. They came back to the hostel dejected, wondering how long it would be before they got news of another body in the river — this time Lolita's. Moti came to Kat's room from her hospital duty, eager to find out if they had good news for her. They had nothing.

"Couldn't get in to see Jambu either," said Kat. "Though the cop at the door was very interested in us. He looks like a younger version of actor Vadivelu but seems to think he's a dude. Asked us several stupid questions and then refused to let us in."

"That figures," said Moti. "We have a criminal undergoing surgery in our hospital. Only family members and hospital personnel are allowed in."

"So they have a list and ask for your ID, is it?"

"Yes," said Moti. "Though they don't ask me and the other staff as we wear hospital scrubs."

"That's it!" said Kat. "You are doing it for us, with your hospital coat. All you need to do is pick up a tray of medicines or a prescription pad on your way in."

Moti was startled. "He's not in my hospital and their rules may be stricter. What if I get caught?"

"Come on, Moti," said Kat. "Can't you take a small risk for the sake of Lolita? I'll tell you exactly where his room is."

"The cops have spoken to him already. Wouldn't he have told them whatever he knew?"

"They say he doesn't remember anything. Maybe he's stonewalling because he doesn't want the cops poking into his dirty dealings."

"Okay, I'll try," said Moti. "Maybe I'll bat my eyelashes at Junior Vadivelu." She knew it was a weak joke, but was just trying to cover up her nervousness. Kat told her the location of Jambu's room and the room number. She practised her lines when she was on her way to the hospital in an auto: what she'd say to the cop and to the nurses or doctors if they caught her.

But she was in luck. The hospital was quiet when she went in. Visitors' hour was over. She picked up a clipboard from the deserted nurses' desk and walked to his room. She smiled at the cop and walked past him with a confident step. He was too busy looking her over to check her credentials. She closed the door behind her and turned to look at Jambu. She was shocked to see his battered face, covered almost completely by bandages. He was hooked to a monitor and opened his eyes with difficulty when she called his name. He seemed to recognise her and tried to say something in a garbled voice.

"What is it?" she asked, bending closer to him.

"Lolita," he said, adding something that sounded like "love her".

As she bent nearer, a heavy hand fell on her shoulder. She straightened up in a hurry. Her eyes widened as she saw from the name tag that it was the head nurse accosting her. "What are you doing here?" asked the stern woman. Moti stood with her mouth open, her wits deserting her. "Student nurses go to H Ward," said the head nurse. "Down the stairs and then past the pharmacy."

Moti bobbed her head and bolted from the room, her thoughts in a whirl. So Jambu did have some information. Maybe Vir or Bishnu could try coaxing it out of him. He might know where Lolita was, or might have seen something. There was hope still.

47

The team at HATCHET was reviewing progress or rather the lack of it. Keegan had met Dev, Aryan's assistant and asked him about the conference at the resort on ECR. Dev confirmed that Aryan had been very active organising the whole event and that they had all travelled and stayed together on those two days.

Vir spoke to Charan Raj and took him through his meeting with Lolita. The politician told him about her seeking his help to stop Jambu from harming her. He also asserted that he had nothing to do with her disappearance. "You must have heard all the stories about me spread by my enemies," he said. "But I'm talking to you now as a responsible leader deeply concerned about the young victims. Ask me for any help you need to catch the bastard. And let me know as soon as you catch him." Vir could not push him further unless he had some evidence against him.

The only new lead they had now was a note left in one of the locked boxes on the college campus. Someone had seen Jambu threatening Lolita on the day she had gone missing. They had described the two thugs who had been with him.

"Maybe that's what he was trying to tell Moti — where she could find Lolita. See if you can match the descriptions to any known members of his gang," said Vir. "What do we know of this Champa Darling who provided his alibi?"

"She is an actress in C-grade movies. You know the ones where a stupid bimbette wearing red lipstick goes clickety clack into a haunted house?" asked Bishnu.

"Then a ghost or vampire pounces on her and tears off her clothes. The camera pans lovingly over her skimpily clad body."

"Exactly. Champa Darling has one of the loudest screams you can ask for," said Bishnu. "And a body that is always bursting through her clothes. Ideal kill material. There's even a Wiki page referring to her role as an angry zombie, killing her lovers after having torrid, inventive sex with them."

"Fascinating," said Vir. "What does Jambu's wife have to say about all this?"

"She lives in his village with their two kids, waiting for his occasional visits. The cop who interviewed her said she didn't seem too surprised to hear about his being beaten up. She was mildly curious to find out who he had been living with when he was attacked."

"So if this guy is a philanderer, there could be other angry husbands or boyfriends on the suspect list, in addition to Charan Raj's men. Isn't he also a suspect in the killing of a rival gang leader?"

"Yes, Punk Raja. The dead man's gang may be out for revenge. Anyway, it's high time we spoke to him," said Bishnu. "Maybe he will reveal something about Lolita's disappearance if we tell him we are not concerned about his other crimes."

Vir's phone rang. "That was Kat," he said. "Looks like there's a lead. I'll be back in a couple of hours."

****

Minx had received a call from Shaitaan. Her first instinct had been to reject it. But then she thought she should blow him off in such a way he never bothered her again. The creep!

"Don't hang up," he said. "This is about your friend Lolita. I have some information for you."

"Why don't you tell the police? Why me?"

"They won't listen to me, but they might listen to you as you are her friend. So please, just ten minutes in a coffee shop of your choice."

Her flesh crawled at the thought, but her mind conjured up a vivid image of Lolita in captivity somewhere. With a depraved psychopath fondling her or sharpening his tools for the torture. "Okay, ten minutes. Aquamarine, at 6 pm," she said and hung up. Kat said she would come with her and ask Vir to join them at the coffee shop. She also called Aryan; the poor man would be delighted to know they had a lead.

Shortly afterwards, Minx was waiting with Kat at a table under the trees, wearing huge sunglasses. The evening sun glinted through the branches. A few young couples were scattered in the far corners, trying to get some privacy to hold hands or steal kisses. Shaitaan strode in, took a look around and walked up to them. He pulled out a chair and sat down, making a face at Kat who was playing the role of chaperon. He was in another of his suits and dangled his Ray Bans in one hand.

"So what's the information you spoke of?" asked Minx in a no-nonsense tone.

"What? No coffee for me?" he asked, then thought better of it as she glared at him. He continued: "Everyone knows that Charan Raj had her kidnapped or killed so that his dark past would not be exposed."

"That's what you have to tell me? Tabloid gossip? Do you have any proof?" Minx's voice rose with each question.

"Think about it. Why do you think Jambu was attacked now? Only because he was telling people that Lolita was Charan Raj's daughter."

"So you want us to do your dirty work. Get Charan Raj in trouble before he defeats your father. That's not going to happen," she said.

Shaitaan shrugged it off. "Okay, I had to give it a try. I'm more interested in what you've decided about my movie offer."

She clenched her fist in answer.

"Okay, no movie." He leered. "How about a friendly visit to my suite in Seven Star Hotel?"

She stood up, ready to leave. She should not have wasted time on this scum.

"No, wait," he said. "If you don't listen to me, I'm releasing your nude photos to the yellow journals."

"There *are* no nude photos," she said.

"Oh, didn't you get your copies?" asked Shaitaan as he went on to describe the photos in graphic detail. He told her his plans for her in his bed and said that he would be recording the sessions so they could watch it together. He laughed uproariously when he saw her horrified face.

Vir walked up from the next table, dragged out a chair and sat down. Shaitaan looked at him with contempt. "Hired muscle, huh?"

Vir touched Minx's arm to stop her from saying anything. "A suit in this heat? Really?" he said to Shaitaan. "You look like a don in a cheap Bollywood flick."

The other man stared back at him. "And who do you think you are? The hero? Want your face rearranged? Shall I call my men or the cops? They'll hang you upside down in a jail cell till you learn your lesson."

"Stop harassing her," said Vir.

"Or else, what?"

"Listen to this," said Vir. He pressed some keys on his Blackberry.

"This is Rakesh," the voice identified itself. "I hacked into Minx's computer and morphed her face onto some nude bodies. I was asked to do this by Shaitaan who paid me twenty thousand rupees for the pictures. I'm ready to provide a signed affidavit confessing to this."

Vir stopped the recording and looked at Shaitaan. The man laughed. "So you get some fool to say something and think you can threaten me with it? Hey man, do you know who you're messing with?"

"Well, let me think," said Vir. "Santhaan, also known as Shaitaan. Education, 8th Standard failed. Expelled from MRM School for selling drugs. Questioned in the 2009 murder of the lottery king Chinnu. On bail now after being charged in two kidnap cases and in the rape of TV star Anjana. Caught red-handed last week bribing the voters in his father's constituency. Shall I go on?"

Kat and Minx looked at him with their mouths open as he continued: "So, to answer your question, I do know who I'm messing with. I also know your Party's going to be mighty pissed when they bite the dust because of something you did."

He nodded to Aryan and Sushil who joined them from the next table. "May I have my sunglasses please?" said Aryan to Minx and she handed it over to him. He pulled out a memory card from the frame and played it on his smartphone. They saw Shaitaan in full colour, blackmailing Minx and asking her to visit him in his suite.

The waiter brought coffee for all of them. Vir took a sip, looking perfectly relaxed. "At last. It's thirsty work," he said.

"So tell me," Sushil said to Shaitaan. "Do you want me to play this on a loop on my channel tonight? I'm ready to share copies with other channels too."

Shaitaan looked hunted. He hadn't expected this. "Okay, if that's what you want," said Aryan as he passed the card to Sushil.

Shaitaan snatched at it. Vir's cup clattered in the saucer. He stood up, took a long stride and let fly with his fist, right into Shaitaan's mouth. The man's teeth were knocked loose and he reeled back. Vir speeded him on his way with a jab from his elbow, with the full weight of his body behind it. As Shaitaan writhed in pain, Vir pivoted on his heels, kicking out at Shaitaan's knee so he collapsed backwards. Shaitaan cracked his head on a big cement pot as he fell. The pot toppled, shattering smaller pots in its wake. A shriek and then silence as he lost consciousness.

Vir dusted off his trousers, sat down and took another sip of his coffee. "Good, it's still hot," he said. He signalled to the waiter for another pot. Kat and Minx looked fearfully at Shaitaan, wondering if he'd get up and come for them. Vir had trained with experts in hand to hand combat and could have snapped Shaitaan's neck in two seconds if he'd wanted. "No fears," he said now. "He's out for the count."

A few minutes later, the group finished their coffee and left the cafe. The head waiter checked Shaitaan's wallet and called his office phone number. His men came scurrying to carry him away. The waiter who had enjoyed the fight from his ringside seat replayed it for the kitchen staff who had not been fortunate enough to witness it. "What a fight — Rajni ishtyle!" he said. "Left hook, right elbow, left kick. Two hundred rupees tip for me. Five hundred for the broken pots. One cup missing. Probably broke in the fight."

All told, it had been a very satisfying evening, in more ways than one.

48

The cop standing watch over Jambu's door was bored. His name was Azhaguraj, meaning 'King of Beauty'. But as he could not pronounce his name right like many others, he usually went by the name Alaguraj: King of the Beak. He did have an impressive nose, long and hooked at the end, so it was quite appropriate. Now Alaguraj was quite a dapper cop, as cops go. His khaki uniform fitted like a glove across his chest and butt and was always ironed to perfection. He thought he would be 'discovered' any day now by one of the new wave of directors who chose newcomers to star in their movies. After all, he was better looking than many of the heroes these days. Maybe one of Jambu's important visitors would suggest his name for a role, even if it was that of a ghoul in a Champa Darling movie.

Unfortunately, no big shot had visited Jambu; not even Champa Darling, who had moved on to a producer of horror movies. This man specialised in movies in which a contorted, semi-nude female body occupied the foreground in most shots.

No wonder then that Alaguraj was bored out of his skull, standing at the end of a deserted corridor in front of a musty room with a dying man. He took every opportunity he could find to visit the nurse's desk to talk to the toothy nurses in their delightful uniforms. In fact, he thought the one who looked like a distant cousin of actress Nayantara was interested in him. He now gave her his best smile as she told him he was wanted at the front desk. He had a visitor waiting for him. She went back to her desk to whisper sweet nothings on her cell phone to the orderly in the

ICU, who was coaxing her to spend her day off in his 'mansion'. This was what working men's hostels were called in Chennai.

Alaguraj was so eager to get away from his uncomfortable stool that he did not notice the man who stood just outside the doors of the ward, watching him race past to the next building. The man walked unhurriedly past the nurse still bent over her phone and down the corridor to Jambu's room. He looked around and saw no one. He put on his gloves, opened the door, closed it quietly behind him and shot the bolt. He looked at the patient swaddled in bandages. "Bastard! You should have died that day and saved me all this trouble," he said. He yanked at one of the pillows from under Jambu's head. Jambu opened a bleary eye that shot open fully as he recognised the man bending over him.

"You... you...," he stammered, gathering his breath to yell for help. Too late. The pillow was pressing down on his face, stifling the sound. Jambu's feet thrashed and his hand knocked down the plastic tray of drugs and syringes on the side table. The killer paused to check if the noise had been heard by anyone. Jambu took the opportunity to push back, pulling out the needle attached to the drip and almost getting away.

The killer jumped onto his chest, holding him down with the full weight of his body. He pressed the pillow down firmly over Jambu's nose and mouth, until his body stopped flailing. The legs twitched one final time and then were still. Still the killer waited, keeping the pressure steady, in case Jambu was trying to trick him. A minute passed, and then another. The deed was done.

He lifted the pillow away from the face, put his fingers to the man's throat to check for a pulse and then got off the bed. He listened at the door for a few seconds, then opened it and peered out into the corridor. Still deserted. He stepped out, closing the door behind him. He then pulled off his gloves, put them into his pocket and strolled quietly away. There was no one at the nurses' station. He made it to his car without being seen.

It was another fifteen minutes before Alaguraj came back to his post. No one at the front desk had known anything about his visitor as the shift had just changed. He enjoyed his time away and did not hurry back. He smoked a cigarette, picked up a sleaze sheet at the small shop outside the hospital gates and then returned to his stool. He sat devouring the story of the young star caught groping his girlfriend in the hotel elevator.

The nurse who came to give Jambu his medicines half an hour later was the one who discovered the body hanging half on and half off the bed. The pillows were on the floor, the medicines scattered around. His tongue was protruding, showing signs of having been bitten. Saliva, blood and tissue cells were found later on one of the pillows, indicating that he had been smothered with it.

The nurse screamed and fainted in a dramatic heap on the floor. Alaguraj came crashing through the door, realising too late that he'd missed his cue to catch the killer red-handed and have his face in the papers. He called his senior, broke the news and watched as the khakis descended. Reddy arrived soon, ripped him to shreds and banished him to traffic duty on Anna Salai. He would have to stand in the hot sun directing fools looking to find their way out of the maze that the road had become with the ongoing work on the Metro Rail.

Jambu's murder was soon topping the news. The TV channels were enjoying the spike in viewership and hoping that the killer wouldn't be found soon. Vir and Bishnu were distressed as they had not had an opportunity to talk to Jambu.

"Do we have the tapes from the closed circuit cameras in the corridor?" asked Vir. "We might be able to identify his killer."

"No cameras," said Bishnu. "These are crowded hospitals where you're lucky if all the patients have beds. We seem to be back where we started. At zero."

49

Kat had been watching reports of Jambu's murder late into the night. Then she'd struggled for several hours to complete a paper without success. How did their professors expect them to concentrate when there was a new death every day? Moti had to sprinkle water on her face the next morning to wake her up. "What is it?" she muttered, then sat up with a start when she saw her friend's face.

"They've found Lolita's body," said Moti, turning on the news. Sushil was standing on the banks of the Cooum, where firemen had just pulled a body out of the water. A sheet had been placed over it and it was being loaded into the waiting ambulance.

Kat and Moti huddled on the bed in silence, too shocked even to cry.

"The police suspect that this is the body of the missing girl Lolita from SS Padmaja College, Chennai," said Sushil. "The face is said to be mutilated beyond recognition and the identity will have to be confirmed through other means."

"My God — this is terrible," said Kat, beginning to cry. Her phone began to ring stridently and she picked it up in order to silence it. She couldn't bear to talk to anyone. Then she saw it was Vir and a wild hope surged through her mind. Maybe he was calling to say there had been a mistake and that it was not Lolita after all.

"Did you see the news report?" asked Vir.

"Yes."

"I need you to come with me to the morgue. To tell us if it is Lolita."

"No, no, I can't!" she became hysterical.

"I'm sorry Kat. But it will take her mother a few hours to get here. We need to find out if it's her or not. What if she's still alive? Don't you want to save her?"

"How can you ask me that? Isn't there anyone else?"

"Unless you want Moti to do it," he said.

She glanced at her friend and felt like crying again when she saw how broken she looked, in a faded T-shirt, her hair a mess. She could not ask her; she would have to do it herself. In just a few minutes, she was sitting by Vir's side in the car. She was silent, caught up in a dark world, dreading the moment when she would see what was left of her friend. She had never seen a dead body up close. Even when her grandfather died in Delhi, her parents had left her at home in order to spare her the trauma.

Vir reached out his hand to clasp hers in a strong grip. "I'm here, I'll help you through it," he said. "You are brave, you can do it."

They parked a little distance away from the hospital morgue, a dreary government facility with strong smells and unpainted walls. Groups of people waited for bodies of their loved ones to be handed over to them; some wailed while others stared with blank eyes. Rude staff pushed them aside each time they entered the nether world behind the doors.

Vir closed his eyes as he remembered the crisp aseptic surroundings of another morgue in another country where he had gone to identify Rima. He remembered how he'd felt as he laid eyes on her beloved face. Her eyes were closed, her arms stretched by her side. The smile that he loved was gone forever.

And then Kat was pulling at his arm. The attendant led them to a small windowless room where the body was laid out on a hard stone slab, covered by a stained sheet. Vir saw that Kat looked as if she was ready to bolt. She was feeling nauseous and did not want the sheet to be lifted. She felt the blood drumming in her ears as she reeled. He grabbed her before she could fall and made her sit on a stool set against the wall. He pushed her head down between her knees and told her to take deep breaths. "You are going to be fine," he told her.

He put a strong arm around her waist, holding her close so she could absorb his strength. She sat up in a few minutes, held tight to him and gasped. Tried to listen to his soothing words and calm herself. He helped her up, pulling her forward to face the body. "Let's get this over with and leave, shall we?" he asked. He lifted the sheet covering the face. She turned away, feeling faint again. The face was a battered mass, with no features visible. "We'll have to check for moles, birthmarks. Does she have any?" he asked as he pulled the sheet down further.

Kat gasped as she saw the green T-shirt with the graphic of an upraised middle finger. "That's her T-shirt," she said, starting to weep.

"There's a ram's head ring on her hand," he said. "Is it hers?"

"Yes, she always wore that."

"We've got to be absolutely certain. I was asking you about birthmarks. Think carefully Kat."

"A tattoo. She has one. A butterfly just below her breasts. It's normally hidden by her clothes." She stood stock still, unwilling to touch the body to look. He pulled up the T-shirt slightly to reveal the girl's chest. There was no tattoo. "It's not Lolita, it's not her," she cried out.

"Are you sure? A hundred per cent sure?" He looked intently at her face while he waited for her reply.

"Yes, I am. I am."

"Then you can leave," he said. "Walk to my car and sit inside. Here's the key. And *don't* talk to the press if they are waiting outside."

"But aren't you coming with me?" she asked. Her legs were trembling and she wanted to curl up and die.

"I need a minute or two here," he said. "And I don't want the press to get pictures of me. If the inspector in the front room asks, tell him that the body is Lolita's. Do you understand?"

His words struck home after a few seconds. "What? Why?" She looked at him, confused. "It's not her body and if we say it's her, the cops will stop looking. And she'll die."

"Listen to me. Just do what I tell you to. I'll explain later," he said, pushing her towards the door. She stumbled into the corridor outside and walked to the front room. The inspector intercepted her.

"Is it your friend Lolita's body?"

She should tell them it was Lolita as Vir wanted her to. "It's not her," she heard herself saying. "It's not Lolita."

She ran out of the room to escape the smell of death that seemed to be clinging to her. She would go back to her room and burn the clothes she was wearing.

When she came out of the darkness of the morgue into the bright sunlight, she blundered right into a line of OB vans. A horde of reporters charged towards her, thrusting out their mikes. "Are you Lolita's friend? Is it her body? Is her face horribly mangled?" The questions came from all directions.

"It's not Lolita," she shouted as she pushed through them. "It's not my friend."

The reporters ran into the morgue to get more details from the inspector. She stumbled towards Vir's car which was parked on the main road. *Why had she said that?* she asked herself. What if something terrible happened to Lolita because she'd made a mistake?

50

Vir came out of the morgue a few minutes later, after he'd checked under the girl's fingernails with his forensic kit. He thought though that the dumping in the polluted river was not going to be helpful in preserving DNA.

He was shocked when he heard the reporters telling the world that the body was not Lolita's. He saw Kat's face on their monitors and felt a pang when he realised she had disregarded him completely. Did she even realise what harm she was doing to her friend's cause?

"Lolita may still be alive! It's time we played a more active role in her rescue," the reporters were saying, raising the decibel level. "We will bring the killer to justice with your help. So talk to us and tell us if you see or suspect anything."

So many vigilantes, thought Vir, *multi-armed monsters hot on the heels of the killer*. They would not rest now till the man was caught or made his escape. He walked slowly to his car, got in and pulled out into the traffic without saying a word to Kat, afraid he would say something he would regret later. He felt her eyes watching him. "Why?" he asked finally. "Why did you ignore what I said?"

"I told you why I couldn't lie, why I had to do something. I'm unable to sleep. I wake up in the middle of the night in terror. Wondering if this is the day I find out my friend is dead, or if I'm next in line. Can you even begin to understand that? Can any man understand?"

"I didn't ask for much Kat. Just that you trust me enough to wait a few minutes till I explained."

"So what is the big explanation? Tell me, damn you. I'm tired of your secrecy."

"Okay listen," he snapped. "Why do you think the killer has gone to all this trouble to fake her death? He wants to stop people looking for her. And if we let him think we're fooled, we get more time to save her. But now... now you've forced his hand. Set the hounds loose on him. Which means he'll have to kill her. Today. Tomorrow. And then escape to a new place to start all over again."

There was total silence in the car. He said nothing more till he dropped her off at the first auto stand he could find.

He cannot wait to get rid of me, she thought. *I've lost his trust forever and killed my friend, almost as if I strangled her myself.*

****

The killer turned off the TV. He had thought Lolita was the one for him, the one who would make him complete. That he could take her with him to Malacca or Malaysia; somewhere no one would look for her. But this girl Kat had destroyed his plan by telling the world that the body was not her friend's. Now he would have to kill Lolita before things got out of hand.

He grew excited at the thought. Blood rushed to his lower limbs. His body stirred. Maybe he could use her before he killed her. Use her as he had wanted to use his mother before she died. He remembered the night he'd killed his mother, by tightening her red silk scarf around her neck. And then he'd covered the ugly red mark with the scarf. After that, he'd cut off the toes with the rings, as the rings were to be worn only by women who were good wives and mothers.

He couldn't let her get away with wearing them, in this life or the next. He had dumped her in the sea late that night, taking her body in the landlord's car that stood shrouded in tarpaulin when the landlord went on his pilgrimage. And the sharks had done the rest; they must have. Or she would have washed up on shore as he'd feared for months.

He had taken her box of scarves that he loved so much. Embossed with mangoes, squares and zari dots. And her silver anklets. The ones that taunted him through the night with their tinkle. He had hidden away her jewels and money; lots and lots to keep him going for the rest of his life.

He came back to the present with a start. It was time to plan his next move. How to kill Lolita and get away to a new city. He went to the next room and watched the girl squirm and strain against her bonds. This one had spirit. She never stopped trying to get away. He moved closer, staring at her chest, clad only in a bra. He'd taken her T-shirt to dress the body he'd dumped in the Cooum, the body of the hooker he'd set up as his decoy.

Then he saw it — a tattoo just below her breasts. How had he missed this? So that's how that girl Kat found out. He stood thinking. Maybe it was a sign that he should take Kat next. Bring her here first so she could watch him kill her friend. Then stash her in the trunk of his car as he drove to the next town. That would be fun. But first, he had to get ready for tomorrow. Tomorrow was the day.

"Ma, can you see how smart I am? I'm not a little boy anymore. You'll be so proud of me ma." His voice rose shrill and sharp.

His mother? Was she here? Lolita sharpened her ears. *Maybe his mother would free her when he left. If he left.* She would try to escape till her last breath. She was not going that easily, not after all that she had struggled to achieve.

51

"Lolita is still alive somewhere. But why are we not able to find her?" Kat was crying as she spoke to Aryan on the phone.

"Now with Jambu dead, it's got to be Charan Raj. The bastard's probably got her locked up in a room at the farmhouse still," he said. "How come your precious friend from Interpol hasn't done anything about him?"

"I don't know. He doesn't tell me anything," she said. *Especially now when he's waiting to blame me if something happens to Lolita.*

"I'm not waiting any longer. I'll go to the farmhouse myself and sneak in when it's dark," he said.

"I'll come with you. And don't worry, I won't tell Vir," she said. She had to make up for her mistake, do what she could to rescue Lolita.

As she waited by the gates for him to pick her up, she began to wonder if she should inform Vir about what they were doing. After all, she had deserved everything he said. She called him, but the call went to his voice mail.

****

Vir was with Bishnu's team at HATCHET. Tension ran high as they all had the same thought in their minds. This could be the last day of Lolita's life and what they did now would determine if she survived. They were working at breakneck speed: making calls, rechecking their records, trying to see if they had missed something.

Bishnu was monitoring TV reports. A programme on the Hollywood film shooting was just ending. He realised he'd forgotten his promise to take the blonde actress shopping. Sushil's interview with Charan Raj was next.

"Yes, I've heard the rumours that are being spread by the ruling party," said the politician. "They know they're going to lose heavily and are hoping to blacken my name. But I repeat once more, I have nothing to do with the girl's disappearance. In fact, all my men are out on the streets, checking if anyone has seen anything. Anything at all."

Bishnu turned off the TV. "This is not helping. The killer's going to panic and kill her right away."

Umang walked into the room. "No usable scrapings — for the DNA testing — from under the fingernails of the Cooum body," he said.

"What about the coffee cup I gave you?" asked Vir. "Does the sample match the killer's DNA that we got from under Deepika's finger?"

"Sorry, still working on it. The sample's contaminated," said Umang. "The cafe is not really five star, is it? Don't think they sterilise their cups. We made sure there's no cross contamination in the lab."

"Damn it! I was counting on the result," said Vir.

"What cup is this?" asked Bishnu.

"The one Aryan used. I took it on the sly when we went to meet Shaitaan. I felt his behaviour and reactions were a little weird when I first met him. And his alibi seemed too perfect to be true. In fact, I planted a bug in his car so I could track him if need be."

"I'll run him on the criminal database while we wait," said Rom. "Also check his photo on the facial recognition software to see if he's using a fake identity."

"But he doesn't fit our profile," said Bishnu. "His parents are respectable middle class folk in Mumbai, aren't they?"

"Got him," said Rom. "He's been lying about that. He's in our database under a different name. Arvind. He was questioned in one of Mumbai's unsolved cases — his mother's disappearance. The body was never found. I'm sending the details to your systems."

"Father unknown. Mother Tarakeshwari, known as Tara, a high class call girl," Vir read out. "A favourite with politicians and rich businessmen. Lots of black money. But the cops found nothing when they turned her flat upside down."

"Here's the police report on the son's questioning," said Bishnu. "Boy was just fifteen, went manic when she went missing and had to be treated for six months. A cousin of his mother's took over his guardianship."

"I tracked down the cousin," said Rom, a few minutes later. "The boy ran away after his treatment. They tried finding him, but not very hard, I think. They never saw him after that."

"It's clear then that he lied about his parents," said Vir. "But didn't Keegan say he had a cast iron alibi?"

"His assistant Dev said he was at the sales conference throughout," said Bishnu. "How did he slip out and kidnap her?"

"Spoke to Dev just now to check the alibi again," said Keegan, who had been talking softly into his phone in the corner of the room. "It seems Aryan ducked out for a few hours saying he had a terrible migraine and that he was going to rest in his room. Didn't want anyone disturbing him."

"He could have called a cab and gone to pick up his car, then snatched her," said Vir. "That was my initial thought but I dropped it as you had vetted his alibi."

"Is he in the showroom now? Let's bring him in," said Bishnu.

"No such luck. Dev says he's not working for them now. He quit 10 days back when pulled up for irregular attendance," said Keegan.

"Was checking out his claim that he studied in MITS," said Rom. "No Aryan or Arvind among the graduates in the last ten years who fits our description. Just an Arvind on the applicants' list. He didn't make it through the interview though. They probably saw something queer about him."

"Damn. We should have given him the third degree, regardless of his alibi," said Vir. "The girls told me he'd gifted Lolita an expensive phone. Must have bugged it so he could track her and the others."

"I've just checked on the other stuff he told you, about Charan Raj's wife being ill as per their cook," said Keegan.

"And...?"

"The wife's in Mumbai now, shopping for a Sabyasachi saree to wear to Charan Raj's swearing in. And their cook is Ellamma, an old woman who's been with them for years. No Selvam in their employ."

Punit came running in, his glasses askew. "It's a match. The cup is a match with Deepika's killer."

"So it was Aryan all along. Let's head to his flat on Usman Road in T Nagar. Keegan, come with me," said Bishnu. "Vir, you look at other leads." The two ran out of the room.

Vir picked up his phone and saw that he had a voice mail from Kat. He played the message: "Going to Charan Raj's farmhouse in Injambakkam with Aryan. Will call when I get back."

He banged his fist on the table. "Dammit! He's got Kat too." He was shell-shocked. Felt guilty as hell. He'd been so rude to her when he'd seen her last and dumped her on the side of the road. Also told her she was to blame if Lolita turned up dead.

Get a hold on yourself. Concentrate on what you need to do, he told himself. "Let me see if the tracking device in Aryan's car is working," he told Rom, his fingers flying on his Blackberry. "Here it is — his car's nearing Triplicane. Not too far from here, is it? You stay here and coordinate the chase. And inform Bishnu."

"I'll put out an alert," said Rom. "Give the cops Aryan's car number and description."

"But why Triplicane if he's headed to Injambakkam? Is it another lie and is Lolita already dead? Or is he planning a double killing?" asked Vir before heading out in a run to his car. *Let me not be too late. Please God. All I need is a fighting chance.*

52

Aryan nodded to Kat as she got into the car.

"This isn't your car is it? What happened?" she asked.

"Some problem with the brakes. I had to hire this," he said.

The car sped along the main road and passed a police station. His lips twitched when he saw that Deputy Commissioner Reddy's car was no longer there. So Vir thought he had been smart planting a tracking device in his car. What he did not know was that Aryan's scanner had detected it the same day. Aryan had let it stay in his car a couple of days in case they were monitoring it, and then removed it and let it sit on a shelf in his flat.

Today, he'd picked it up, checked its batteries and brought it along to dump in another vehicle. He'd seen Reddy's car with the trunk open, parked in front of the station. The driver was nowhere in sight. He had been unable to resist the crazy idea that popped into his mind.

He'd parked a few metres ahead, dashed back, hidden the tracker under the mat in the trunk and driven off.

Good luck to Vir if he was planning to follow him now. He would love to see his face when he ended up nose to nose with Reddy. And even if they gave the cops Aryan's car number to track, they would find he had dumped it and was long gone. He was too intelligent for these dumb fools. Even more satisfying was the fact that he'd managed to grab Vir's girl.

Yes, I saw the spark in your eyes whenever you looked at her. Too bad your Interpol skills aren't going to help save her, he thought. He remembered he had something to ask Kat, a loose end that he needed to tie up. "It was you who went to the morgue to check the body, wasn't it? That must have been tough," he said.

She shuddered. "Yes, I hated it. But fortunately, it turned out to be someone else, some other poor girl."

"You were really smart to figure that out. How did you do it? Was it the missing tattoo?" he asked.

"Yes," said Kat. "Thank God for that." She turned to look out of the window as memories of that horrible day washed over her. The road signs were flying by and she saw they were nearing Anna Nagar.

"Wait. Where are we going?" she asked, surprised. "This isn't the way to Injambakkam."

"Oh, didn't I tell you? Sushil called to say that he'd checked the farmhouse and that it was deserted. We're going to check another property owned by Charan Raj." He seemed to trip over the words, making them up as he went along. Was he lying? Kat turned towards him and saw him look quickly away.

Was he hiding something? she wondered. *Wait. How did he know about the tattoo under Lolita's clothes*? Lolita had joked often enough that Aryan was too gentlemanly; that he'd not gone beyond holding her hand. And that he'd kissed her only that once before he left for Mumbai. *So how did he find out about the tattoo? Unless he saw it on Lolita after she was kidnapped, which meant that he was the kidnapper.* Kat's heart thudded. Calm down, she told herself and ran through her reasoning again. Yes, there was no other explanation. He had to be the killer.

She gasped aloud and tried to cover it up by pretending to sneeze. She had been a fool, placing herself in his power. Where were they going? A godforsaken hideaway where he tortured and killed his victims? Maybe she could get away by jumping out — but not at this speed. Even if she shouted for help, he would have sped past before anyone saw her. *Vir, where are you? Did you get my message? Do you know the killer's got me?*

She had to act normal and pretend she didn't know the truth till she came up with a plan. She opened her handbag, fumbled inside it, took out some chewing gum and popped it into her mouth.

****

Bishnu called Vir with some bad news. "The watchman at Aryan's flat says he vacated the place yesterday. He said that he was moving to another city but the watchman doesn't know where."

"So if we miss him now, it's not just Lolita and Kat. Young girls in yet another town are going to get killed too," said Vir.

"I'm heading to Triplicane now," said Bishnu. "Let's hunt the bastard down."

Traffic was getting heavier. Vir kept his eye on the flashing light that indicated the tracker's position. The signal was now close by and had become stationary. He pulled up by the roadside and homed in on the signal. It was coming from a police car with a beacon.

Vir stopped short. *My God! I know this number. This is Reddy's car. How did the tracker get here? The creep must be laughing now at the thought of my following the cop. He's been two steps ahead of us all the time.... I have to turn around, check in with Rom.*

He got back into his car, found that he was now wedged in and could move neither forward nor backward. No way to make a

U-turn either. What the hell was going on? He was on Wallajah Road near Chepauk stadium. God. Chepauk. The final cricket one-dayer where India and Australia were fighting for the cup. What had he been thinking?

His phone rang. "Aryan's car is parked near Padmaja College," said Rom. "He's probably switched cars. How come you tracked him to Triplicane then?"

"The bastard found the tracker and dumped it in Reddy's car. That's who I've been following all this while. We need to find out what car he's driving now, maybe he stole one. Check for reports of stolen vehicles in the vicinity where he dumped his car. We might get a number and a description."

His phone rang again. It was Kat. Had she managed to escape or was she still in Aryan's clutches? He picked up the call but stayed silent, just in case. He heard her speaking to someone, asking where they were headed.

"To Sholavaram, where they used to hold races some decades back," Aryan's voice replied. "Do you know there's a lovely lake on the way?"

The monster is playing with her, thought Vir. *Hinting that he is going to dump her body there. But he has underestimated Kat. She's been smart enough to call without his finding out, and has left her phone on so they can be tracked. Maybe we still have a chance.*

He thanked God he was a gadget freak and had an iPhone in addition to his Blackberry. He called Rom and asked him to track Kat's phone. "Already on it," said Rom. "I've been waiting for her or Aryan to use their phone, so I could ping their location. Hers just popped up. I told Bishnu and am patching him in now."

Bishnu came on the line. "I talked to the Commissioner," he said. "I wanted to find out if he has some good guys on that side of town. But his top cops are either in Chepauk or at Sriperumbudur."

"Oh, right," said Rom. "The PM is paying respects at the Rajiv Gandhi Memorial in Sriperumbudur. So we're on our own then. What's your location Bishnu?"

"Anna Salai," Bishnu replied. "With all the diversions for these two events, it's going to be a nightmare to get to Sholavaram, and Aryan's already there. He has enough time to do whatever he wants to the girls."

"You're 30 km away from them Vir," said Rom. "That'll be a solid two hours, if you even manage to get out of the Chepauk area. And then Poonamallee High Road's a bitch, man."

"Let's gun for it," said Bishnu. "Vir, leave the car and look for a cop. Put him on the line with me and I'll wangle a cop car and siren for you."

Vir got out of the car with his iPhone and Blackberry. He ran a few yards ahead looking for a policeman, but there were none in sight. The other drivers looked at him scurrying around in the heat and grinned, thinking he was trying to buy a ticket in the black.

He ran on the pavement, almost breaking a leg as he tripped over an uneven edge. *Should I call Reddy? No, the man's an ass and I will need Bishnu to intercede for me. Better leave him free to get to Sholavaram on his own.*

He ran round pavement artists who were painting the Indian colours on the fans' faces. There was a tight mass of blue India jerseys moving towards the entrance of the stadium. Loud voices talking, laughing and looking forward to a cliffhanger. Why hadn't he reached the end of this queue of cars yet? Maybe he could hire a vehicle if he made it past this jam. But a rickety auto wasn't going to get him to Sholavaram in time. He felt dejected, thinking that he might as well have stayed back in the US for all the good he was doing here.

"Coming to get you." Bishnu's voice rang out in his ear.

"What? Where? Don't get into this gridlock," Vir shouted.

"Hey, don't think ordinary. Look up."

Vir moved the phone from his ear and caught the sound of a helicopter's rotors. *Was he here? Could he have really?* He felt the faint stirrings of hope. He looked up and saw a big helicopter with 'FBI' painted in huge letters on its sides, hovering over his head. Bishnu was hanging out of the side and waving. A hefty white guy was at the controls. The 'whomp, whomp, whomp' of the blades grew louder. *God! He must have grabbed the chopper from the Hollywood movie crew*, he thought. *Smart thinking!*

"There's an entrance to the stadium 100 yards ahead. Get inside the field. Your ride's two minutes away," Bishnu shouted above the noise.

Vir sprinted to the entrance and was hauled to a stop by the security personnel. Metal detectors, sniffer dogs, frisking. It looked like Fort Knox. No way was he going to get through without an armoured tank. He looked at the surly faces of the security guards. The cricket fans standing in the queue abused him for trying to jump the queue. His shoulders slumped.

A senior police officer was rushing towards him from inside the stadium. "A pleasure to meet you sir," he said as he shook his head and ushered him in. "We just got instructions from the Commissioner. A matter of life and death I'm told. Follow me."

Vir sprinted behind him and saw the helicopter hovering at the far right of the field. The players, who had been warming up for the match, had moved to the perimeter, away from the airborne intruder. A packed audience of 50,000 watched with bated breath, while many more streamed in, craning their necks to see the action. They were being treated to much more entertainment than they'd paid for. All cameras were trained on the live action. The TV commentators were in a frenzy, asking questions to which no one had the answers. Was it a terror strike or just a mock drill to handle an attack? How did an FBI chopper get here from the US?

Bishnu was shouting instructions into his headset. The guy at the controls gave him a thumbs-up from the cockpit. A rope ladder tumbled down. Vir ran to the helicopter and clambered up, even as the ladder swung wildly in the wind. The crowd screamed in delicious anticipation of a fall. Bishnu reached out to pull him in.

He introduced him to Jeff, the genial giant at the controls. "I hijacked the chopper from the film crew on Island Grounds. They were shooting a hostage rescue. Had a brainwave when I was inching through Anna Salai. Jeff's handy with his fists too if we need him."

"You must have seen me in 'Death Warrior 6'. The fight on top of the train?" Jeff grinned.

"You've met Keegan, of course," said Bishnu. "And this is Dr. Prasad with his paraphernalia. I picked him up in case Lolita is... you know?"

The helicopter lifted off, but not before Jeff dipped the nose of the helicopter in a salute. The masses in the galleries hooted and cheered. Total *paisa vasool*.

No one cared much anymore about who won the one-day match. Today would always be remembered as the day the helicopter swooped down on Chepauk stadium. And they had been there to witness the high drama. When the Indians romped home with the cup, it was just the icing on the cake.

53

Kat was desperate. The car was speeding down dirt tracks and side roads. There were hardly any houses now, just an occasional shed or shack. No wonder Aryan had got away all these months. There was no one here to see or hear anything. A sob escaped her throat.

He turned to look at her. "So you know, don't you? You guessed. I was wondering why you were so silent."

She looked at him with tear-filled eyes. She couldn't pretend any longer, and what was the point anyway?

"Don't try anything," he said. "Or I'll have to kill you."

"I won't, I won't. Let me go. Just tell me where Lolita is and I'll find her myself. No cops. I promise I won't tell."

His strange, high-pitched laugh made her shiver. "Of course you'll tell — when you think you're safe. You'll tell Vir and Bishnu and anyone who will listen. I'm not letting you go. Stay with me and be my love," he mocked.

"You sick bastard! You think I'll make love to you?"

"You have to, don't you understand?" He laughed his strange laugh again. "Your friend couldn't and so she's going to die. Just wait... I'll show you how much I love you." He was talking as if in a trance, as if he couldn't hear anything she said.

"You will be caught and hanged, you psychopath. Vir is coming. He'll kill you," she screamed.

He was silent for a few seconds, then turned to look at her with eyes that chilled her to her marrow. "Give me your phone," he said. She shook her head in refusal. He slashed at her, cutting her lip open with a backhanded slap. "Give me your phone," he repeated in the same monotone. She opened her handbag and took it out. He saw her call to Vir was still open and realised she must have hit the speed dial when she took out the gum.

"You bitch," he screamed and slapped her again. Then he stopped the car on the sand track, removed the battery from the phone and threw it out. Then he took out the SIM card, snapped it in two and flung it away. And then the instrument went flying, shattering against a tree trunk. "Let's see how he finds you now. You'll pay for this, bitch."

He slowed down as he went down another side road, towards a ramshackle house shrouded in creepers and the spreading branches of an ancient neem tree. Barren land on all sides, with patches of wild grass, littered with plastic covers, empty bottles and weeds. He pulled up in front of the house, opened the car door on her side and dragged her out.

She did not run; she had nowhere to run to and he would be upon her in an instant. He opened the huge padlock on the door and dragged her into a dark room. She realised she was still clutching the heavy torch she had brought from her room. She'd thought it would come in handy to search Charan Raj's farmhouse. She had been such a fool.

Her heart slowed down, as if her body had accepted that she could do nothing, go nowhere. Her fate was to die here. She could see nothing in the darkness inside the house, but felt something cold being slapped around her wrist. He had handcuffed one of her hands to a wooden post supporting the roof, just inside the door. Her torch dropped to the floor.

He turned on the light and she gasped at what she saw in front of her. A bare room with dirty walls and cobwebs, a dusty floor with rat droppings. And Lolita, tied to a reeking bed, gagged and blindfolded, wearing her pants and bra. Squirming as she heard sounds of her captor returning to torture her. She heard an eerie tinkle each time Lolita moved her feet.

My God! He's put anklets on her, she thought. Somehow that seemed more disgusting than anything else he'd done. She reeled and was brought up short by the handcuff.

He moved to the bed and removed Lolita's blindfold and gag. She could barely open her eyes after days of total darkness. Her face was dirty, gaunt, bloody. Her eyes were swollen, with deep shadows under them. "Aryan? Thank God you found me," her voice trembled. It was torture to talk through her parched lips. But she was so happy she had been rescued at last. "Where is Jambu? Untie me, we must get away." Kat listened in despair, fighting waves of dizziness.

"That bastard? He's long dead," Aryan replied. "He was following you around like a love-sick fool and threatening me. I beat him up and left him for dead, but he survived. Then I had to finish him off in the hospital."

Lolita gasped, realising at last that the author of her nightmare was the man standing in front of her. The man she had trusted to keep her safe for the rest of her life. Her eyes moved past him and she saw Kat shackled to the post. *My God! Not you too.*

Kat had pulled herself together and was staring at her friend with intense eyes. A burst of adrenaline kicked through her veins as she determined the man wasn't going to get away with his depravity. She was going to do everything she could to defeat him.

He was talking, in the high thin voice of a little boy, turning to a corner and addressing someone who wasn't there. "Yes ma. I brought her for you. Do you like her, ma?" He paused, listening to a voice that only he could hear. His voice rose higher: "Why do you hate me, ma? Why? All those men, everyday. Am I not good enough? I love you, ma."

Kat watched his face, the spittle running out of the corner of his mouth as he worked himself into a frenzy. He was getting ready for the slaughter.

He was still talking. "Yes ma, I remember. First, a picture for my album." He opened the wooden cupboard next to the bed and took out a camera. It whirred as it captured Lolita's terrified face. Kat was horrified when she saw close-ups of several other girls taped to the inner walls of the cupboard. There was something else that made her stomach churn, something that looked like toes. Grisly specimens bathed in formaldehyde, floating in glass jars.

"Pity there's no time to take a video," he was saying. "I wanted to record the light going out of your eyes, little by little," he said. "So much fun to watch." He put the camera back in the cupboard, took out a red silk scarf which he laid out on the table next to the bed. "A pretty scarf for your throat," he told Lolita. "You'll look so pretty when you're dead." He spoke calmly now, as if he was reciting a verse. As if he had said it many times before. A flame was leaping in his eyes.

"And here's the knife, nice and sharp." He ran his finger over the edge. "You won't feel a thing when I cut off your toe. Oh, of course. You'll be dead by then, won't you?" He laughed.

Lolita wailed — a weak, ragged sound. "Please let me go, let me go. I'll do anything you want. Anything."

Kat added her voice to the appeal. "You don't have to do this. Just lock us in and leave. It'll be days before someone hears us, or we'll die of hunger and thirst. Why kill us and have our blood on your hands?"

"Yes, beg, beg. I like it when pretty girls beg," he said.

"How can you do this to me? I thought you loved me," said Lolita.

"I thought so too, till I found out you were a slut. Like my mother and yours. It's time I got rid of the filth." He picked up the scarf, held it between his two hands like a garrotte.

"No, please," she begged. He put the scarf round her neck, preparing to knot it in front.

"At least let me pray before you kill me," she screamed. "Untie me and let me kneel."

"Oh, you want to pray? Maybe God will come to your rescue." He laughed, looking forward to a little more fun before she died. He untied her hands and legs. She staggered as she tried to stand and fell on him. He pushed her down to her knees.

Lolita had what she wanted by then. Her hand had flashed into his pocket, retrieving the key to Kat's handcuffs. She tossed it to Kat with a quick flick of her wrist as she fell to her knees. Kat grabbed it with her free hand, turning the key in the handcuff with trembling fingers. The click sounded loud to her ears. She bent, picked up the torch and took a quick step towards Aryan.

But he'd heard the click and was turning towards her. She raised her arm, then swung the torch forward. He blocked her with his left arm while lashing out at her face with his right fist. She fell back against the wall with a sickening crack. He had already turned to face Lolita, pushing her down as she tried to get up. He would kill them, both of them. One after the other. The she-devils.

54

The signal from Kat's phone had died. Rom refreshed the screen, wondering if his computer had frozen. Nothing. "She's gone," he told Vir. "Either the battery died or Aryan found out she called you."

Vir's heart sank. He raised his voice above the insane whomping of the blades. "Is there a house anywhere near the place where you saw the signal last?"

"No, nothing for a few kilometres," said Rom. "Can you see any vehicle from the helicopter?"

"Nothing, we're still a few minutes out," said Vir. *Damn. He couldn't lose her now after coming so close.*

"I checked for any property listed in his name or his mother's," said Rom. "No luck. What next?" Time was skittering past and every minute mattered now.

"What about his mother's known customers?" asked Bishnu. "Propertied guys with roots in Chennai?"

"Cross-referencing now. Yes, I found one. Sethupathy, a moneyed landlord with four properties in Chennai."

"Focus on Sholavaram."

"Right. Two properties a few kilometres apart. I'm sending you the locations now."

"Set Vir down near the first one," Bishnu said to Jeff. "Keegan and I will take the other place." He turned to Vir and said, "Want a gun? No questions will be asked on this one."

"No," said Vir. "I got this. Death by bullet is too good for him. I need to make sure he's hanged for his crimes." *Unless we're too late and he's gone, taking the bodies with him.*

****

Kat slid down the wall to the ground, senseless from Aryan's blow. He flung the scarf round Lolita's neck, ready to twist it tight. This was what he had been waiting and planning for.

And then he heard it. A loud clattering noise above their heads. He paused and looked up. The noise increased in volume, seeming to shake the foundations of the house. What was it? A helicopter? Had someone caught up with him already?

The door crashed open. Vir charged in, taking in the scene with a swift glance. Aryan turned towards him, dropping the scarf and straightening up. Vir's right fist crashed into the bridge of his nose. Aryan reeled back screaming, blood streaming from his nose. Vir pushed him down and drove his knee into his stomach, preparing to finish him off with a blow to his larynx. He was now in killer mode. Ready to kill without emotion if that was what was needed.

But Aryan seemed to have the strength of the devil. He lashed out with his fist, landing a hard knock on Vir's jaw. Even as his head rocked back with the force of the blow, Vir's knee was in motion, slamming into Aryan's groin with a force that sent him staggering.

"Run outside and call Bishnu," he shouted to the girls, throwing his phone to Kat. He turned to smash Aryan's head in, only to find that he was no longer there. The man must have armour-plated guts to have moved so fast after the attack. He looked around. No place to hide in this room. He could see under the bed and the cupboard stood open displaying its macabre contents.

There was another room that could be entered through a doorway on the right. It was dark and he would have to enter blind to finish him off. He had no idea what lay beyond the doorway and Aryan had shown himself to be capable of anything. The room had no door or he could have locked it and imprisoned the killer. He had the option of waiting for reinforcements: Bishnu, Jeff, the cops. He could call for guns, powerful lights, tear gas. But that was not his style. He needed to finish what he had started.

Maybe he could draw him out, make him show himself. He knew just the right prod. He moved to stand to one side of the door and spoke in a clear, steady voice. "Her name was Tarakeshwari, wasn't it? Your mother. You tried so hard to win her love and approval, but she wouldn't give it. Instead she abused you, abandoned you. Made you feel small and worthless. Less than a man."

"Stop talking. You know nothing. Shut the crap or I'll shut it for you." Aryan's voice came screaming through the doorway.

"She is to blame, isn't she? She made you impotent. You wanted to show her you were in control but couldn't — even after you tied her up. You tried and failed and she laughed at you, didn't she? You got mad and choked her. Kept squeezing till her life escaped through her eyes."

"I'm warning you. I have a gun. A big powerful gun," shouted Aryan.

"Judging by how angry and bitter you are, I'd say it isn't that big, is it?" asked Vir. He knew it would all be over in a matter of seconds. The gun had changed the equation. He had only one chance to come out of this alive. He must grab Aryan's gun hand as he charged out.

Running steps approached the doorway. Aryan came out shooting, spraying bullets in all directions. What saved Vir was that he had begun to move to the other side of the door after his final taunt.

Blam. Blam. Blam. The gunshots at close quarters made his ears ring. He felt a searing pain on his cheek as a random bullet gouged through his flesh and shot past. But his hand was already flashing towards the gun hand, knocking it out of Aryan's grasp with a powerful swipe.

Then Vir knocked him down, slamming into his chest with his knees. He grabbed his head by his ears and bashed it on the floor, again and again. Aryan had his hands round his throat, choking him. Vir saw blood clots obscuring his vision, but he still continued to bang the monster's head on the floor. The fight seemed to go on and on, as if in slow motion.

And when Vir thought his head would explode and that he could not draw another breath, he felt the man's grip loosening. At last. The hands fell away and Aryan's head settled with a final crunch on the hard concrete.

Vir fell back, wheezing and coughing. No longer caring if Aryan was alive or dead. And then Bishnu raced in with Jeff and Keegan. "Just like a bad Hindi movie," whispered Vir through his ragged throat. "The cops rushing in when it's all over."

Keegan went to check Aryan. "Still breathing. Do you want me to…?"

"No," said Bishnu. "Leave him for the law." And then to Vir, "So he had a gun and you had to play hero. Let me see your face."

He examined it under the light. "A flesh wound — you'll live. And if you're lucky, you'll have a scar to impress the girls."

"Are you angling for a movie role too?" Jeff asked Vir, giving him a friendly thump on his back. Vir saw stars. The giant didn't know his own strength. Keegan dragged the unconscious man by his leg like a piece of meat and handcuffed him to the wooden post near the door and threw away the key.

They went outside to where Kat and Lolita were waiting.

55

Kat had taken Lolita out of the shack and wrapped her upper body in her dupatta. She hugged her and held her close while she heaved with dry sobs. Then she had given her water from the bottle she had snatched on her way out. She called Bishnu on Vir's phone and he told her he would be there with the helicopter in a couple of minutes. They'd found no one in the dingy shed at the other location.

When the chopper landed, he and Keegan helped Lolita climb in. The doctor dressed her wounds and asked her to take slow sips of water to rehydrate herself. He reassured Kat that there was nothing a hot bath, nourishing food and rest couldn't set right. Lolita needed to give her body and mind some time to recover from the trauma.

Kat saw the men coming out of the house. No Aryan. Maybe the monster was dead. Vir stopped to make a call. "He's down and the girl's safe," he said. "I'm sending you the location. You know what to do."

Bishnu and he got into the helicopter and Jeff lifted off. Keegan was standing guard till he could hand the man over.

****

Much later, they all gathered in Vir's suite at the Taj. The table was loaded with comfort food. Buttery croissants, glazed doughnuts, chocolate cake, strawberries with whipped cream, fresh fruits. And, of course, a pot of strong aromatic coffee for Vir.

Bishnu dropped in after tying up the loose ends and regaled them with a colourful version of how he had coaxed the film unit to lend him their helicopter. "I'm sure our stunt is still playing," he said, turning on the TV. And it was, for the benefit of those who'd missed the live action.

It did make for great viewing. The helicopter descending into the stadium. The players and cricket fans watching with bated breath. The rope ladder tumbling down. Vir doing his Spiderman act as it swayed in the strong wind. Bishnu hanging out to pull him in.

"Don't miss Jeff executing a bow to the audience before leaving the stadium," said Vir.

"The wiseass wanted to do a triple barrel roll. Always the Hollywood showboat!" said Bishnu.

The channel cut to show the cops taking away Aryan. "Do you feel okay about watching this Lolita?" asked Kat. "I'm fine," she replied, huddling under a thick blanket.

Sushil was reporting from the killer's house. An ambulance stood by with its red light revolving. Police cars and policemen were everywhere. A stretcher brought out an unconscious, bloody figure. A medical orderly walked alongside, holding a drip aloft. "The kidnapper is being moved to hospital," said Sushil. "He's in pretty bad shape. The doctor says he may not fully recover, or even walk again."

"But he wasn't that badly hurt when we left, was he?" asked Kat. "You said you'd knocked him out and handcuffed him."

"Well, I told someone to send his guys to take care of him till the cops came, and take the credit too," said Vir. "Someone with a big stake in making sure Lolita wasn't killed."

"Charan Raj?" she asked.

"Yes. He's quite the hero now. Pollsters are predicting a landslide win for him."

"But what's Lolita going to get out of it?"

"A big fat cheque from one of his trusts. Enough to pay for her education abroad or to set up her own outfit. Whatever she wants."

Lolita was unable to fully grasp her good fortune. Tears slid down her cheeks as she realised she and her mother need no longer live in poverty and fear.

Moti was not talking about it, but she was beginning to hope that perhaps Dr. Gaurav, her mentor at the hospital, was growing interested in her.

Minx and Sushil had had a fight again. He had lectured her on taking unnecessary risks and she had called him a wimp. Both of them were too strong-headed to apologise. Maybe they'd work it out... or not.

Vir had taken Kat to the rooftop balcony so they could look down at the twinkling lights of the city. "I had no idea when I came to India that I'd meet someone like you," he said.

"Same here," she replied. "No way was I going to settle for the Bheem Boys and Gajendrans of the world."

"Seems like you have a lot of goofy tales to tell. Maybe later? After we get rid of all these hangers-on?" He smiled into her eyes.

"That's a date," she said. "Now we'll have to break the news to my mother."

"I've a confession to make," he said. "The day I came to your college? It was to meet you, armed with the pictures your mother sent me. It was easy once I spotted your face in the photo on your principal's desk. And it was easier still to manipulate him."

"So the course you were starting...."

"Primarily an excuse to get in to see you. Scoping out campuses where the killer operated was a bonus."

So you've been playing me with the help of my mother, is it? thought Kat. "No problem," she said. "I'd like to pick your brain for my script, maybe join you as assistant. You know how brilliant I am — calling you so you could track us down and all that?" She looked into his face with an innocent smile. *Now stick that in your pipe and smoke it.*

Hmm, life just got more interesting, thought Vir.

****

Later, much later, he was fast asleep, dreaming pleasant dreams. A strident ringing woke him up just when things were getting interesting. He opened a bleary eye. The time was 4 am. What the heck?

"Took you long enough," said Bishnu. "How soon can you come to the office? Looks like we've got another one."

Glossary

Aiyyo — an exclamation of lament, such as 'alas!'

Anna — big brother

Asura — demon

Bajjis — vegetable or chicken pieces dipped in batter and deep fried

Beti — daughter

Bhai, Bhaiyya — brother

Bhoot — ghost

Bindi — a dot on the forehead, worn mainly by women in India

Biriyani — a rice dish prepared with vegetables or with meats

Chai wallah — tea seller

Dhoti — a garment wrapped around the lower limbs, worn by men in India

Dupatta — a long scarf worn by a woman over her shoulders

Ganja — cannabis

Gulab jamuns — a type of sweet

Hijra — eunuch

Izzat — honour

Kabab — meat roasted on skewers

Kajal — traditional Indian cosmetic used as eyeliner

Kanyadaan — a ceremony to 'give' one's daughter in marriage

Muhurtham — an auspicious moment

Murukku — a snack of crunchy twists

Naan — a type of bread

Neta — leader

Paan — betel leaves

Paisa vasool — to get your money's worth

Parisam — groom's engagement gift to bride

Pyaari — beloved

Ras malai — a type of sweet

Salwar kameez — loose, pajama-like trousers and long tunic

Shaitaan — devil

Shamiana — marquee

Sindoor — vermilion, auspicious red powder

Zari — fine thread made from gold or silver, used in brocade